Something Wicked This Way Comes

By

Joanna Larum

Copyright 2017 Joanna Larum

For Thomas, Coco and Luke who all believed in me.
And for Olive who kept my nose to the grindstone week after week!

Something Wicked This Way Comes
Prologue 1898

It was a noise which woke him - a noise which he had never heard before and it reverberated through his four-year-old head in a very unpleasant way. He opened his eyes and stared up at the dark ceiling, realising that his mother wasn't in the bed with him and aware that the noise was continuing unabated.

He sat up, disturbing the single, thin blanket which was his only covering on that cold night. As his eyes adjusted to the lack of light, he was able to make out the curly tendrils which Jack Frost had painted on the inside of the window and he shivered with the bone-jarring cold that was seeping into his tiny frame. He wished that his mother would come to bed and save him from the terrors which were starting to creep into his mind. What if the noise came from a monster which was hiding under his bed? No, the noise wasn't in the room with him. So was the monster on the landing and only waiting for him to blink before it jumped into the room and ate him? Why didn't Mam come and look after him? He couldn't remember a time when his Mam hadn't shared their single bed, so where was she when he needed her most?

It crossed his mind that he could get out of bed and peep round the door to see if the monster was on the landing. If it wasn't, he could go downstairs and see if his Mam was in the kitchen and then he would be safe but he rejected that thought as soon as it came to him. If Grandad was in the kitchen he would get slapped for getting out of his bed. He could remember the only time he had gone downstairs after bedtime when Grandad had slapped him so hard that the pain in his bottom had still been there the next day. So, what could he do to find his Mam?

Then the noise increased and he heard his Granny's voice.

"Stop with your noise. You aren't the first person to go through this and no-one else screams like a child."

The voice was as harsh as the words and Daniel knew, suddenly, that the noise was coming from his Mam. There was something wrong with her and he panicked, worried that she might be ill and he would lose her. If his Mam died, then who would look after him? His Granny and Grandad hated him and they would both hit him at the slightest opportunity. How could he live without his mam's cuddles and love? Then all thoughts of himself were washed out of his mind when the loudest noise yet battered at his eardrums and he finally recognised his mother as she screamed in pain.

There was a harsh banging from Granny and Grandad's bedroom and his Grandad shouted.

"Keep the noise down, you slut. I'm trying to sleep here."

Then there was silence and suddenly a small cry, so quiet Daniel wasn't sure he had actually heard it. Then it came again and he recognised it as the cry of a baby. Was that what had happened? Had his Mam had another baby? With the realisation came a tidal wave of emotion. He would have a little brother or sister, like the other children who played in the streets, but would his Mam still love him like she had always done, if she had another child to cuddle and love? He felt suddenly so alone and desperate for his Mam to put her arms round him and keep him safe from the grandparents who had terrified all his years on this earth. How he wished he was older so that he could take his Mam and this new baby and live somewhere where people were kind all the time and nobody slapped or punched him when he spoke.

Eventually, Daniel fell asleep, despite his fears and the biting cold and when he opened his eyes the next morning, his Mam was in bed next to him. As he turned to wrap his arms round her, he heard a snuffling noise and he sat bolt upright in case it was a rat trying to find a home in the bitter room. He would never forget the rat which had invaded the kitchen or Granny chasing it with a frying pan in her hand. He had laughed outright at that sight, finding his harsh Granny funny for the first time in his life. She had dealt with the rat and then spanked his backside with the pan for laughing at her. He had never laughed in front of her again.

It was daylight now and he immediately saw the source of the noise, but it wasn't a rat. It was a tiny baby wrapped in a threadbare blanket and lying in a cardboard box on the floor. He moved to put out his hand to touch the baby and this movement woke his mother. She wrapped her arms round his skinny body and hugged him as though she was trying to squeeze the air out of him. Daniel hugged her back, overcome with relief that she still loved him even though there was now a baby for her to hug. His mother understood without speaking that he had been worried about her and she rocked him in her arms and crooned to him. He though his heart would burst with the joy of having her back and decided that it was the happiest he had ever been in his life.

When his mother bent over and picked up the baby and put it between them, he looked at his sibling properly for the first time.

"This is Martha, your new sister." His Mam whispered to him and he nodded and smiled to show that he had understood and then he carefully took hold of one of the tiny hands which had escaped from its meagre wrapping. The fingers were tiny and the hand was cold and Daniel covered the minute hand with his to try and force some warmth into it. His Mam smiled again and then Daniel looked into the face of his baby sister for the first time. Her eyes were closed but her little mouth was pursed, as though she was dreaming about food and Daniel felt his heart melt at sight of her. When she opened her eyes and seemed to look into his face as though she recognised him, he felt his whole stomach turn warm and the warmth spread up to the top of his head and right down to his toes. That was the moment when Daniel Coleman knew that he loved his sister Martha Coleman and that it would continue until he breathed his last.

His mother watched the emotions rush across her son's face and she knew that, whatever happened to her, Daniel would look after his baby sister until the cows came home. Her fear that he would be jealous of a new baby dissipated and she wished with all her might that she had brought them both into a kinder world.

The bedroom door slammed open and hit the wall behind it as Grandad entered. He crossed the tiny room in one stride and slapped his daughter across her face so hard that her head bounced against the wall behind her and tears began to slide down her cheeks,

"That's for bringing another bastard mouth into the house." Grandad growled. "Get your lazy backside out of that bed and get downstairs to cook breakfast for us. You have to earn your keep, you know, and not on yer back."

He cuffed Daniel for good measure and then stormed out of the room, leaving Daniel and his Mam both in tears. For the first time in his life, Daniel questioned his grandfather's attitude towards his daughter and grandson.

"Why does Grandad hit us both, Mam? Daniel asked, so quietly that Mam had to tip her head towards him to be able to hear him. "What have we done that he hits us all the time?"

His mother wrapped her arms round him again and whispered back to him.

"We cost him money to keep us and he doesn't like spending any money," she replied. "When you are older, you will understand it better. Come on; get up before he comes back for another go."

It was only as they were descending the stairs that Daniel remembered his mother's cries in the night and whispered to her again.

"Are you poorly, Mam? Will you be able to work today?"

"I'm not poorly, just tired." His Mam answered, also in a whisper. "I'll feel better when I've had something to eat."

Daniel knew that he would feel better too, when his empty little stomach had taken some food on board. He knew that he hadn't had any food the night before cos Grandad had shouted ' lazy tarts don't earn money, they don't eat' before making them both leave the kitchen while Granny and Grandad had their tea. His Mam had cried again when they were sheltering from the icy rain against the wall in the back yard while Grandad and Granny Coleman ate their tea in the warm kitchen. Daniel hoped that there would be some food that morning but how could his Mam work when she was so tired? For the first time in his short life, Daniel wished that Grandad and Granny Coleman would stop being so mean to him and his Mam. Why could Grandad have food when his Mam couldn't? Grandad often didn't do any work but he never missed a meal. Daniel discovered that the world wasn't fair, that morning after his baby sister was born, and it was a lesson he never forgot.

"She won't be doing much work today, will she?" Grandad snarled as Edith, Martha and Daniel entered the kitchen. "I don't reckon she's earned enough this week to have any more food from our table. And there's another mouth to feed now, don't forget about that."

"She'll not manage to do any work if she doesn't have some grub inside her." Granny Lillian snarled back. "She's no use to me if she faints from hunger when she's supposed to be stirring the poss tub."

"Well, don't feed the other two." Grandad added. "They don't earn their keep."

"Don't be daft, man." Granny Lillian was as abrupt with her husband as she was with her daughter and grandchildren. "They won't grow up to be able to work if we don't feed them enough. We'll need them when we're too old to work. They can run the laundry and look after us. That's the only reason I haven't put them in the workhouse before now."

Daniel felt his insides shrivel at this mention of the workhouse. He didn't know what it was but he knew that threats to put her in it terrified his mother. He didn't know that houses could work because all the houses in their street didn't do anything except stand still. The thought of a house that could work worried him no end and it was one of the monsters that he thought about when he was alone and frightened.

Chapter One
1901

The church bells were ringing all over the town, but it wasn't for a celebration. The bells were all ringing their deepest notes and they rang slowly and with great emphasis because it was to mark the death of the old Queen. The town had taken on a display of deep mourning with some of the old die-hards closing their curtains as though they had lost a member of the family, although others said that the Queen hadn't even known that they existed so why should they mourn her passing? Whatever their private feelings about the dead Queen, the town intended to have a proper wake for her and then a party to celebrate their new King's accession to the throne. It had been a miserable few years for South Bank with its fairly-new industries and no-one had had any money to spare. Life had been one long round of tightening belts and doing without and everyone wanted to forget the lean times and think ahead to a new reign and a new future for themselves. One old codger even admitted to thinking of the Queen as the 'most miserable person in the kingdom'. Was it any wonder that life had been so bleak when the Queen had spent the last thirty years mourning the death of her husband? Now, they could all turn their thoughts to the future and who knew what that future could bring?

In the end house of the terrace which was York Street, Daniel didn't know who this Queen was who had died and he couldn't understand what all the fuss was about. Neither a dead Queen nor a new King would make any difference to his life of drudgery and fear, no matter how many people were mourning the one's passing or celebrating the one's arrival. He would continue to watch his mother as she grew evermore frail and depressed while his Granny and Grandad Coleman grew fat on their labour - for Daniel worked very hard as did his baby sister Martha. She was only three years old but she carried dirty laundry about the backyard, even though she could only manage to carry a small basket. Bless her, she thought it was a game that they played every day and didn't realise that it was actually slave labour. Daniel didn't know the name for what he did, but he knew enough to realise that his grandparents were exploiting him and his mother and his sister, even if he couldn't put it into words.

He was worried about his mother. She never had any energy these days and she didn't smile anymore. He could just remember her before Martha was born when she used to whisper about the wonderful life they would have when they left his grandparents' house and set up home on their own, or possibly with some prince-like gentleman who would look after them all. His mother used to smile at him then and they would giggle over shared jokes, but she didn't whisper to him anymore at bedtime because she was so tired all the time. The joy of life had gone out of her and Daniel missed her smiles so much. Although he was too young to understand properly, he knew that she was at the end of her tether and he worried what would happen when she finally snapped.

It was the day of the old Queen's wake that Daniel made a promise to himself, a promise he fully intended keeping for the rest of his life. He began to mark off on the backyard wall every time Granny or Grandad cuffed either his mother or himself, every time they yelled at either of them and every time they said something disparaging about either of them. He didn't understand the meaning of many of the names that Grandad, particularly, called him or his mother, but he could tell by the tone in which they were spoken or shouted that they weren't what he called 'nice' names. He was only seven years old and he couldn't be expected to understand all the names, but he knew a nice name when he heard one and he knew a few of the swear word names and these latter he marked on the backyard wall with a chunk of an old brick. Nobody noticed what he was doing and nobody asked why he was marking the wall so he continued to do it.

By the time of the new King's coronation in 1902, Daniel had quite a pattern of brick marks on the wall and they were being added to at the rate of about ten a day. This number increased whenever Grandad spent his evening in the local hostelry because being drunk made him even more bad-tempered than usual and having a hangover made him into a perfect monster. He never took his ire out on Granny Lillian, however, only on Daniel and his mother and Daniel had already come to the conclusion that it was because he was afraid that his wife would fight back.

They had a party in the street for the Coronation although Daniel and Edith were refused permission to go to it. Daniel did look out of the bedroom window and was intensely jealous of the children who had been allowed to attend because they were treated to party food and Daniel could hardly remember the last time he had eaten a cake. It had been when one of the neighbours had seen him staring into their backyard as she gave her children the fruits of her baking. Daniel couldn't help staring at the children as they had eaten the cakes and the neighbour had felt sorry for him. She had her own ideas of the treatment he and his mother received at the hands of the elder Colemans and she had handed him a cake and told him to eat it in her backyard so that his grandparents wouldn't see what he had. In more modern times, she would have reported them to the authorities but in 1902 most people turned a blind eye to child abuse, whatever kind of abuse it was.

Coronation Day in 1902 was the day Grandad Joshua Coleman drank even more of the strong beer for sale in his local hostelry than he usually did and, when he finally rolled home past midnight, he was in a terribly bad mood. He had played cards with some other older men and had lost spectacularly time after time until he had no money left in his pocket. Ordinarily, he would have gone home when he ran out of cash, but he had been irritated by a new member of the group playing cards whom he accused of cheating and he had given an IOU for the last few hands of the game. It had been a mistake, because the new member had turned out to be a policeman from Middlesbrough whose job it was to stop illegal gambling and he had arrested Joshua at the end of the game. Joshua had been taken to Middlesbrough Police Station and been charged with illegal gambling and then released with a notice to appear in court in ten days' time, where he knew he would be fined and so lose even more money. He arrived home just as Martha woke from a bad dream and had laid about him with his walking stick, indiscriminately hitting furniture and walls and, twice, his daughter because he couldn't stand the sound of the child's cries. He hadn't stopped Martha's tears but had made his wife shout and his daughter and grandson cry, so the noise level had got even worse, at which point he had kicked the kitchen wall and put his foot through it, twisting his ankle badly which had pained him immensely.

Edith, Daniel's mother, had forced herself to stop crying even though she was in great pain from the blow she had received to her head and she had whispered to Daniel that he had to stop crying before his grandad turned on him, so Joshua had finally gotten the peace he had requested, although he was making enough noise to drown them all out because of the pain in his ankle. Daniel stood in the kitchen doorway, halfway behind his mother so that Grandad wouldn't see him, and had watched his grandfather as he had been waited on by his wife. Granny Lillian had brought a bowl of warm water and had soaked his ankle in it to bring down the swelling which had already appeared above his heel. She had then soaked a cloth in very cold water drawn from the pump in the backyard and wrapped the offending ankle in it before drying as much of his leg which was still visible and then she provided him with a cup of hot tea, well-sugared and blown to his favourite temperature.

Grandad had settled back into his chair and fallen asleep when the combined effects of the cold compress and the few drops of laudanum which Granny had put in his tea worked their magic and reduced his pain to an ache. Daniel watched the hated face relax as the laudanum took effect and wondered why it was possible to hate another human being as much as he hated his Grandad. When he glanced at his Granny, she was watching him and he hoped that his hatred didn't show on his face. She didn't make any comment, apart from telling Edith to take the children back to bed before she banked up the fire and put out the one candle, leaving her husband now fast asleep in his chair by the fire and backlit by its glow like a demon from Hell.

The next morning, the full meaning of his visit to the Police Station dawned on Joshua Coleman and he mulled over it while he played with the fried bacon which his wife had given him for his breakfast. He found his stomach rebelling at the thought of the grease from the dripping that the bacon had been fried in and he pushed his plate away without eating a bite. His wife ignored his muttered curses and his abandoned breakfast, merely pouring him a cup of tea into which she had already poured some drops of the laudanum she had secreted in her pinny pocket. Daniel watched with interest as his Granny performed her sleight-of-hand with the small bottle and hugged the knowledge of the bottle's position to his chest, not even letting his Mam know what he had seen.

The laudanum didn't put Grandad Joshua to sleep that morning but it calmed him down enough that he didn't shout, scream or lash out with his cane while the rest of the family were in the kitchen with him. When they had finished their breakfasts (Daniel had snatched Grandad's sandwich and shared it with his mother while Granny had her back turned), they all trooped out into the yard where Daniel began his first task of the day which was to light the fire under the big copper drum which held the water for heating. His mother and Martha began sorting the piles of clothing which constituted their day's work while Granny Lillian put the irons next to the fire to heat so that she could press yesterday's washing before Edith took it back to its owner and got their payment for the task.

Life continued in this same way for a few months. The marks that Daniel was making on the yard wall grew in number in direct correlation to the moods that Grandad was in, although it had to be said that his black moods grew fewer as his ankle mended and he was no longer in pain. This didn't mean that he stopped taking every opportunity to belittle his daughter or to roar at his grandson but at least it was done without the heat that his pain had engendered.

The weather stayed warm and dry throughout August but, as September marched into view, the rain clouds gathered and South Bank was sprinkled with raindrops quite regularly. The wind moved round and began to blow at the North East coast having travelled across the Russian Steppes and floated over the North Sea, so that by the time it arrived at South Bank it was cold and managed to find a way through every gap in window and door frames and every gap in clothing. People shivered and shook while they were out in the wind and only the richer of the inhabitants were able to pile coal onto their fires to keep their houses warm.

In York Street, the only room in the end house that was warm was the kitchen. Grandad and Granny Lillian didn't seem to feel the cold and none of the other fireplaces in the house were ever visited by coal, so Daniel, Edith and Martha shivered their way through every night. Martha's box had disappeared and the three of them shared the same single bed that Daniel had shared with his mother before Martha's birth, even though there wasn't enough room in it for the three of them. There had been no increase in the number of blankets on the bed and so it was only their own body heat which kept them warm enough to be able to sleep at all. Usually, they all fell asleep quite quickly; especially when they had spent most of each day in the cold back yard, getting wet every time that washing was transferred from the poss tub to the mangle but some evenings Daniel couldn't fall asleep. These were the evenings when Grandad had refused to allow them anything to eat and Daniel couldn't sleep for the painful emptiness of his stomach.

It was during evenings like this that Daniel began to make lists in his head of the different types of punishments which his grandparents visited on Edith, Martha and Daniel. He was now seven years old and able to question the events which occurred in their house and measure the differences between their lives and the lives of other families in the street. He had recently realised that, although he was well-endowed (even over-endowed he thought) with grandparents, he was sadly lacking in the number of parents that he had and it was this discrepancy that bothered him during the nights that he found it difficult to sleep. This realisation had come to him the day that his Grandad had belted his mother after the grown-ups had held a discussion in the kitchen while Daniel and Martha were told to remain in the yard. Despite the noises coming from other houses, both Daniel and Martha had been able to hear the argument which had raged in the kitchen, although it had passed over Martha's head because she was too young to understand what was being said. Daniel, however, had understood every word and had stood, transfixed, as he listened to it.

"Why didn't you come straight home after you had delivered the laundry to the Miller's house?" Granny Lillian's voice was low but there was always a hard edge to it.

"I told you, there was no-one in at the Miller's house." Edith's voice was low and pleading and Daniel felt the anger grow in him because they had made his mother frightened of her parents. "I waited for a few minutes then I went round to the front of the house to see if I could see them coming home. I couldn't, so I went back round to their yard, which is when I saw Mrs Miller coming back from the shops. She wanted to have a chat so I talked to her for a couple of minutes while I waited for her to pay me."

"A couple of minutes?! You've been gone a good half hour! Plenty of time for you to spend it on your back making another mouth for me to feed! Is that what you were doing, you lazy tart? Trying to find another man to bring even more disgrace on our house?" Grandad was shouting now and Daniel winced at the noise he was making. In his mind's eye he could see his mother cowering away from her father and he was seized with such rage that he wanted to batter the back door down and attack his grandfather.

"I couldn't force Mrs Miller to pay me more quickly." Edith sounded resigned to her fate. "I couldn't stop her talking to me."

This quiet answer seemed to increase Grandad's rage, rather than smooth over the argument and Daniel heard him lever himself out of his chair. He waited with bated breath for the sound that he knew would come next, when the older man grabbed his thick ash stick and used it to such effect on his mother. It was his mother's scream that he heard next, which seemed to come even before the whistle that the rod made as it was swung through the air. Then Daniel heard the thuds as the rod made contact with his mother's back and she screeched with the pain and the terror she was feeling. Daniel forgot who he was, where he was and what he was doing. He flung open the back door and tore into the kitchen, straight towards Grandad Joshua who was so shocked at his intrusion that he stood stock still with the rod raised above Edith's back.

Daniel jumped and grabbed the rod and brought it down on his Grandad's ankle as a way of causing him the most pain. Grandad let out a bellow of pain and shock and tried, unsuccessfully, to regain possession of his weapon but Daniel had danced away from him and was holding Edith as she sobbed into the child's head. From outside in the backyard, they all heard Martha's wails as she reacted to the sight of her mother being beaten by her Grandad and her brother fighting back. At this point, Mr Davis who lived next door to them appeared in the doorway of the backyard and quickly entered the kitchen, addressing Grandad as the head of the household.

"I don't know what you are arguing about, but you are putting the fear of God into those two bairns and no mistake, as well as keeping the whole street entertained with your bullying. It's none of my business why you think you're such a big man but it becomes my business when me and the wife can't have a conversation in our kitchen for the noise that's coming from next door. If I were you, I'd be careful how free with my fists I was being cos there's a lot of folks in this town would take a great deal of delight in giving you the same treatment you're dealing out to this young lass. We don't like bullies round here, particularly bullies who only pick on those littler than themselves. Any more carrying-on like this and I'll be calling the police."

Having delivered this speech, Mr Davis turned on his heel and marched out of the kitchen, giving Daniel a pat on his back as he passed him. When Mr Davis had gone, there was silence in the small kitchen, apart from the muted sobs coming from Martha, until Granny Lillian pulled Martha into the kitchen and slammed the back door closed.

"See what you've done now?" Granny hissed at Grandad. "Just think about the numbers of customers we could lose if word gets round that Jack Davis thinks you are a bully. Folk'll go to that new laundry on Middlesbrough Road and we'll lose a lot of money. You are going to have to put a stop to these beatings, or we'll lose our business.

"What! Are you going soft, woman? This tart deserves to be beaten at least twice a day for bringing two fatherless brats into the house and no-one has the right to stop me punishing my own daughter. I've a good mind to go next door and give Mr High and Mighty Davis a good hiding for his cheek."

"Well, you won't, you stupid great lump or you'll make a bad situation even worse. Don't forget that Jack Davis is the one who writes letters for us when we need it and reads anything official-looking that comes through the letterbox. We could have got into a lot of trouble when that man came about filling in the census form last year if we hadn't had Jack to explain what it was. We need to keep on the good side of him."

Grandad Joshua grunted over this but he didn't have an answer to it because he knew his wife was right. Neither of them could read and write and nor could Edith who hadn't been allowed to attend school with the other children because her father thought he could get more out of her by making her work in the laundry. As a consequence, they relied on Jack Davis to help them out and couldn't afford to alienate him. Grandad had to bite his tongue and keep his feelings to himself, which wasn't something which came naturally to him. There was a silence and a stillness in the kitchen that had rarely been seen in that small room, until Daniel marched across to the back door, opened it and made his way across the yard to where the copper boiler stood, waiting for its next task for the day. With great deliberation, Daniel hefted the ash rod which his Grandad had used to beat his mother and pushed it into the fire underneath the boiler. With a growl, Grandad moved to run and rescue his weapon, but his wife held him back by the simple expedient of grabbing his earlobe between her finger and thumb. Grandad Joshua couldn't move without inflicting hurt and pain on himself and Granny Lillian had no intentions of letting him go.

It was a stalemate until Grandad turned his face to his wife and, slowly and deliberately, spat into her face. Granny didn't give any indication that she had seen or felt this disgusting show of temper from her spouse; she merely tightened the grasp she had on his earlobe and then began pulling gently downwards. It wasn't long before Grandad was on his knees in front of his wife, furious with himself for falling into her trap, furious with his wife for using those tactics and furious with his daughter and grandchildren for being witnesses to his humiliation. It didn't bode well for the weaker members of his family because Daniel knew that Grandad would take his shame out of his daughter and grandson's backs, even without his ash rod.

Granny, it seemed, had other ideas. She had been doing a lot of thinking while Grandad had been displaying his temper and while Daniel had been showing his independent spirit and she had decided that it was time to inform the rest of the family of the fruits of her considerations. She let go of Grandad's ear, which he wasn't expecting, and pushed him towards his fireside chair.

"Sit down there cos I've got something to say." Granny Lillian snapped and then jerked her head towards the table. Edith rightly took it to mean that she and the children were to sit down at the table and they hurried to do as they were told.

"Right." Granny Lillian said. "You can all listen to me. I've decided that Daniel is going to go to school so that he can learn to read and write. That way, we won't need Jack Davis anymore which will stop us having to kowtow to his moans. It will also mean that Daniel will be able to take over the laundry when you and I get too old to work and he can provide us with a comfortable home for our retirement. I don't imagine that Edith will ever find a good man and get married because what good man is going to take on a lass with two bastards tied to her apron strings? So, the boy is going to have to earn us enough money to keep his mother as well. I've worked in this laundry for too many years to not get something out of it for my retirement. Right you lot, back to work and Daniel, you'd better make sure you learn all the lessons those teachers can teach you."

"Hang on, lady. There's something I want to say before this little meeting is over." Grandad got out of his chair, struggling a bit with his injured ankle which was still paining him from Daniel's attack. "I'm not having any laziness from any of you so don't think that what Jack Davis said will stop me from belting any of you if I think you deserve it. Nothing's changed here. I'm still in charge and I will be until they plant me in the ground."

"On the contrary." Granny Lillian snarled. "You gave up any rights to ruling this household when you got yourself caught gambling. You'll need to work ten times harder than you've ever done to repay what the fine will be when you go to court and don't dare raise either your voice or your hand to me cos you'll pay for it fifty times over."

Granny Lillian obviously considered the matter closed because she opened the back door and made her way across the yard to the copper which had built up a good head of steam while they had been in the kitchen. She turned once to make sure that the rest of the family were following her then she started throwing washing and orders around in equal measure. Even Grandad Joshua couldn't withstand her strong personality and he joined them as they began to empty the hot water into the poss tub ready for the next load of washing.

Amidst the confusion of the steam and the movement, Daniel sidled up to his mother and asked her if she was hurt. Edith looked down at his concerned face and she managed to find the time to stroke his cheek before Granny yelled at her to get the scrubbing brushes. She even managed a weak smile, heartened by the thought that Daniel was going to get some schooling and so may one day be able to leave the house on York Street and go out into the world and earn himself a decent living. At the same time, she prayed for the strength to carry on until her children no longer needed her.

Chapter Two

Granny Lillian was well satisfied with her plan for Daniel to get some schooling although she had no intentions of letting the boy give up his share of the work that he did. Recently, she had been feeling her age and she had worried about what would happen to her when she could no longer work as hard as she had always done. She had no illusions that her husband would be by her side to support her in their old age because she knew, none better, the totality of his selfishness. He would abandon her to poverty in the same way that he would abandon a pet dog, of no use if it couldn't provide for his needs. Daniel learning to read and write would give her the support she would need and if her husband didn't like it then that was too bad. He could leave if he didn't like what was happening. As far as she was concerned, he had given up any rights to her loyalty when he had been stupid enough to gamble away her hard-earned money. The miserable old dog had never worked as hard as she had and he didn't deserve a comfortable old age. He could go to the workhouse for all she cared. One thing she knew for certain, he was going to have to start working harder than he had ever done before because she had carried him for too long. It was time he earned his keep.

It was still very early the next morning when they heard the army of men tramping past the backyard gate on their way to their early shift at the works. Daniel, Edith, Martha and Granny Lillian were already in the back yard, sorting through the washing and getting everything ready for their day's work. Grandad hadn't appeared as yet and it was obvious that Granny Lillian wasn't happy with his tardiness. Eventually, she threw the washboard onto the ground and stomped across the yard to the kitchen door. Edith and Daniel heard her shout as she went upstairs and they heard the deep growl that was Grandad's reply. Then there came an almighty bang and then Grandad shouted again. They had no idea what Granny had said or done but it wasn't long before they could see Grandad through the kitchen window. He had taken a seat at the table and was obviously waiting for his breakfast. He soon realised that this wasn't forthcoming when his wife batted him across the head with the frying pan and told him he would get his breakfast after he had lit the copper and started the water heating for the washing. Nobody spoke to him as he erupted into the back yard but they all watched him surreptitiously as they went about their own tasks.

Daniel was worried that nothing more had been said about him going to school and he kept flashing glances at Edith, trying to communicate his fear to her without actually saying anything. Edith knew what was worrying him but she didn't dare raise the subject, so all she could do was nod at him and smile slightly to show that she understood his worries. When the copper was bubbling merrily and the irons had been put to warm next to the fire, Granny put an end to their worries in her abrupt way.

"Right, breakfast and then Daniel can go to school."

"Why should he get breakfast if he isn't going to do any work today?" Grandad grumbled, but Granny put him in his place immediately.

"He'll not learn anything on an empty stomach, so shut your mouth. I decide who gets fed in this house, not you. Be careful that you don't have to go without breakfast, cos you won't get any tomorrow if you don't get yourself out of bed when the rest of us do."

This comment closed Grandad's mouth as nothing ever had before and Daniel had to turn his head away so that no-one could see his smile of delight. The day was turning into the best he had ever had and he was looking forwards with great anticipation to having a day in school. To top off his joy, Granny Lillian handed him one of Grandad's rashers of bacon, wrapped in the crust off the loaf. Daniel had never had such a fortifying breakfast in his life and he ate it more slowly than was usual because he wanted to savour the taste. All the way through breakfast, Grandad glowered at Daniel but, that day, Daniel wasn't as bothered about it as he would normally have been. The thought that he was going to school, leaving the house where his life was one long round of beatings and hunger and cold, kept his spirits so high that he could ignore his Grandad and concentrate on enjoying his breakfast. His mind raced with the possibilities that were opening up for him but part of his mind was also thinking about the change in the relationship between Granny and Grandad. Granny Lillian had always been the more vocal of his grandparents but she had never shouted at Grandad before or treated him in the same way that she treated her daughter and grandchildren, but that had now changed. Daniel wondered if his mother's situation might improve now that her parents were no longer a team. That was another warm thought to hug to his chest on this good day.

After breakfast, they all trooped out into the yard to continue their work and Daniel's stomach began to roll as he feared that Granny might have changed her mind about him going to school. He found that the unaccustomed richness of his breakfast bacon was sitting very heavily in his stomach and he hoped that he wasn't going to be sick. It would be criminal to waste such a breakfast. However, once the bulk of the washing had been sorted into piles and the first load had gone into the tub, Granny put Daniel's mind at rest.

"Get yourself off to school then." Granny barked at Daniel. "Make sure you take note of what that teacher learns you and prove to me that it's worth you missing work to go."

Daniel couldn't believe his ears and it was only when his mother took the bucket of water off him that he was holding and smiled into his wide eyes that he pulled himself together and shot out of the yard as fast as his legs could carry him. It was so rare that he went to school, he wasn't sure which classroom he should go to but when one of the teachers caught sight of him standing alone in the hall, she called him to her and pointed towards a door. He crept quietly into the classroom and seated himself at one of the pairs of desks which stood in rows facing the teacher's desk and the blackboard. Unbeknown to Daniel, the teacher who had directed him to the classroom made her way to the teachers' room at the end of the hall and had a quiet word with one of the other teachers.

"Daniel Coleman's turned up for school today." Miss Johnson said to Miss Swift. "I haven't seen him for months. I showed him where to go and he's got himself a seat towards the back."

"Is he any cleaner than he was last time he came to school?" Miss Swift asked.

"No, you wouldn't think that the family ran a laundry if you looked at the dirty state he's always in." Miss Johnson commented. "I feel sorry for the little mite. He looks half-starved and he wears cast-off dirty clothes. The poor child will never make anything of himself with a family like his."

Miss Swift nodded in agreement but didn't make any other comment. She picked up her pile of books and made her way rapidly to her classroom. Miss Johnson was right. Daniel was sitting right at the back of the classroom and nearest to the side wall. The other children had given him as wide a berth as possible in a classroom inhabited by nearly sixty children. It was to be expected because Daniel never played out in the street with the other children and had no idea how to play any games. He didn't know the names of any of his classmates because he had only ever spent the odd day at school. Miss Swift had attempted to call on his mother when Daniel had first attended school but had been stopped by the large frame of Grandad Joshua who had refused to let her into the house. He had told her it was none of her business who Daniel's parents were and that she could see the boy next time he went to school. Miss Swift had abandoned any idea of chatting with Daniel's mother and had been sad to see that Daniel hadn't attended school since that day. But now he had turned up again and she was curious to see if he was actually as bright as she had thought that he was the last time she had seen him. That day, she had been astounded at the ease he had shown in understanding what letters and numbers were and how they could be grouped together. She had been convinced that she was teaching a very intelligent child and had looked forwards to showing him the wonders of books and number work, but he hadn't reappeared at school since that day. She hoped that this time he would attend for longer so that she could properly measure his capabilities and bring out the latent intelligence that the child had.

   Miss Swift set the rest of the children some copying work to do and then called Daniel over to her desk. It was all she could do not to draw back from him at the odour which emanated from the boy's clothes and body but she manfully refused to give in to the messages she was receiving from her nose and smiled at him. Daniel didn't smile back because he was too wary of any person in authority to ever smile at them and he was wondering if she had called him over in order to either berate him for not coming to school or hit him for some unknown rule-breaking mistake which he had committed. Miss Swift did neither of these things but began showing him how to form his letters on the wax tablet which was on her desk in front of them. Gradually, Daniel began to relax when Miss Swift didn't shout or lash out and, after half an hour, was prepared to smile at his teacher when she told him he was a very clever boy.

   Miss Swift sent Daniel back to his desk with a large piece of paper covered in small words and phrases and he spent the rest of the morning copying them onto his tablet with ease. The afternoon was given over to learning times tables and Daniel enjoyed learning these, to him, very easy small sums. He could naturally add numbers onto each other and had no difficulty in understanding the concept of addition and subtraction. He was heartbroken when the school bell rang to signal the end of the school day and hoped that Granny Lillian would allow him to return to the sanctuary of the warm classroom the next day.

   Miss Swift also hoped that Daniel would be in her classroom the next morning but she knew that the boy's family life was strange, to say the least, and she wasn't sure that he would be allowed to return the next day. She was therefore pleasantly surprised when she saw Daniel in his place the next morning when she called the register. She didn't know how or why the old man had been persuaded to let the child attend school but she had every intention of using every minute of the time she had been given to make sure that he had a grounding in schoolwork so that he could carry on himself when the grandparents withdrew their consent to his appearances at school.

   Miss Swift wasn't the only one who had been surprised to learn that Daniel was allowed to return to school the next day. Neither his mother nor Daniel had expected that Granny Lillian would be as amenable the next morning but she had put a plate bearing a slice of bacon in front of him and then told him to get himself to school when he had lit the fire under the copper boiler. Edith had smiled at Daniel and nodded to him to do as he was told until Grandad Joshua had opened his mouth.

   "Why is the little waster getting my bacon to eat?" Grandad had demanded to know. "And what's this about him going to school? He should be out in the yard earning the food that you are pushing down his throat, Lillian, not having a day off to go to school again."

Both Edith and Daniel held their breath while Granny stared at her husband with a sneer on her face.

"He's learning his letters so that he can be of use to us in the running of the laundry, you old bat." Granny was never one to mince words. "And he's going to learn reckoning up so that no-one can diddle us out of any money. I reckon he's earning his keep by learning, so keep your fat mouth shut and let me get on with running the household."

Grandad Joshua grumbled under his breath but they all knew that he wouldn't argue with Granny when she had spoken like that. Daniel wolfed down the bacon and shot out of the kitchen to go and light the boiler. Grandad Joshua aimed his walking stick at him as he ran past (the only weapon he still had since Daniel had burnt the ash rod) but Daniel dodged out of the way and Joshua grunted with the pain of his ankle as he jarred it trying to catch Daniel. He let out a bellow that had Martha crying into her bowl of milk and bread offcuts, so Edith snatched her up and carried Martha and her milk and slops out into the backyard to get away from him. Let her mother deal with her moody husband.

"Did you enjoy going to school then, Danny boy?" Edith asked as she started to sort the pile of washing that was in the basket next to the boiler.

"Yeah, I really did." Daniel confessed. "The teacher is really nice and the classroom is so warm! I'll tell you all about it when we go to bed tonight, if you're not too tired."

"I'll make sure I'm not, precious. Thank God for small mercies but I reckon this schooling will be the making of you."

Daniel kept his promise and, when they had gone to bed in the icy, tiny bedroom that night, he gave his mother a full description of his classroom and the lessons he had done the day before. Edith was exhausted with the work she had done that day, but she wanted to listen to her son as he described his school experiences and she forced herself to stay awake, remembering the few days when she had attended school herself. Her school career had been very short but she could remember the warmth and the happiness she had felt while she was there and she looked back on it with nostalgia.

But describing his first day at school wasn't the only subject that Daniel wanted to raise with his Mam that night. There was another subject which had been on his mind a lot over the last few months and, while he had his mother's attention, he wanted to ask some questions.

"Mam, why don't I have a dad like the other kids? I heard them talking about their mams and dads when we were in the playground and they all seem to have both. One of the lads asked me what my dad did and he seemed surprised when I said I didn't have a dad. He said that all kids have dads, otherwise we wouldn't be here. So where's my dad?"

Edith shrivelled inside because this was the one question she had dreaded coming from his lips. She had known that he would, eventually, need to find out about his father, but she had hoped that it wouldn't be for a few years yet. She also knew that her boy was as bright as a button and would be bound to question everything in his life, but she didn't have an answer for him.

"Your Dad was the best thing that ever happened to me but he died before you were born." Edith spoke very quietly so that her parents wouldn't be able to hear her from their bedroom. The walls in the house were as thin as paper and sound travelled well in the silence of the night. "He was a tall, handsome man who wanted to protect me and look after me for the rest of his life but, unfortunately, that didn't happen. Now, go to sleep cos you'll need to be well-rested for school tomorrow."

Daniel snuggled further down into the bed and then rested his face against his mother's shoulder.

"What was his name, Mam?" he whispered before he fell asleep.

"His name was Daniel, just like you and I loved him as much as I love you."

Daniel was happy and proud to bear the name of the man who had treated his mother so well and it was only as his eyes closed in sleep that he thought of Martha. If his dad had died before he was born, then who was Martha's dad?

Chapter Three

Daniel didn't ask his Mam who Martha's dad was. He felt he had got more answers than ever before to his questions and at least he now knew his father's name. In Daniel's mind, this older Daniel took on something of a hero figure, murdered by some villain before he could arrive in York Street on his white horse, ready to rescue his beloved princess and his namesake and son, Daniel. This romantic picture grew in his mind because he didn't get any more details from Edith about his birth and he had to have some details to fill the void. He knew that mentioning his father to his grandparents would be a waste of time, so he hugged his picture of his Dad to his chest and embroidered it ever more, every time he thought about him. Edith didn't realise that her son had such a breadth of imagination, although she knew that his intelligence already far-outstripped hers because she would have been deaf and blind not to have noticed, but she didn't know that he held such a romantic view of his father.

Granny Lillian continued to allow Daniel to attend school, impatient as she was for them to be self-sufficient in their dealings with anyone in authority and his thirst for knowledge while he was there continued to amaze his teacher. Miss Swift had come to the conclusion that this little bundle of rags and dirt was the most intelligent child she had ever had the pleasure to teach and she began to give him extra lessons at lunchtime, so that he could catch up with the rest of the class. It was only a matter of months before this aim was realised and then Daniel began to outstrip every single one of his classmates. This didn't make him very popular with the other children, but as he didn't mix with any of them outside school and always had his head down in a book whilst in school, Daniel wasn't really aware of what his peers thought of him. If he had known, he wouldn't have cared because he knew that he was different from all of them and that none of them would ever figure largely in his life. He was still only interested in his own small family and that didn't include his grandparents.

Despite his concentration on his schooling, Daniel was aware of the changing circumstances in his home. Grandad was as belligerent as ever with his daughter but he no longer wasted any time in disagreeing with his wife. Her attitude to her husband had changed since he had been charged with illegal gambling and it was only inflamed by the fine he received when he attended court for his sentence. It had cost them the equivalent of two weeks wages for a steel worker and was a large enough sum for it to have consequences to the family budget. Grandad Joshua had been disgusted to realise that he had to do without any meat meals for two weeks after his sentencing and that he no longer received any pocket money to pay for his visits to the local hostelry. When he had tried to argue with his wife about this, she had brushed his comments aside and told him that things were going to be very different in their household for the foreseeable future. He took this to mean that she was going to spend his money on their daughter and grandchildren and he began to take an equal amount of pay out of their backs by walloping them with his walking stick for any imagined slight or back-sliding. It was only a matter of time before he turned his attention to Martha, whom he had mostly ignored since the night she had been born.

Daniel came home from school one Friday afternoon to find both his mother and his sister bruised and battered and standing in the autumn rain in the backyard. His mind had been full of the story his teacher was reading to the class about King Arthur and the

Knights of the Holy Grail. His father had taken on the persona of Arthur in Daniel's mind and Daniel was in the middle of imagining a scenario where one of his father's knights came to the laundry to rescue the little family when he walked into the back yard and found Edith and Martha in tears with Edith attempting to clean the blood off Martha's face where Joshua had split the tender skin. Daniel was brought up short by the sight of his sister's pale face covered in blood as she stood in front of the wall with Daniel's brick marks on it.

Granny Lillian had gone to do some shopping but his mother told him that Grandad was in the kitchen and wouldn't let them into the house. Daniel, who had just turned ten the week before, drew himself up to his greatest height and barrelled his way through the back door, intent on retribution for this latest display of temper from his grandfather. Edith and Martha followed him through the door as quickly as they could; Edith because she was convinced that Daniel would be floored by one almighty blow from her father and desperate to stop him from killing his grandson and Martha because, unlike her mother, she had inherited some of her grandfather's belligerent personality and wanted the price of her blood out of her grandfather's skin.

When Daniel entered the kitchen, Grandad Joshua was in his chair next to the range, calmly eating a piece of the pie which Granny Lillian had made for their tea for that day. He knew that his portions of food had been reduced since his sentencing and he was trying to rectify this imbalance while his wife was out. He looked up guiltily as Daniel pushed the kitchen door wide open, thinking it was his wife returning from her shopping trip, having already put out of his mind the fact that he had drawn blood from his granddaughter's face. He wasn't prepared for the whirling dervish which entered the kitchen, howling his hatred of his grandfather and wanting payment in kind for what he had done to his sister.

Daniel picked up Grandad's walking stick from its place next to the range and crossed the kitchen in two strides with the stick held aloft above his head. When he reached Joshua, he brought the stick down with all the force that he could muster onto Joshua's forehead, which knocked what little sense the man possessed totally out of his head and the bully folded onto the floor. Daniel, unaware that he had knocked Joshua out, continued to hit his Grandad's head as he lay defenceless on the floor and only stopped when his Granny Lillian, who had returned from the shops to discover her grandson trying to murder his Grandad in the kitchen, snatched the stick from his upraised arm and pushed the boy into the chair which stood on the other side of the range.

Granny Lillian was short-tempered at the best of times and that day wasn't the best of times for her but it was her husband she was angry with, not Daniel. Despite having entered the kitchen in time to see Joshua being beaten about the head by his grandson, it wasn't Daniel who attracted her ire. She had taken in the scene with one glance, noting the blood on Martha's face and the tears on Edith's face and had jumped to the only solution possible; that Joshua had been laying the law down yet again but had, this time, come off the worst. She was a strong woman whose muscles had been built up by years of lugging wet washing around the back yard and had no problem in lifting Joshua off the floor by the scruff of his neck and dumping him into his usual chair next to the range before she turned to ask Edith what had been going on.

Between sobs, Edith managed to explain that Martha had dropped her side of a heavy washing basket and some of the clothing had been dragged across the yard floor. Joshua had lost his temper with the little mite and had slapped her across her face, making her nose bleed. Daniel had come home from school in time to see the blood and had gone for Joshua in a fit of temper at what Joshua had done to his sister. Grandad Joshua regained his wits as Edith was explaining this and he tried to butt in but Granny Lillian was having none of it.

"Keep your mouth shut." Lillian snarled at Joshua. "You've cost me too much money recently for you to have any say in this. Boy, what made you go for your grandad like that?"

"He'd hurt our Martha and she's too little to be picked on by him." Daniel replied, for once in his life standing up to the grandparents who had made his and his mother's lives a misery for years. "He's a bully and the only way to beat a bully is to give him what he gives you."

Edith was terrified that her mother would turn on Daniel now but, at the same time, she was proud of her son for trying to protect his sister and for not backing down when his grandmother challenged him. She knew, even though she was ashamed of herself for it, that she had never found the strength to stand up to either of her parents and that there had been times when she should have done. Her pride and her fear warred within her and she prayed for the argument to end, even though she couldn't think of a way that it could end happily for her and her children. But she hadn't allowed for the sea-change which her mother had experienced over the last few months and she was amazed to hear what Lillian had to say next.

"You are right, lad. He is a bully." Granny admitted. "But I don't want you following his example and thinking that shouting and lashing out is the answer to any argument. I'll do any of the beating that he needs in future, so you keep out of it, right?"

Daniel was surprised that he wasn't going to be punished for attacking his Grandad but was happy to be allowed to get away with turning on him. He filed Granny Lillian's change in attitude towards Joshua away in his mind, to be dwelt on at his leisure. He was sure that Granny had her reasons for abandoning their previous joint hatred for their daughter and grandchildren and he thought that he knew what those reasons were, but he needed to work through it in his mind before he decided that he was right. For the moment, he was happy to accept that there were changes afoot in the household and he resolved to wait and see if he was correct.

Edith and the children retreated to the yard and continued with the work which was waiting for them. Edith took a customer's shirt and wet it at the pump in the yard before wiping the blood away from Martha's face, even though Martha squeaked with the pain when she rubbed at her nose.

"Nasty man." Martha declared when Edith had finished cleaning her up. "Nasty and stinky."

"Shush now. You'll get us all into trouble if you say things like that." Edith scolded her gently.

"Don't care. Nasty man." Martha repeated. "Daniel smacked him."

Edith was about to scold her again when she noticed the grin which had spread across Martha's face and she couldn't help joining in with the merriment of the memory of seeing Daniel whacking Joshua with the stick which Joshua had used so often on the three of them. Daniel giggled too and soon, all three of them were laughing as they filled the copper with the washing and then began the arduous task of scrubbing the clothing clean. Their hands were red-raw from the hard soap but the atmosphere was so different from what they had all been used to that they ignored their hurts and enjoyed re-living the moment in their heads. It was this mood of merriment which Miss Swift came upon as she knocked at the yard gate.

Having being rebuffed when she had knocked on the front door the last time she had called, Miss Swift had resolved to try the only other entrance to the house, which was by way of the back yard. She had steeled herself for another meeting with Joshua Coleman and was surprised to find that he didn't answer the yard door when she knocked. After a couple of minutes of delay, Miss Swift was readying herself to knock again when the door slowly opened and Edith peeped out. Never in her life before had anyone knocked on the back yard door and she had debated about answering it. In reality, she was afraid that whichever course of action she took, be it to answer the door or not, she would be wrong and bring her mother's ire down on her head again but, as the day had already been unusual, she decided to go with it and she opened the yard door. She didn't recognise the woman who stood there and was about to close the door in the woman's face, when Daniel pushed past her.

"Miss Swift, what are you doing here?" Daniel asked and Edith realised that this was Daniel's teacher. She was horrified that this genteel young lady should have arrived at their house when Joshua and Lillian were having a loud argument in the kitchen and both Daniel and Martha were wet and dirty and obviously working in the back yard. She wished with all her might that she hadn't opened the door but she had been aware that it could have been a new customer who was knocking and she couldn't turn custom away. But while Edith dithered over what to do, Daniel had taken charge of the visitor and opened the door wide to let her into the back yard. There was nothing that Edith could do short of pushing the woman out of the yard and she knew she couldn't embarrass Daniel in such a way.

Miss Swift was well-aware of Edith's thoughts and she hastened to reassure her that she hadn't come visiting to judge their lives or their lifestyle.

"I wondered if I could have a word with you about Daniel's schoolwork." Miss Swift said, doing her best to avoid looking around the yard or listening to the noisy argument emanating from the kitchen. "I don't know if he's told you but he's doing very well at school and I would like him to be able to attend school until he is at twelve years of age. That will give him another four years of schooling which I am sure would stand him in good stead for the rest of his life."

Miss Swift's conversation with Edith came to an abrupt ending when the argument in the kitchen ceased when Joshua realised that Miss Swift was inside their back yard and talking to Edith. He pointed through the window to show his wife that they had a visitor and then he erupted out of the kitchen door to demand why she was there. Edith and Daniel were appalled at the aggressive stance which Joshua took but he was roughly pushed to one side when Granny Lillian made her presence felt.

"I'm glad to hear that Daniel is doing well at school but there is no need for you to call on us." Granny said, when she had reasserted her dominance over the whole family. "Daniel is at school to learn to read and write so that he can carry on the family business when we are no longer able to work. There is no need to discuss his progress or anything else, unless you are here to inform us that he isn't paying attention when I shall take what measures I deem necessary to change his attitude. Thank you for calling."

Granny Lillian opened the yard door and stood holding it open so that Miss Swift had no option but to say goodbye and leave, although she bestowed a smile of such sweetness on Daniel that he blushed to his toes with the warmth of it. Granny closed the door very quietly after Miss Swift had stepped over the threshold and turned to look at her family. In reality, she was listening hard to see if she could hear Miss Swift's footsteps as she walked away from their house. When she was sure that the teacher had left the street she curtly told them all to get back to work.

"Hang on." Grandad Joshua was still feeling belligerent as well as having a headache from being hit over the head by his own walking stick. "I'm not finished with that young man yet. He hit me and yet no-one seems to be offering to give him his proper punishment. There'll be no more work done in this yard until I see him being punished."

"Stop your mithering tongue, man." Granny was very short with her husband. "He hit you because you had hurt his sister, so you deserved what you got. You're such a big man, hitting a little girl but you can't cope with a boy of eight. Stop your whinging and get some work done, otherwise you won't be getting any tea."

Granny turned to walk back into the kitchen but some devil had entered Daniel's soul and he couldn't stop himself from telling Granny what else his grandad had done that afternoon.

"If our tea is the meat pie you made yesterday, then none of us is getting any. Grandad was eating it when I came home from school, while you were at the shops."

Granny Lilian was furious at her husband's greed, especially as she had been anticipating eating that meat pie herself and she turned on her husband like an avenging fury. She lashed out with the nearest weapon which came to hand, which happened to be the washboard she had leant against the house wall in order for it to drain. It was a heavy object and the blow caught him under his chin, jerking his head up and knocking it against the kitchen wall. For the second time that afternoon, Joshua saw stars and blackness before his head stopped spinning and the bluster went out of him as he slid down the wall and landed with a crunch on the yard floor. The blow had opened his lip and he wiped the blood away with one hand before he used the bloody hand to point at his wife.

"You think you rule the roost round here but you couldn't be more wrong." Joshua's voice was low and laden with poison as he glared at Lillian. Anyone else would have been terrified at the level of rage and hatred emanating from the older man but Granny Lillian was made of stronger stuff than that.

"Shut your moaning mouth." Granny hissed at Joshua. "You'll need to save your strength cos you won't be getting any tea tonight. I hope you enjoyed that pie because it's going to have to last you until tomorrow. Isn't it lucky that I made two of them so the rest of us will eat well tonight while you go hungry? Change your attitude, man, or you will learn what it's like to go without food for longer than one meal."

With that threat, Granny went back into the kitchen and slammed the door shut behind her. Edith and the children carried on with the jobs that they were doing although both children had smiles on their faces until Edith whispered to them to stop smiling in case Grandad lifted his hand to them again for laughing at him. That sobered the pair of them so they went about their work in silence and with straight faces although Daniel was still the happiest he had been in that yard. He hugged to his chest the thought of Miss Swift's smile and the sight of his Granny hitting his Grandad with the washboard. It had been one very strange day but it had certainly had its compensations.

Miss Swift moved quickly, as her name implied, but she could also move very quietly as well. She had noticed a gap in the boards of the yard door and had looked through this before she had knocked on the door. She had seen the two children as they helped their mother with the heavy washing and she had heard the tremendous argument coming from the kitchen. When Lillian Coleman had invited her to leave, she had stepped outside and then trotted away from the house to make sure she could be heard from the yard. What Lillian hadn't heard was the very quiet steps which had brought Miss Swift back to the yard wall where she had listened to the rest of the conversation between Granny and Grandad Joshua. It was only when Granny went back into the kitchen after hitting Grandad with the washboard that Miss Swift had, very quietly, moved away from the wall and walked out of the end of the street.

She took with her the picture of the two children working like slaves in the yard and the memory of the bile and hatred which constituted the older Colemans' relationship. She knew that some of the families in that area were very poor but she had never before come across a family which was so full of loathing and aversion amongst its members. She was shocked to the core but at the same time she couldn't help but admire the little boy who was growing like a rose on that particular dung-heap.

Chapter Four

Life became more difficult for Joshua Coleman from then on. Lillian never forgave him for wasting money on gambling and strong drink and she fought a running war with his greed, particularly when it involved stealing food which had been prepared for the whole family. At the same time as her hatred of her husband grew, her treatment of Edith and the two little ones altered perceptively and life, as a consequence, became a lot better for the three of them. Lillian needed an ally once she had alienated her husband and the only other adult was Edith. For her part, Edith had always been too weak-willed to stand up to any adult and she welcomed her mother's change of heart with open arms. Martha was still too young to be able to understand any of these relationship changes but had inherited enough of her grandparents' greed and strong will to make sure that she suffered as little as possible. Daniel, however, was old enough and clever enough to be able to see what was going on within the family and was irritated by his mother's ready acceptance of Granny Lillian's softer attitude towards the three of them, knowing that it was for Granny Lillian's own ends and not meant to improve life for her daughter and her children. Although he didn't say anything about these changes, he watched and absorbed every detail and marked every change down on a mental scoreboard which he transferred to paper when he had the time. Secure in the knowledge that no-one else in the house could read what he'd written, he didn't hold back with his conclusions.

Grandad Joshua knew that he had crossed a line with his wife the night of the new King's Coronation but he had no idea how to put his mistake right. Every time he tried to talk to her, she wouldn't listen to him or she made some sarcastic comment in reply to his opening gambit which, more often than not, irritated him immensely and he wasn't able to hide it. He wasn't feeling genuine remorse; he just preferred it when it was his daughter and grandchildren who were the hated ones in the family and he couldn't cope with being the butt of everyone's jokes (or nastiness). His attitudes throughout the whole of his life had always been driven by his own selfish ends and he was incapable of putting anyone else before himself. His wife, who was remarkably similar in nature to her husband, had decided that he was a liability rather an asset to the laundry and the family and she couldn't have cared less if he had disappeared in a puff of smoke. In fact, there were times when she wished that he would just disappear in a puff of smoke and make his way down to the hell that was waiting for him.

It wasn't only the mistake that Joshua had made which coloured Lillian's view of her family. Recently, she had been feeling rather under-the-weather and knew, deep within, that it was an advance warning that all was not how it should be with her. She didn't tell anyone about it because she wasn't the sort of person who dwells on every ache and pain but she knew that she had to heed the warning and make arrangements for running the laundry when she was no longer able to do so herself. She envisaged a time when she would be able to sit and watch the others work and have her meals made for her every day. She was realistic enough to know that Joshua would never spend any time caring for his wife if she were ill, so she easily transferred her attentions from her husband to her daughter and grandchildren. It didn't cross her mind that her relatives may not want to care for her, even if her attitude towards them had softened in recent months. She was convinced that she only had to demand and Edith and the children would obey.

Lillian's plan could have worked if Daniel and Martha had been made of the same stuff as their mother, but that wasn't the case. Martha was more like her grandfather than her mother and Daniel, with his intelligence and his quick mind, had spent all his short life hating his grandparents for the way they treated his mother. Lillian's plan was based on inaccuracies and wishful thinking and was doomed to fail from the outset.

For the next few months, life in the laundry on York Street moved on much as usual. The only change at first was Joshua's behaviour and that was usually as a result of him either missing a meal or being served a smaller portion than the other adults in the house when Lillian didn't think he'd worked hard enough to deserve more. Because he knew he was wasting his time by bringing his problem to his wife's notice, he reacted by taking his temper out on his daughter. He left Daniel alone now, ever since Daniel had whacked him with his own walking stick but he had no qualms about hitting Edith. She did her best to keep out of his way whenever she knew that he was on the warpath but, like other bad-tempered people, it wasn't always easy to predict when his temper would boil over and she made many mistakes in her judgement of his mood.

The back yard as a place of work was small, although there was ample room for the copper, the poss tub and the mangle and even the open-sided shed which ran along one of the walls, but it was too small to avoid anyone else who was working there. So on days when Joshua was looking for any excuse, whether real or imagined, to hit Edith, she was always within range. He didn't swipe at her when Daniel was around but he still looked on Martha as a baby and often forgot that she was perfectly capable of informing her brother if Joshua had hurt their mother while Daniel was at school. Martha, who had hated her Grandad since he had made her nose bleed and carried that hatred undiluted into every day, was happy to tell tales when Daniel came home from school and Daniel found many ways of taking his mother's pain out of Joshua's hide. Daniel didn't lash out at his Grandad because he knew that the older man was still capable of hurting him if he ever managed to catch hold of him but he had other little ways in which to inflict punishment on him. He was a past master at gathering dirt from between the flagstones in the back alleys and the streets and concealing it in his trouser pockets. If Grandad had hurt Edith during the day, Daniel would scatter this dirt onto Grandad's plate or into his tea cup, making sure that Lillian and Joshua didn't see him doing it but that Martha and Edith did. Edith tried to stop him but she hated her father so much it wasn't long before she gave in and enjoyed the spectacle as much as Martha.

Daniel also wasn't above gathering some of the urine from the nightsoil bucket into the empty laudanum bottle which Granny Lillian thought she had thrown out when she had emptied the last few drops from the bottle into Grandad's tea. Daniel had retrieved it, along with its stopper and kept it permanently to hand, also in his trouser pocket. As his trousers were never washed, it was unlikely that anyone else would find it and throw it away. On days when Daniel had got some urine in his little bottle, he would empty it into Grandad's tea and watch in squirming delight as Joshua drank it. Twice, Grandad had been sick during the night after this prank, but Daniel considered it a just punishment for him. Daniel didn't let anyone see him emptying urine into Grandad's tea because he knew that his mother wouldn't overlook that act and he didn't want to upset her.

Daniel found many other ways of exacting retribution from Joshua, usually without the man knowing that he had been punished but Martha outdid everybody in her way of dealing with her Grandad. He had committed an unforgivable sin in Martha's eyes, the day that he had slapped her face and made her nose bleed. She had been extremely shocked, both by the pain of the slap and by the sight of her own blood dripping down her face and onto her dress and her anger at what her grandfather had done to her had boiled white-hot. Even though she forgot what had happened to her as she grew older, she never forgot her hatred of her grandfather and this hatred never boiled at any other temperature than white-hot in her veins.

One day during that winter, when Martha was cold because of the weather and because of the fact that she was soaking wet from trying to carry the wet washing from the tub to the mangle, she showed them all how hot-tempered she could be. It was a Saturday, so Daniel wasn't at school and was doing his best to take the heavy lifting away from his mother and his sister. Grandad, who had stolen money from his wife's purse the day before and had spent the evening in the local hostelry, had woken late with a stinking headache. He had missed the milksops which his wife had put out for his breakfast and had had his knuckles rapped when he had tried to make himself a sandwich which had made his bad mood even worse. The weather was cold and sleety and his job for that day was to hang the clean washing over the wooden slats which hung in the roof of the open-sided shed. The wind was making this task difficult in that it kept blowing the wet washing into his face as he moved around the shed and this, with the knowledge that the washing wouldn't dry because the sleet was getting into the shed through the open side so making the task a waste of time, made Joshua's irritation ever greater until, finally, he boiled over.

Martha had crept into the minor shelter of the shed to try and escape from the sleet which was making her hands, already sore from the detergent, sting with the cold. She had recently had her fourth birthday and was very small for her age and could easily hide amongst the drying racks in the shed. Unfortunately, Joshua had his head tipped back so that he could see the racks in the roof and didn't see that Martha was behind him. He stepped backwards and fell over the child's slight form. He grabbed the washing hanging nearest to him to stop himself from falling but the racks couldn't take the heavy pull that he put on them and the fixings came away from the ceiling. Three rows of racks dropped from the roof and spread the washing out of the open side of the shed and across the yard's dirty floor.

Martha had rolled herself into a ball and managed to get away from Joshua, so she wasn't hurt by his fall but Joshua had landed on the brick surround of the copper boiler's base and was sure that he had broken his shoulder. He screamed in agony, bringing Lillian out of the kitchen and Jack Davis from next door. Mr Davis laid Joshua flat on the ground, ignoring the mess of ash and water and soap suds and then tested Joshua's shoulder. He could tell that Joshua's shoulder had slipped out of its joint and was aware of how much pain the man would be in. Without telling Joshua what he was going to do, Mr Davis rolled Joshua onto his front, put his own knee behind Joshua's shoulder and gave it a massive yank backwards, which neatly slotted the shoulder back into its proper position in relation to the rest of Joshua's bones but making Joshua scream in agony as the shoulder made its rapid journey to its proper place.

Joshua's language should only have been heard down the docks but he continued to swear and cuss and scream until Lillian came to stand next to him.

"Get up you moaning moron." Lillian said without any heat in her voice. "Thanks for putting him to rights Mr Davis. That would have cost a pretty penny if we'd have had to call for the doctor."

"No problem." Mr Davis brushed his wet trousers where he had knelt on the ground and then wiped his hands on one of the sheets which was half hanging up to dry amongst the wreckage of the drying racks. "He'll be fine now. A bit sore I would imagine but he's a strong man and will soon recover from the pain. I reckon a few drops of laudanum will soon put him right. It'll give him time to get over the shock, anyway."

"Yes, I'll nip and get some from the shop." Lillian answered. "I used the last we had when he banged his head a few months back. Could you give me a hand to get him into the kitchen?"

Mr Davis virtually carried Joshua into the kitchen and then left hurriedly, before Lillian could think of anything else that he could do. Lillian gave Edith some curt orders to retrieve the now-dirty washing, fix the drying racks back on the ceiling and get the washing back into the poss tub, while she went to get some more laudanum. They all trooped out of the kitchen, leaving Joshua sitting in his usual chair next to the range. It was warm and dry in the kitchen and Joshua took the opportunity while he was alone to filch some of the bread which was on the kitchen table, smother it in butter and top it with a large dollop of jam from the jar in the pantry. His pain had subsided immediately when Mr Davis had returned the joint to its proper place and the only pain Joshua still had was his hangover from the night before and a bruise which was now appearing on his arm. What he did have, however, was a great deal of bottled-up anger over Martha's presence in the shed when she should have been outside in the yard, doing her fair share of the work. In his mind, the fault for all of it rested on the child and she should be punished for what she had done. He didn't make the connection between this thought and his own insecurity now that he was no longer part of Lillian's team, although he knew that no-one else had made the same connections he had because Lillian hadn't punished Martha for hiding in the shed. Joshua decided it was up to him put this right and he stepped out into the yard, the glower on his face enough to warn Edith that he was once again on the warpath.

Martha was doing her best to put the washing through the mangle, even though she had to stand on a box in order to be able to reach the handle to turn it. Edith was at the poss tub, beating the ash and the dirt out of the sheets which had already been washed once that day and Daniel was putting logs into the boiler fire to heat yet more water. Nobody noticed him as he crossed the yard, making a bee-line for Martha where she was wobbling on her box. When he reached the mangle, he lifted his hand and brought it down on the child's legs so that they were swept out from under her and she fell sideways onto the ground. She started to cry with the shock and the hurt but, when she turned her head to see who it was who had knocked her off her box and she saw Joshua, her anger flashed and she grabbed his leg to stop him walking away. Joshua looked down at the little mite and then grabbed her by her jumper and lifted her off the floor until she was level with his face.

"That'll teach you to hide, thinking you won't have to do any work." Joshua growled, with his face inches away from Martha's, expecting to frighten her even more by being so close to her. He hadn't allowed for the fact that Martha was as belligerent as he was and that, unknown to him, she hated him with a passion. Being held by her jumper on a level with Joshua's face, Martha couldn't kick out at him with any force or use her hands to hit him, so she did the only thing she could think of to hurt him as much as he had hurt and shocked her, she bit him. The only part of him that she could reach while she was being held in mid-air was his face, so she calmly fastened her teeth round his large nose (the nearest part of his face to her) and bit down as hard as she could. Her little teeth, although only small, were as sharp as a razor and she could immediately taste Joshua's blood as her teeth broke through his skin. Joshua yelped with the shock of this unexpected assault and dropped Martha immediately. She landed awkwardly on the ground but, as soon as she had got to her feet, she turned and began kicking the nearest of Joshua's shins. She was only small but she was so angry with this brute of a man that she kept on kicking him until she was grabbed once more and Edith pulled her away from Joshua.

Joshua was bellowing with rage at his feisty granddaughter and hadn't realised that Lillian had come through the back yard gate and was watching him as he struggled to reach Martha to wallop her as hard as he could. His face was purple with anger and there was a roaring sound in his ears which drowned out any other noise in the yard so he didn't notice that Lillian was back until she walloped him across the back of his head with the washboard and he measured his length on the yard floor once again. He rolled over to glare at Lillian, his ire inflamed by the blood from his nose which was now running into his eyes and his mouth, but Lillian stepped forward and clouted him once again with the washboard to shut him up. His brain reeled from the onslaught and he tried to roll away from her in order to regain his feet. Lillian put one hand on the shoulder he had hurt when he fell and almost whispered into his ear.

"Stop your mouth now or we'll have Mr High and Mighty Davis back in here in a second. I saw what you did to the lass and you only got what you deserved when she bit you. It seems you can't even pick on the littlest person in this family. Now, stop wasting time, clean your nose and get on with washing those sheets again. I want them finished before dinnertime so that they can dry in the kitchen overnight tonight. We don't get paid until we deliver them washed, dried and ironed."

Lillian walked away from Joshua, leaving him to get to his feet on his own. Edith, Martha and Daniel ignored him as he grunted and huffed and puffed, making a dramatic performance out of standing up. Eventually, he wiped his face with the tail end of someone's shirt and then moved to help Edith as she began lifting the heavy sheets out of the tub. Immediately he joined her, Edith moved over to the mangle and helped Martha turn the handle to squeeze the bulk of the water out of the washing. She then caught it as it moved through the mangle and directed it into the washing basket which was waiting for it. Nobody spoke to Joshua; nobody went near Joshua and nobody helped Joshua. By the time Lillian called them all in for a quick sandwich at lunchtime, Joshua had decided that he needed to regain control of his family before he found himself out on the street. Unfortunately, he had none of his grandson's intelligence and couldn't think of a way to reassert control, which only served to make him even more bad-tempered.

When the day's work was over, the family moved back into the kitchen to eat their evening meal. It was eaten in silence because Joshua was sulking, Lillian was doing her best to ignore the pain in her chest which had been making itself felt much more often recently and Edith and the children knew that their best course of action was to not draw attention to themselves. Daniel, who had watched the day's events with a very critical eye, watched his granny closely during the meal because he could tell that there was something wrong with her, over and above her usual temper. He noted that the bottle of laudanum was back in her pinny pocket and that she put a couple of drops in her cup of tea when she thought no-one was looking. She didn't offer any of it to Joshua and he didn't ask for any. Daniel mulled over what this secret laudanum-taking was for, making a list in his head of the possible reasons why his Granny should need to take it. Whatever the reason, he didn't think that it boded well for him and his mother and sister.

Chapter Five

Granny Lillian continued to have the odd pains in her chest but they weren't permanent and weeks often passed between one bout of pain and the next. Daniel had watched her when she took the laudanum in order to relieve this pain and he knew that she now kept a stock of it, hidden in the pantry behind the large dish which was used for making bread. No-one else in the household made bread apart from Granny Lillian so she wouldn't expect anyone else to move the large bowl and find her secret stash. Daniel stored this piece of information away because it meant he could have access to the laudanum without having to steal it from Granny Lillian's pinny pocket.

Over the next few weeks, the weather turned ever colder as winter settled on the town and life became harder again for everyone. At the laundry, drying the washing was the major bugbear because it meant that it had to be hung on the racks in the kitchen to dry overnight with the heat from the fire. Consequently, the fire used up more coal than normal which added extra cost to the laundry procedure but Lillian knew that she couldn't charge her customers anymore because they would simply go elsewhere. So the business had to absorb the extra costs which meant that Lillian took the extra out of the housekeeping budget and Joshua's favourite meals were the first ones to be abandoned in favour of cheaper alternatives. Edith and the children were now being better fed than they had ever been, simply because Lillian was aware that she would get more work out of them if they were well-fed than if they were half-starved but as Joshua wasn't pulling his weight, then his share was dramatically reduced.

Joshua wasn't slow in realising that he was getting the thin end of the wedge and he made it his business to mentally compare the sizes of every meal served at the kitchen table, with a view to making up the difference by stealing food from the pantry when there was no-one else about. This may have worked if Lillian had been a sloppy housewife but that was the last thing that she was. All food ingredients were weighed and measured for every meal and Lillian never bought even an ounce more of anything if it wasn't needed. Butter, lard and cheese came into the house wrapped in a greaseproof paper package which never weighed more than four ounces and often weighed only half that. Tea came in a paper bag, two ounces at a time while flour (to make bread and pies) came in a sack weighing three pounds. Lillian marked the level of every container, packet, jar and bottle every time that she used it, so the opportunities for theft were remarkably few and easily noticed. Joshua was on a hiding to nothing and, deep-down, he knew it. He was never going to be given the amount of food that he wanted and he was alternately angry and depressed about it because he couldn't think of a way to get round all of the stops which Lillian put in his way.

Joshua had never been the kind of man to let things fester in his mind. If a situation displeased him, he lashed out at the person he thought was causing his problem which, in the past, had always settled any argument in his favour. Now, he ruminated on every slight he received, whether real or imagined, and this, eventually, totally changed his character. He brooded on his woes every minute of his day, noting every time that he came off worse in comparison to other members of the family and his deep-seated anger grew until it filled his whole being. He could chew on it; he could feel it as it fought with his empty belly; he could taste it as it made every mouthful bitter and he could smell it as the dirt which was encrusted on his skin grew because Lillian would no longer fill the bath with hot water and give him any soap to use in it. He could have given the whole matter some thought and then decided that he needed to change his attitude and be prepared to work for his keep like the rest of the world but he was basically a lazy, indolent man with a chip on his shoulder as big as the church on Normanby Road and he wasn't going to change for anything or anyone.

Over that winter and as they moved into the new year of 1907, the weather continued cold, wet and windy. It didn't snow, it didn't freeze, it was just always raining and the wind came galloping over the Russian steppes or down from the Arctic wastes, bringing a bone-chilling cold with it that was a typical 'lazy' wind - it couldn't be bothered to work its way round a person - it just blew straight through each and every person who put a nose out of doors. The coal consumption at the laundry in York Street had reached its greatest height ever and then, when the little business was beginning to struggle, a new laundry opened on Middlesbrough Road. It was owned and run by a family who already had a laundry in Middlesbrough and they were quick, efficient and had the newest equipment. It was also cheaper than the laundry in York Street and nearest to the largest population in the town. The fact that it was also on one of the busiest retail streets, so it picked up any passing custom, made it odds on to be very successful.

Lillian nearly gave up the day that their biggest customer, the landlord from the Station Hotel which had letting bedrooms and so used a large number of sheets and towels which constantly needed washing, called round to say that he had decided to take his custom from them and place it with the new laundry. He was perfectly polite but he pointed out that he had received a few sheets which hadn't been properly dried in recent months and that some of the creases in them hadn't come from an iron but from the washing and drying procedure. He had standards to keep, he said, which the bedding received from Granny Lillian fell way below, so he was going to try the new laundry. Granny Lillian would understand, the landlord thought, because she had been in business long enough to know that standards had to be high in every business these days.

This meeting with the landlord form the Station Hotel depressed and angered Lillian. She was depressed because she could see that this could be the start of her own business going down the pan and angry because, whatever else she was, she had her own standards as far as her work was concerned and she had always considered them to be superior to anyone else's. To hear that the new laundry was better (and cheaper) than she was, frightened and angered her, but she didn't know what she could do to improve the reputation of her little business. But she had to think of something and quickly, before their situation became so dire that nothing could be done and they lost the laundry and the house and all ended up in the workhouse.

Daniel had listened without interrupting to Granny Lillian's conversation with the landlord and had come to the same conclusions that Lillian had reached: that their business was in danger of collapsing, but where Lillian was unable to think of a rescue plan, Daniel had some ideas of his own which he had been considering over the last few months. He knew that Granny Lillian was worried about the business but he wasn't sure if she would be open to taking on some changes, especially changes suggested by an eight-year-old boy. He considered discussing the problems with his mother and instructing her to pass on his recommendations but he brushed that idea aside virtually as soon as he had thought of it. Edith was even more depressed than she had been over the last year and Daniel didn't think that she was capable of lifting her own mood in order to sound enthusiastic about anything connected to the laundry. She considered the laundry to be a source of hard work and punishment and nothing else. She couldn't see a time when she would be running it without her parents and able to gain a good living from it, but Daniel could. He might only be thirteen, but he had an adult head on his shoulders which was perfectly capable of looking at numerous angles of any subject and deciding which course of action would be the best. Miss Swift had remarked on his cognitive ability only the week before, amazed that he had understood the problems the Romans had undergone when they were losing their Empire and retreating from Britain.

Daniel decided he would take Granny Lillian to one side and try to encourage her with his thoughts on how they could improve their laundry's business and therefore turnover. Daniel waited until an early evening when Joshua had been sent with a large load of laundry to one of the other public houses in the town. Lillian had decided that he should be the one to deliver the load for a number of reasons, the main one being that she was too tired to go out again that day but there was also the fact that it was a very heavy load which neither Edith nor Daniel would have been able to carry and she worried that they would drop it on the wet ground and ruin the work that they had done on it. She wasn't happy about Joshua going to a pub to deliver a load and be paid for it, but she thought that she had put the fear of God into him with her warnings of what would happen to him if he dared to touch a penny of the payment, so she hoped that he wouldn't be tempted to spend any of the payment on ale and gambling.

Daniel sidled over to Granny Lillian where she was sitting in her chair next to the range and put his hand on her arm to get her attention. She had been sitting staring into space, worrying about the business and if Joshua would return home minus the money he was supposed to collect, when Daniel touched her. She looked him up and down as a way of discouraging him from chattering to her, but he was used to that sort of treatment and wasn't that easily cowed.

"I've got some ideas about the laundry." Daniel declared, not wasting his breath on any niceties of conversation before he got to his point. "I understood what that man said when he called to see you today. He doesn't want us to do his bedding and towels anymore, so we'll lose money and you're worried that more of our customers will move to the new laundry."

Lillian was taken aback by Daniel's grasp of the details of their problems and was unable to answer him until she recovered from the shock of hearing these words coming from a little boy. Joshua didn't realise how deep a mire they were in but Daniel seemed to have his finger right on the pulse. She decided to listen to his 'ideas' before she pushed him away.

Daniel took her silence for interest in what he had to say, so he continued with the little speech he had prepared.

"The problems we have are because of getting the washing dry, especially in weather like we are having now." Daniel began. "If we had a way of drying the washing more quickly, so that it can be ironed and returned to its owner more quickly, we would soon get back the customers we have lost to the new laundry. I also think we should start checking all of the washing bundles last thing before we take them back to the customer. That way, we would never deliver washing that hadn't been properly dried or ironed, so no-one could complain and we wouldn't lose those customers."

Daniel paused for breath and, for the first time in his life, his grandmother smiled at him.

"That's very good, son." Lillian said." But we need to find a way of actually getting the washing dry more quickly and I don't know how we would manage that. I don't know about checking every bundle before it goes out. That would take time and it would have to be done properly, otherwise it would just be a waste of time."

Daniel wasn't put off by his Granny's lukewarm reception of his ideas. He knew that he was right and he had every intention of forcing his ideas onto the old woman.

"I think I've thought of a way to dry the washing more quickly and more cheaply than we do now." Daniel said. "It was something Miss Swift told us about in our lessons last week. We were talking about Roman Britain and what the Roman houses were like that they built when they were living here in England."

"I've no idea what you are talking about, son." Granny sounded as though she was irritated but Daniel knew that he had hit on a good idea and he wasn't going to stop until he had explained it all to the old woman.

"Have you heard of the Romans?" Daniel asked, realising that she probably had never heard of them.

"No, lad. Did they live past Middlesbrough, then?"

"No." Daniel was as patient as he knew how to be because he knew that Lillian would just slap him and turn away if she thought he was being cheeky. "The Romans came to live in England hundreds of years ago, when we were all living in wooden huts and never getting washed. Well, that's what Miss Swift said, anyway. But they came here from Italy where it is warm all the time and they didn't like our cold, wet weather."

"Well they should have gone home again, then." Granny Lillian snapped, starting to lose her patience with this story of people she had never heard of.

"They couldn't go home cos they were soldiers and had to stay where they were told." Daniel was worried now that he was losing Granny Lillian. "But they found out a way of making their houses warm cos they were clever people. They put pipes under their floors that had hot air running through them from a fire under the floor and these pipes warmed the rooms. I think we could put another side wall on the shed in the yard and run a pipe from the copper all round the shed so that the hot water would fill the pipe as well as the copper. That would heat the shed and dry the washing that we had hanging from the racks. Our teacher told us that hot air rises so it would get up to the ceiling. It wouldn't take much in the way of extra coal to keep the water hot, well, less than it takes to keep the fire in the kitchen going all night."

Daniel came to a stop, unsure whether his Granny understood what he was saying. He couldn't tell from her stony face if she thought it was a good idea or not and, now that he had had his say, he waited to see if she would laugh at his idea or worse, take the mickey out of him for thinking they should do what some foreigners had done hundreds of years ago. Silence fell on the kitchen and Edith, Martha and Daniel all watched Lillian's face for any sign that she was thinking about what Daniel had said. Edith was so proud that her little boy could come up with such a good idea but she was also amazed at what he was capable of understanding and she waited with bated breath for her mother to respond.

The silence stretched out and, just when Daniel had decided that his Granny was going to ignore his idea, she spoke.

"We'd need someone who was clever with his hands to run a pipe from the copper round the bottom of the shed but I don't suppose they would charge too much for that little job. The pipe wouldn't have to go underground, would it? You said these Roman soldiers put their pipes underground."

"No, it wouldn't have to go underground." Daniel replied. "The Romans put their pipes under the floor tiles as they were building the houses but we could just run the pipe round the bottom of the walls. If anything, I think that it would make the pipe heat the room faster with it not being under the floor."

"Would we need anything to make the water run through the pipe?" was Lillian's next question. She was obviously giving it a great deal of thought.

"Well the Romans didn't have pumps to push the hot water through their pipes cos they just let the hot air move through them but we could have hot water which would warm the shed more quickly. I think the heat would spread through the pipe and warm the water as it went. Our teacher said that water always finds its own level."

"Mmm, I think you might have hit on something there. Give me chance to have a good think about it and I'll let you know in the morning. You're a good lad. I reckon letting you go to school was one of my cleverer ideas."

It was the first time in his life that Daniel had received a compliment from the woman who was his grandmother and his chest swelled with pride at her words. He couldn't help it. Even though he hated his grandparents for what they had done to his mother, he couldn't help but respond when she praised him. He walked back across the kitchen and snuggled down next to Edith on the wooden settle that was their seat when they were allowed to sit down in the kitchen. Edith wrapped her other arm round Daniel, not taking away the arm she had round Martha's shoulders and smiled into his face.

"You are so clever, Daniel." Edith stroked his face and took note of his bright eyes and the smile on his lips. He had never been a particularly happy child, small wonder when you considered the life he had led so far, and she was thrilled to see him so happy. She wished with all her heart that she could give him a better childhood but she felt that it was impossible. As far as Edith was concerned, the only way her and her children's lives would improve was if she found a young man to look after all of them and that was make-believe. What man would look twice at her with her straggly hair and patched clothes? She'd never had a proper dress in her life, so what chance did she have of finding a knight on a white horse in the back yard of a laundry? Edith never considered the possibility of surviving without her parents so it was unusual that Daniel thought of nothing else. He couldn't wait to grow up, get a job and take his mother and his sister away from this hell-hole that was laughingly called their home.

Nobody had chance to discuss Daniel's idea anymore that evening because that was the moment that Joshua rolled into the backyard, knocking over the yard brush and various containers as he tried to make his way to the kitchen door. No-one in the kitchen could see him because the door was closed against the cold weather and the scrappy bits of cloth which served as curtains were closed over the window but they all knew that it was Joshua. When he finally found the door handle and opened the door, Joshua was greeted by what felt like a sea of faces, all watching and, he thought, condemning him. He was as drunk as he had ever been in his life but, at that moment, he was the happiest he had been in a long time. He tripped over the doorstep and catapulted himself into the middle of the kitchen. He had intended greeting them all as normal but, before he could draw his addled wits together, his wife spoke to him. It was like being doused in ice water.

"Don't come in here as drunk as a skunk." Lillian didn't pull any punches. "Get out in that back yard now."

Lillian stood up and crossed the room in two strides. She grabbed Joshua by the ear and dragged him outside into the yard. Edith, Daniel and Martha gathered in the doorway to watch what Granny Lillian was going to do next. It was dark outside, but there was enough light coming out of the open door for them to see Joshua and Lillian clearly. Lillian picked up a large jug which they used to carry water and filled it from the pump in the corner. She then threw the jug-full of icy water at her husband's head and finished by whacking him across the back of the head with it when it was empty. Joshua went down as though he had been pole-axed, measuring his length across the back yard floor and staying there in the wet and the grime. Granny Lillian lost her temper at this and beat him about the head, over and over again until Daniel grabbed her arm to stop her. She turned a face of such fury onto him that he shrank backwards and stepped towards his mother for protection, although his movement had seemed to bring her to her senses. She bent and grabbed hold of Joshua's hair at the back of his head and stared into his face. His eyes were closed and there was blood running down into his eyebrows which flicked away when she shook him. He didn't open his eyes.

Edith drew in a short breath and almost whispered.

"You've killed him."

"Don't be daft, lass. He's not dead, just dead drunk. I've a good mind to leave him out here for the night."

Lillian let go of the hair that she was holding and Joshua's face hit the floor once more. She pulled at his clothes and finally managed to work her hand into his trouser pocket from which she removed a penny and a farthing.

"He's drunk the lot." Lillian said, her voice totally expressionless. "The payment for the laundry. It's all gone. He's drunk the lot."

She wiped her hand on the back of Joshua's jacket and walked round Edith and the children to get back into the kitchen. She stopped as she reached the door and looked back at them.

"If it bothers you, you can drag him into here. I'm not lifting a finger to help him." Lillian said and then turned her back on them and made her way upstairs to bed.

Chapter Six

Daniel and Edith manhandled the old man into the kitchen. Neither of them was strong enough to get him into a chair so they dumped him on the floor in front of the fire where the wet and the dirt soaked off his clothes and formed dirty puddles on the floor. Edith hovered over Joshua, as though deciding what to do but Daniel grasped her hand and led her towards the stairs, refusing to allow her to attend to Joshua's hurts. Martha, who still bore Joshua an enormous grudge, took the opportunity to kick her grandfather in the face as he lay, unconscious, on the floor. Edith tried to stop her but Martha was too quick and too determined on getting her own back on the Grandad who had hit her to be stopped by Edith's ineffectual attempts. Edith hesitated again when she got to the foot of the stairs and this time, Daniel couldn't drag her any further.

"What if he's seriously hurt?" Edith whispered to Daniel. "He could die on that floor during the night and we'd be none the wiser."

"Good riddance." Daniel hissed back at her. "He's never done you any good turns so why should you help him? You'll get no thanks for it."

Edith had to admit that Daniel was speaking the truth and she couldn't think of any other reason to hesitate any longer so the little family made their way to bed, leaving Joshua to manage on his own. Daniel hated to admit it, but he hadn't really wanted to leave his grandfather in such a state but his analytical mind told him that it was what the old man deserved and that he and his mother and sister would be better off if they left Joshua to his fate. Martha still wanted her pound of flesh from Joshua so she followed her mother upstairs with great regret but promised herself that she would take more of her revenge out of his skin in the near future, in any way she could.

It might have been the cold weather or the fact that they had eaten well the night before but Edith and the children slept well and didn't wake until it got light the next morning. They were all surprised that Lillian hadn't called them and Edith hurried them all downstairs as quickly as she could, worried that Lillian would take her bad-temper out on them for being late and not give them any breakfast. They slept in their clothes because that was all they had, so it didn't take them long to get downstairs but Lillian was already in the kitchen with the fire going and bacon frying in the pan. The smell was delicious and Daniel's stomach growled loudly in response to the delicious odours. He was only interested in looking at the frying pan to see how much bacon was in it and didn't see Joshua at first. It was only when Edith spoke that he tore his gaze from the pan.

"Oh my God! What's happened to him?" Edith spoke in a whisper but in a whisper heavy with fear and shock.

Daniel glanced to the side of the range where Grandad Joshua usually sat and saw him in his usual chair. He couldn't work out why his mother was so shocked until he gave his Grandad a second glance and realised that the old man's face didn't look normal and that he wasn't sitting upright in the chair. Joshua was slumped to one side and his face looked as though it had been turned into clay and pulled until one side of it was totally out of shape. His mouth drooped down towards his chin and his tongue was slipping in and out of it, as though Joshua had lost control over it. He kept mumbling and one hand moved up and down, although the other one was hanging below the level of the chair seat and didn't move at all. Martha took all of this in with one glance and then moved until she was behind her mother, frightened by the change in Joshua and scared that he would leap out of the chair and attack her like a monster would.

"There's no need to hide, lass." Granny Lillian barked what might have been a laugh in other circumstances. "He's never going to hurt or frighten anyone ever again. I remember his father going the same way, years ago. He never walked or talked again and he was dead within a couple of years."

Lillian seemed to be taking a great deal of satisfaction out of her husband's condition, almost as though she was enjoying it. She spoke as though he was incapable of hearing her and wasn't human anymore. Daniel looked more closely at Joshua's face and was sure that there was understanding in his eyes and he wondered if Granny Lillian knew this. Would she deliberately make him worried about his condition if she knew that he could understand what she was saying? Daniel knew that she would. It was from her that Martha had inherited her vengeful streak, so Granny was doing this deliberately. Daniel shuddered at the depths of the human soul, even though he couldn't put the concept into words.

Edith and the children weren't sure what they were supposed to do so they stood awkwardly in the centre of the room, occasionally looking at Granny and, less occasionally, glancing across at Grandad Joshua as he mumbled and burbled in his chair. Granny didn't seem to see anything strange in the tableau laid out in the kitchen, but continued to fry bacon as though her life depended on it. When the bacon was cooked, she signalled to Edith to take her place at the table and the children followed her over, all the time trying to avoid looking at Grandad. Lillian distributed the bacon onto the plates which were already waiting on the table, then she took the large bread knife and sliced a thick round of bread for each of them. Finally, she wiped out the frying pan with another slice of bread and cut this into four, sharing it amongst the four of them as they sat down to eat.

For a while, the only sound in the kitchen was the crackling of the fire and the munching of four pairs of jaws as they all enjoyed the unaccustomed largesse, but then Grandad began mumbling again. At first it was a very quiet mumbling but then he got more and more agitated until he managed to lift one foot and slam it down onto the floor. All four heads at the table turned towards him, but nobody spoke and he was incapable of doing anything else so they turned back to their food and continued to ignore him. Joshua's hand waved a little bit and he mumbled some more, but then he seemed to go to sleep, as though the effort of mumbling and banging his foot had exhausted him and he had to sleep before he could regain any more energy.

When breakfast was over, Lillian stood up and addressed them as though she was a general giving orders to her troops.

"Daniel has come up with a scheme to try and improve our drying rate and so get back the customers we've lost. I intend to find someone to fit a wall to the open side of the shed and put a pipe around at floor level, joined to the copper, so that we can warm the shed and so speed up the drying. It's a brilliant idea and I'm glad that I thought to let the boy go to school. While I'm out, you three carry on as usual because we still have a few loads to do. We haven't lost all our customers yet and I intend getting back every single one that we've lost so far. Right, I'll go and get my coat."

Daniel never knew what spark of courage had entered his mother but, after Granny had finished speaking, Edith spoke voluntarily to her mother for the first time in years.

"What about Dad? What are you going to do about him?"

"There's nothing anyone can do, so there's no point mithering about him. Just get on with your work."

Edith was so taken-aback at this high-handed attitude that her voice was silenced and she dropped her gaze to the ground. But Daniel was made of much stronger stuff than his mother and he knew how to deal with Granny Lillian. There was no point in telling her what she should do but there were ways of introducing a topic so that Lillian didn't feel that her superiority was being threatened.

"It won't take long for word to get round that there's something wrong with Grandad. He's always spent a lot of time going round the town with the washing loads. People will ask what's wrong when they don't see him or when they see us struggling to carry it. If the doctor comes to see him then we won't have to explain to everyone that he's poorly cos everyone will know he is when they see the doctor."

Daniel deliberately didn't suggest that Lillian should call the doctor. He knew better than to try to force her but he had said enough to put doubt in her mind. She stood looking down on her grandson with a frown across her forehead and then she suddenly tapped him on the shoulder and smiled at him for the second time in two days. Daniel knew that he had the measure of the woman now, even though his child's mind couldn't have articulated that thought and he waited to see what result his words had on her. He didn't have long to wait.

"The boy's right again." Lillian said, taking her coat from where it hung on the back of the kitchen door. "After I've found a plumber, I'll call in at the doctor's office and ask him to come and see Joshua. Then people will think that I've done all that a grieving and concerned wife should do and we won't lose any customers who might have finer feelings than me. A wise man once said that if you work with the public, you don't have to be two-faced, you have to be two hundred and two-faced. Clever man that. Right, I'm off, you lot get that copper lit and the washing started. We're fighting a war against the competition here and I'm determined that we are going to win it. So, no slacking when I'm not around."

Edith committed the unforgivable sin of questioning her mother's wisdom which had Daniel shaking his head over her soft heart.

"Shouldn't we try to give Dad some breakfast?"

"Don't be daft lass. There's no point in wasting good food if he's going to pop his clogs today. We're not made of money, you know."

With that closing statement, Lillian picked up her purse and left through the gate in the back yard wall. Edith stood staring at her father until Daniel gently took her hand and led her outdoors.

"There's no point in causing an argument cos you'll come off worse." Daniel said, as they set about lighting the boiler. "Granny Lillian only cares about herself not about any of us and that includes Grandad. She doesn't care if he lives or dies and there's no point in upsetting her by going against what she's said cos she'll take it out on you. You must know that."

Deep down, Edith did know that but she couldn't understand how her mother could have been married to her father for so many years if she didn't love him. Why had she married him if she hadn't ever loved him? How could she be so callous? But then Edith remembered all the times she and Daniel had been put outside into the yard while her parents ate a meal which they weren't invited to share and she realised that her mother had never loved her either. Edith couldn't understand her mother's attitude because she loved Daniel and Martha with a passion which frightened her at times, it was so strong. She would have cut off her hands herself if she thought that her children would benefit from such an act but her mother wouldn't waste food on her father in case he died that day. Edith shook her head at the impossibility of understanding her parents' relationship and did her best to put her father's predicament out of her mind, at least until her mother returned.

Lillian returned when they had finished the first wash of the laundry and were preparing to put the washing through the mangle before they began rinsing. It was an arduous task because the laundry was thoroughly wet and weighed very heavily, making it impossible to lift it all in one go. They had to repeatedly grab handfuls of wet washing and squeeze it through the mangle before they then grabbed more handfuls, getting ever wetter and colder themselves as they worked. Daniel was convinced that there must be easier ways of making money and resolved to set his mind to finding out how other people earned their livings.

They hadn't been back inside while Lillian had been out so they all took the opportunity to follow Lillian into the kitchen where the range was lit and keeping the room warm, but as they opened the kitchen door, an absolutely horrendous stench greeted them and they all gagged at it as they entered the kitchen. At first, no-one knew what it could possibly be but then Lillian looked at Joshua as he hung, sleeping, in his chair. At his feet was a thick, dark mass which came from the chair seat and was splattered down his leg and it was from this mass that the smell emanated.

"Oh my God. I never thought about that." Lillian exclaimed, the first to realise what had happened. It took Edith only a couple of seconds longer to understand but then she turned and went back out into the yard.

"Don't run away from it. We'll have to clean it up." Lillian barked at her, but Edith was already on her way back, carrying the shovel from the coalhouse and a bucket of hot, soapy water from the copper. Daniel and Martha stood and watched as Lillian and Edith stripped the trousers from Joshua and carried his clothing and the chair cushion outside. Then they proceeded to clean the old man down before Lillian dressed him in his pyjamas, shoved another cushion onto the chair and pushed him back down on his seat. Through it all, Joshua did nothing to help, although one of his legs seemed to be performing a dance on its own without his volition. Daniel, however, was sure that Joshua was fully aware of what was happening to him. Daniel was sure he could see it in his Grandad's eyes that he knew what had happened and what the others had to do. Daniel was convinced that he could see petty triumph in those eyes and that Grandad was relishing making his family have to undertake such an unpleasant task.

Edith finished by scrubbing the area of floor which had received the unholy mess and, at last, the smell in the room began to dissipate.

"When's the doctor coming?" Edith asked.

"He said he'll be here when he's finished his morning surgery, so it shouldn't be too long now." Lillian answered. "I reckon we're going to have to put him in the parlour cos I can't be doing with him fouling the kitchen every day. We'll have to bring the bed down from the spare room and push the furniture over to make room for it. At least then it won't matter what he does cos there'll only be him suffering from it. Have any of you been back in the kitchen while I was out?"

None of them had so they couldn't tell how long it was since the deed had been done. The old man could have been sitting in his own mess for at least a couple of hours. This distressed Edith but Lillian didn't have her finer feelings. She set about moving the furniture in the parlour so that there was room for the spare single bed to be brought downstairs, but the doctor's arrival brought a halt to that.

Doctor MacMillan opened the kitchen door and breezed straight in without knocking. He never stood on ceremony in any house in South Bank and most people appreciated his kindly, if abrupt, approach to his patients.

"Right, what's happened here then?" Dr MacMillan boomed, his loud Scottish voice scaring Martha and making her hide behind Edith's skirts. "Is he drunk or daft?"

Lillian answered his questions as abruptly as he asked them.

"He went out drinking last night and we left him in his chair, asleep, when we all went to bed. When we got up this morning, he was on the floor and in the state that he is now. I reckon he tried to stand and couldn't manage it and fell, knocking his head as he went down. He can't move one of his arms and one of his legs and his face is all lopsided. He can't talk either."

Daniel listened, amazed at how his grandmother had altered the facts to make Joshua's injuries appear to be accidental but even more amazed that the doctor seemed to be falling for her lies. At any rate, the doctor didn't question anything that Lillian told him and, after taking the old man's pulse and listening to his heart, pronounced his judgement on the cause of Joshua's illness.

"Apoplexy." Dr MacMillan said. "He's not going to get any better, lass, so you'll need to prepare yourself for a lot of nursing. He might stay like this for a long time or he might have another seizure within a couple of days and that'll be the finish of him. How are you going to manage him?"

Lillian accepted the doctor's diagnosis without batting an eyelid.

"His father went the same way." Lillian said, as abrupt in her manner as the doctor. "We're going to bring a bed downstairs for him and put him in the parlour cos that'll make the nursing easier. Then, we'll just have to wait and see what happens, won't we?"

The doctor agreed, seeming satisfied at Lillian's reaction to the news, possibly even admiring her down-to-earth and practical attitude.

"If he gets agitated, which most patients like him do, then put a few drops of laudanum in his tea. I'll leave some with you before I go. It'll relax him and make handling him easier. No matter what you do, he isn't going to recover from this and you might have a long road in front of you until he finally succumbs. You'll need help although I suppose your daughter and grandchildren will be able to help you with the lifting and moving of him."

"We're well-used to heavy lifting in this house." Lillian answered. "You don't work in a laundry without developing muscles with all the heavy lifting we have to do. We'll manage, no doubt about it."

The doctor obviously felt that Lillian was telling the truth so he patted her arm, gave her a bottle from his doctor's bag, asked for his fee and then left, leaving them to finish getting the parlour ready for Joshua.

It was no easy task, even with the two women and Daniel helping, to get the bed downstairs and into the parlour. The parlour was a room which was never used, in fact, Daniel had never walked into it before and he was amazed at the heavy furniture and the dark wallpaper which it contained. It was a dark and dismal place and Daniel wouldn't have wanted to spend any time in it. He almost felt sorry for Joshua having to stay in it for the rest of his life. When he grew up and had a house, he promised himself, every room would be bright and cheerful and dust wouldn't be allowed to settle anywhere. The parlour was inches thick with dust and the whole room smelled very stale and dead. That was the word, Daniel decided. The room was a dead room.

It took the three of them, Lillian, Edith and Daniel, a long time to get Joshua into the parlour. He was impossible to lift easily because parts of him kept flopping towards the floor and he occasionally moved one of his limbs which would then get stuck on a door frame or a wall. They dropped him repeatedly which didn't seem to hurt him as he fell in such a relaxed manner, folding onto the floor as though he belonged there. Eventually, they abandoned trying to carry him and dragged him along the floor instead. It took a concerted effort to get him onto the bed as he seemed to be so much heavier than they had thought. Daniel had heard of the phrase 'a dead weight' and he felt Joshua qualified as such.

All three of them stood back from the bed and stared at Joshua, who was once again asleep. Edith shivered, not from the cold because they had all worked up such a sweat trying to move Joshua but because she felt as though someone had walked over her grave.

"Shall we light the fire?" Edith tentatively asked.

"Don't be ridiculous." Lillian barked. "He's in bed with blankets on him. He doesn't need the fire lit as well. Right, we've got work to do."

Lillian marched out of the parlour without giving Joshua a second glance. Edith hesitated but Daniel, once again, took her hand and led her out of the room. They both backtracked when Lillian shouted from the kitchen.

"Shut the door. We don't want to be able to smell him if he messes himself again."

Chapter Seven

Daniel's idea for the shed was, literally, a roaring success. Once the fourth wall had been built and the pipe run around the floor, the shed warmed up spectacularly and it became a pleasure to have to work in there. Edith wished that it had been done years before and she wouldn't have had to suffer with the cold all her life and Martha wouldn't have had the hacking cough which came upon her every time the weather turned wet or cold. Daniel was pleased that his idea had given his mother a much happier life and he was rewarded by seeing the return of some of their customers who, once they had changed allegiance to the new laundry, discovered that their bills rose every time they used it. Lillian had suspected that this would happen because she knew (none better) the cost of washing every load and she had known that the new laundry had been working at a loss for the first few months of their enterprise. She didn't make any remark about her customers' return but just accepted their laundry and acted as though they had never been away.

Martha was proving to be the lynch pin for Daniel's second suggestion for improvements for their business. She was able to tell if every load was fully dry when she ran her hands over it and she could fold and stack the laundry with a skill which would have been the envy of any other laundress, even though she hated the work that she had to do and was beginning to demand that she be allowed to attend school like Daniel. She wasn't afraid of telling Granny Lillian her wish and Edith was surprised when her mother agreed to Martha starting school, remarking that they had gained from Daniel's attendance and could likely gain from Martha's as well. Martha wasn't as intelligent as her brother but he was exceptional and Martha was capable of holding her own with any other child in her class.

The fact that the children were now both at school for a large part of the week meant that the bulk of the work in the laundry now fell to Edith and Lillian. Lillian had always been a hard worker but Edith had never managed to reach her mother's level. However, the improvement in her diet and the warmth of her working environment meant that Edith became much stronger than she had been before and was capable of far more than she had achieved in the past. Lillian even praised her a couple of times which was an experience that had been very rare in previous years. Neither of them missed Joshua's input because he had always been a past master at avoiding doing the bulk of the work. He had always been a lazy man who could hide it by looking as though he was busy when in actual fact he wasn't. If a spectator had watched him closely, they would have seen that he could carry the same basket of washing across the yard and back repeatedly, giving the impression that he was moving mountains rather than the same pebble over and over again.

The only fly in the ointment at this time was Grandad Joshua. Slowly, during the weeks which followed his seizure, his health began to improve. He still couldn't walk or talk but he had regained some of the use of his left arm, so he could now feed himself which reduced the time that Lillian had to spend in caring for him. After the doctor's visit, she had realised that she would have to feed him and had done so with the finesse of a cook stuffing a chicken, but at least the man had gained sustenance and it had helped in his recovery. Edith and Lillian shared his personal care which Lillian carried out in her usual no-nonsense way but Edith hated to touch her father in any way, especially as she could see in his eyes that he was fully aware of her distaste at the task. Edith was sure that he gained some sort of pleasure from manipulating the people around him, even though he was trapped in his bed.

Problems had arisen when Martha started school because of her inability to get on with the other children. The class had over fifty children in it and the teacher simply didn't have the time to give much attention to each child, so Martha often found that she had to ask others what she was supposed to be doing. As she had never played in the street or mixed with any other children, Martha was unaware of the unwritten rules of getting along with her peers. At home, Edith and Daniel treated her as a baby and gave her any help she needed immediately. Martha couldn't understand why the other children in the class didn't jump to her call, but she didn't hesitate to repeat her demands if they weren't fulfilled instantly. These demands for immediate attention made her very unpopular with her peers and they weren't backward in letting her know this. She responded by using her fists and her feet to hurt the children who made it known that they didn't like her and this twice resulted in her being made to stand outside the classroom in the corridor until she had 'calmed down'.

As the years passed, Martha's behaviour at school didn't get any better, but she learned how to make sure that she wasn't caught by any of the teachers when she was doling out their punishment to those children who had annoyed or irritated her. In front of anyone in authority, she behaved like a veritable angel, but once the teacher's back was turned, Martha could behave like the devil incarnate. Most of the other children learned to leave her alone but, occasionally, a child would turn on her and she would prove, once again, that it wasn't wise to upset Martha Coleman. Eventually, of course, the teacher caught her when she was in the middle of punishing George Stokes, one of her classmates, who had had the temerity to pull her pigtails and tell her that she smelled like their outside privy. Martha had reacted instantly, unaware that her teacher was crossing the school playground, and had pushed the boy into the yard wall, grabbing his hair and banging his head against the wall when he stumbled from the force of her shove.

Miss Johnson, who was Martha's class teacher, had been appalled at Martha's behaviour, especially when George's head had started to bleed profusely and she resolved to visit Martha's mother to let her know that they couldn't accept that level of thuggish behaviour in school. Miss Swift, Daniel's teacher, had a much better idea of Martha's home circumstances and would have advised against that course of action if she had been consulted but Miss Johnson was sure that she could deal with the situation herself and didn't need to confer with the rest of the staff.

Two days after Martha had attacked George Stokes, Miss Johnson arrived at the front door of the laundry on York Street and knocked loudly upon it. There was no reply simply because Lillian, Edith and the children were all in the washhouse in the yard and didn't hear the knock on the front door. After a few minutes, Miss Johnson knocked again, unaware that the only person who knew that there was someone knocking at the door was Joshua, who could do nothing about it. Miss Johnson was sure that the family would be at home because she knew that they ran a laundry from the address and she began to wonder if they had seen who was at the door and were ignoring her. Like Martha, Miss Johnson didn't like to be ignored and she reacted in her own way, which was to make sure that she did what she had come to do. It crossed her mind to open the front door and walk straight in but she abandoned that idea when she realised that she would be committing a terrible faux pas. Her only other idea was to go round to the back alley and see if she could gain entrance that way.

Of course, when Miss Johnson got round to the back alley, she found that the backyard gate was standing open and she could cross straight into the yard, where she found Edith and Martha struggling to put some washing through the mangle. The mangle was the only piece of equipment which still stood open to the elements, although Daniel had ideas about making a separate small shed to enclose it and make all their work weatherproof. Edith saw Miss Johnson as soon as she appeared in the doorway but she had no idea who she was. She stepped forwards to speak to her, expecting her to be a new customer looking for the laundry.

"Have you got work you want us to do?" Edith asked, eying up Miss Johnson's clothes and seeing a moneyed background which spoke of a lucrative deal.

"Are you Mrs Coleman?" Miss Johnson asked, extending her hand to shake that of Edith. "I'm Martha's teacher, Miss Johnson, and I've come to see you about her behaviour."

Edith could tell by the tone of voice which Miss Johnson was using that she hadn't come to praise Martha and her hackles started to rise. She owned nothing in the world but her two children and she had had to fight for them all their lives. She didn't take criticism of them very well and she was ready to respond in kind if Miss Johnson was going to be unpleasant.

"I'm Martha's mother." Edith replied, unwilling to admit that she was Miss Coleman, not Mrs, to this well-dressed and socially superior being. "What about her behaviour?"

"I'm not sure if you are aware that Martha isn't comfortable in dealing with her peers in the classroom or playground. If she wants help, she expects one of the other children to help her immediately and, if they don't, she can be quite aggressive with them. This last week, I caught her fighting with one of the boys who had said something to upset her and she banged his head against the yard wall until the boy bled from the blows. I can't have that sort of behaviour in my classroom."

Miss Johnson paused to give Edith time to answer her but Edith couldn't think of anything to say. Miss Johnson's words had only served to bring a picture of her father to mind, laying about him with any weapon he could put a hand to and beating anyone who crossed him. It was Daniel who sidled up to his mother and answered Miss Johnson's remark.

"Our Martha isn't used to playing with other children, only with me. She's my baby sister so I look after her. I'll tell her that she shouldn't hit other children so that will sort it."

Miss Johnson eyed Daniel and waited for Edith to answer but Edith merely stood and stared at her. Truth to tell, Edith couldn't think of anything to say because the phrase 'she banged his head against the yard wall until the boy bled from the blows' was playing over and over in her head. In her mind's eye, she relived the times that she had seen Martha give her grandfather a sly kick when she thought no-one was looking and she knew that Miss Johnson spoke the truth, even though she didn't want to admit it even to herself. Despite having been brought up in abject poverty, Edith and Daniel had spoilt Martha and that had played into Martha's inheritance of her grandfather's bullying personality. She was appalled that she hadn't noticed it until Miss Johnson had brought it to her attention and she was incapable of providing Miss Johnson with any answer.

Lillian, who was incapable of seeing bullying in either her husband or her granddaughter, was determined that this cocky little madam in her smart suit wasn't going to get the better of her family and stepped in to intervene in her own inimitable fashion.

"Daniel has explained Martha's situation and told you that he will sort the problem. Is there anything else you want?"

Miss Johnson may have had a high opinion of her own worth but she wasn't old enough or experienced enough or brave enough to stand up to Lillian. She mumbled her thanks to the air over Lillian's head and hastily removed herself from the backyard. Lillian and the children turned back to their duties immediately, but Edith continued to stand and stare at the back gate, lost in her thoughts and her shock at Miss Johnson's revelation. It took a shout from her mother to get her moving again but, even so, she still worried about what Martha had done until work was over for the day and they were sitting in the kitchen getting warm by the fire before bedtime.

Lillian was in the sitting room, seeing if Grandad Joshua needed anything before she retired for the night and, while Edith had the opportunity to do so in private, she spoke to Martha without her mother listening in.

"Do you really hit the other children if they don't do what you want, Martha?"

"I don't hit them a lot." Martha answered, totally open in her reply because she couldn't see anything wrong in what she did. "I only hit George Stokes because he said that I smelt like their outside privy. That was very rude and he deserved to be punished for saying it."

Edith drew in a very ragged breath and glanced at Daniel to see what he made of Martha's reply. Daniel was staring at his mother's face, aware that the news had come as something of a revelation to her, although he had known what Martha's character was from before Martha had been able to crawl.

"Don't you see that you aren't supposed to hurt the other children?" Edith asked, still being very gentle in her questioning. She still didn't want to believe that her beloved little angel could be capable of such terrible behaviour. Having been bullied by her own parents almost since birth, Edith had a horror of bullying and she didn't want to believe that Martha wasn't of the same temperament as herself. If Martha was a bully, it meant that she had inherited the trait from her grandparents and Edith wondered what other aspects of her character had been tainted and in what way.

Martha wasn't aware of her mother's thoughts and was still of the opinion that what she did at school was perfectly fine.

"But if they are nice to me, I don't hurt them." Martha declared, convinced that her reasoning was correct. "If they are nice to me then I am nice to them, but if they won't do what I want or if they are rude to me, then I hurt them back because they have hurt me."

To Martha, there was nothing wrong with this tit-for-tat behaviour and she was beginning to get irritable because her mother wouldn't leave the subject alone. Edith now realised that the subject was broader than she had at first thought, as Miss Johnson had said nothing about Martha being violent when she had been teased by any other children.

"Who laughs at your clothes and hair?" Edith asked, taken aback by such a statement, given that no child in South Bank was dressed like a manikin in a shop window. This was a working class area with working class ethics of hard work and hard play. Clothing was to keep a body warm and allow movement, not to make a child look like a London toff. Best clothes were kept as such, for church on Sundays and for family occasions like weddings and funerals. Why would the other children laugh at Martha's clothes?

Daniel answered for his little sister because he had undergone the same treatment at the hands of some of his peers. His way to cope with the jeering over his threadbare clothes and oversized trousers was to stick his nose in a book and ignore the teasing. Martha, who desperately wanted to be a pretty girl with clean hair and pretty dresses, couldn't rise above the torment of being laughed at and she was now close to tears, aware that her only answer to being teased was to be taken from her.

"You know that we never have clothes bought for us." Daniel stated, as calmly as he could. "We get what Granny Lillian picks up for us at the rag-and-bone man's yard. They don't fit us and we look stupid in them. All the other children wear clothes that have been bought or made for them or their brothers and sisters. They all have a bath and get their hair washed on a Saturday night but we've never had a bath in our lives. Don't you realise that we stink? You, me and our Martha. We all stink to high heaven. Even I can smell me when it's summer and our classroom gets hot. The other kids move as far away from me as possible, but they still moan about the smell. Have you never wanted to be clean?"

Edith was horrified at this litany of complaints from Daniel, especially as he had never mentioned any of it before. She could vaguely remember one of the rare days when she had attended school and the teacher had crouched down to talk to her and make her feel secure. The teacher had smelt like an angel in Heaven and she had been wearing a spotlessly-clean white blouse with lace ruffles and Edith had thought that she had looked, as well as smelled, almost delicious. But the days she had gone to school had been very rare and she had spent her time scrubbing laundry and not thinking about her appearance so she hadn't built up a store of hatred for her clothing. She was devastated that both her children were ashamed of their clothing and hygiene and she didn't know what to say or do to make it better for them. She couldn't go and buy them any clothes because her mother didn't give her any money, unless she was going a message and she was trusted with the cost of some flour or milk. But that wouldn't buy the children a set of clothes each. Her other thoughts were of Daniel's desire to have a bath. There was a tin bath hanging on the yard wall, but she had never thought to take it down and put the children in it, simply because her mother had never wasted hot water or soap on giving Edith a bath when she was a child. Her arms were constantly wet when she was working and she had supposed that it was enough to keep her clean. She hated herself for being such a bad mother that she had never thought to do these simple things for her children, even though she had never been bathed and dressed nicely herself as a child. That was no excuse.

Daniel and Martha moved closer to Edith, both aware that she had undergone a sea-change in her thoughts and wanting to show that they both knew why they had been bereft of simple cleanliness and that it wasn't really Edith's fault. Edith put her arms around the two of them and drew them closer, tears springing from her eyes at the way they had to live. For once in her life, she made her own decision and sprang up from her seat.

"Come on. We're going to get the bath off the yard wall and you can both go in it, even though you will have to put your dirty clothes back on. We haven't got any more for you but by God I'm going to get you both some."

Lillian chose this moment to enter the kitchen, having finished with Joshua for the night and heard what Edith said.

"What do you think you are doing?" she growled. "You're not going to waste good hot water on them are you?"

"Damn right I am and if you don't like it, you can stick that tin bath where the sun don't shine." Edith snarled right back at her mother. "And it's not a waste of water. It's better than the boiler going cold overnight. We might as well use the hot water cos we've already paid to heat it."

Edith didn't hang around to see if Lillian had anything else to say. She stormed out into the back yard and they could all hear her running water out of the boiler into the bath. Daniel went out to help her carry it into the kitchen where only Martha remained.

"Where's Granny?" Daniel asked, wondering if she had gone to get a tool to break the bath. It would have been her way of dealing with Edith's rebellion until very recently. They were all staggered when Lillian re-entered the kitchen a couple of minutes later and handed Edith a large bar of soap wrapped in tissue paper. A wonderful smell emanated from it.

"Here." Lillian spoke gruffly. "Your Dad bought me that thirty years ago and I've never used it. It'll get those kids clean."

Edith took the proffered soap, amazed at what Lillian had just done. She knew, immediately, that this was a form of victory and her chest swelled with delight. It was as though a whole new world had just opened up in front of her, but she knew better than to look smug in front of her mother.

"Thank you." Edith said. She left it at that, determined not to seem as though she was exulting in her small victory but equally determined that this was going to be the beginning of a new way of life.

The children had no idea how to take a bath. It was a totally new experience for them both but they enjoyed it immensely. Martha, particularly, enjoyed the feeling of washing her hair and loved the lavender smell of the soap.

"We should launder the bedding with this soap." Martha commented. "All our customers would love to go to bed in our clean sheets if they smelled like this."

Lillian didn't speak while the children were enjoying their bath but she was thinking long and hard about their lives, their business and the prospects for the future, both for her and for her child and grandchildren. She didn't pass on then the fruits of her considerations but she made a few major decisions that night, sitting in front of the range listening to the children's squeals of delight while the aroma of the lavender percolated through the room. They were decisions which were to have major repercussions for them all.

Chapter Eight

The children slept like logs that night from the relaxation of having a bath for the first time and got up in a rush the next morning when they realised how late they were. Edith had taken advantage of the full tub of hot water and had taken a bath after the children had got out. The water had been a bit scummy and it had been no longer as hot as it was for the children but Edith had luxuriated in it and in the opportunity to wash her hair. The whole experience had been so relaxing that she still felt in a happy daze the next morning and she was finding it difficult to concentrate on what she should be doing.

The happy surprises continued into the next morning. Lillian wasn't angry that they had all slept in nor did she refuse to let them have breakfast as she would have done in the past. Instead, they each had a slice of bacon with an egg nestling on top of it and a slice of toast with some of Lillian's jam on it. Daniel was convinced he must have died and gone to Heaven but Martha merely nodded her head and tucked in as though she had been having breakfasts like that all her life. When the plates had been cleared and the washing up done, Lillian announced that she had a few things to say. Edith, Daniel and Martha were at the back door, just about to step out into the yard and start the day's work. Lillian had never stopped them working before so they all waited, Edith with her hand on the door handle, to hear what Lillian had to say,

"I've been thinking about the business and the work we all do." Lillian began. "I'm not getting any younger, your Dad is just a liability now, making extra work for us for God knows how many more years but you three are in the prime of life. I think it's time for you to take on more responsibility, Edith, so that you can run the place when I'm no longer up to it. I've decided to pay you a regular wage so that you are getting something out of the work that you do. I reckon it'll make you more determined to put your heart and soul into the work, if you get some sort of reward for your labours. It would also mean that you would be able to save up and buy the kids the clothes and things that they want."

Lillian paused, obviously waiting for Edith to reply and expecting her to jump at the chance to have some money of her own, even if she had to work even harder than she had been for the last few years in order to get it. Edith was unable to reply at that moment because she had stopped listening to her mother after she had heard the word 'wage' and was imagining buying the children presents and possibly a decent dress for herself. Daniel, however, had been waiting for this conversation ever since he had noticed that Granny Lillian was sometimes unwell and took laudanum, because he had already realised that she would need to be cared for when she became too unwell to work. He had already noted how much work it took to look after Joshua and he knew that Edith would be overwhelmed by the task of caring for two elderly, frail parents never mind running the laundry as well. Daniel, unlike Edith, was prepared for Lillian's speech and had his own comments ready and waiting to add to the debate.

"How much longer do you think you will be able to continue working?" Daniel asked Lillian, knowing that his mother would never dare to ask such questions. Edith, however, came out of her vision of having money to spend and looked at her son with admiration in her eyes. She did have questions she would like to ask, it was just that she was used to a life where she didn't ever answer back or be expected to have an opinion and things were moving too quickly for her to be able to keep up.

"I don't know how much longer I'll be able to work." Lillian admitted. "I know that the laws of nature are such that the body gives out eventually but none of us know when that is likely to be. I'm just planning for the future, that's all."

"You are planning for your future." Daniel remarked. "You don't want to get old and find out that you haven't got anyone to look after you, that's all. You've never cared about any of us in the past, so why should we care about you in the future?"

Edith was shocked that her son could be capable of such thoughts, never mind brave enough to give voice to them to the person who had terrified Edith all her life. She stood, open-mouthed, staring at Daniel as though he had grown an extra head or sprouted wings on his back and too scared to even glance at her mother. Lillian was also shocked at what Daniel had said but, deep down, she had to admit that the boy was right. Why should Edith and the children care what happened to her when she had put them outside in the yard so that she didn't have to feed them? She had never given Edith a moment of mother's love but had spent years beating her whenever she was in a bad mood, never mind what she had done to her when Edith had made a mistake or broken something.

But Daniel wasn't finished. He had watched and taken note of every time his mother had been badly treated. He had marked on the yard wall every time Joshua had beaten or hurt one of them, which Lillian could have stopped if she had wanted to. He had gone hungry when he would have, quite happily, eaten a table leg and the cause of all this suffering, his grandmother, was now offering treats in order to ensure that she would be cared for in her old age. She didn't deserve it and he wasn't going to let his mother take a pittance to ensure that she would be tied to the laundry for the rest of her mother's life.

"I think a lot of things will have to change round here before our Mam can be expected to promise that she will look after you when you get too ill to work. Cos you are already ill, aren't you? You are pretending that it will be a long time in the future before you will be too old to work but you are already poorly and you might have to stop working very soon. How do you expect Mam to be able to look after you and Grandad and run the laundry?"

Lillian looked into her grandson's eyes and saw the utter contempt in which he held her, visible for all with eyes to see it and the brains to understand it. She knew that this boy wasn't going to allow himself to be browbeaten into doing what she wanted and she quailed at the thought of getting old and frail alone.

"Yes, you're right." Lillian admitted. "I do keep getting pains in my chest and I think it's because my heart isn't very strong anymore. And I admit to feeling scared at being left alone to die without anyone to care for me. But can't you accept that I'm offering to improve your lives if you'll promise to care for me when I am too ill to work?"

This is the point where Edith caught up with all that had happened that morning and the full realisation of what her mother was asking burst into her brain. She couldn't keep her temper any longer and she butted in before Daniel had chance to reply to his grandmother's questions.

"You expect to butter me up with the promise of money for working like a slave so that I'll spend the rest of my life waiting on you hand and foot so you don't suffer! Where was the offer of a wage when I was working my guts out and given a single bed to share with my two children? Where was my wage when I didn't get fed because I hadn't half-killed myself scrubbing other people's dirty sheets? When did you ever care tuppence for me? Or my children? Those kids had a bath last night for the first time in their lives and now you want to pretend that life has been hunky-dory for all of us for years when the reality is that I've lived like a slave for all that time and my children have never been allowed to be children and play in the streets. I knew you were a selfish, hard-hearted, cold woman but I never thought you were that stupid. You can stick your wage cos I don't want it. Me and the kids are leaving and we're never coming back. I hope it takes you years to die, lying in your own mess and with no-one to care for you, cos that's what you deserve."

Edith grabbed Martha's hand and dragged her towards the stairs so that they could collect what few possessions they had and leave immediately. She expected Daniel to follow her but when she glanced behind her, she was amazed to see Daniel still standing staring at his grandmother.

"Daniel! Come on! We're leaving here now."

Daniel didn't move a muscle but continued to stare at Lillian. When Edith spoke his name again, he merely shook his head, not even turning to look at her. Edith dropped Martha's hand and walked back into the kitchen. Martha trailed along behind her, not sure what was happening but not very happy at the idea of running away. She still had points to score off Joshua who was now a sitting duck for her nasty little pranks, unable to stop her, and she didn't want to lose the sense of satisfaction she got when she was being malicious towards him.

"Why aren't you coming upstairs?" Edith asked. "Don't tell me you want to stay here to wait on her for the rest of your life. I don't believe that you are that stupid. You must know what she's like."

"Oh, I do know what she's like." Daniel replied. "I have known her through and through ever since I started school and discovered that I had a brain and I could use it. I'm waiting for her to work out that she could improve the situation by apologising for what she has done to us, but that hasn't clicked with her yet. I'm also waiting for her to improve her offer of a wage cos I reckon she has started at the lowest level of what she is prepared to offer, just in case we were daft enough to fall for her lies immediately and take her at her word. I'm not moving a muscle until I hear what her top offer is."

Edith was stunned that Daniel could be so mature for his age. She had known for a long time that he was much more intelligent than she was but she had never realised before how old a head he had on such young shoulders. It would never have crossed her mind that her mother had a sliding scale of offers which she had been considering ever since she had decided to drop this bombshell on them that morning. Despite her anger, she decided to wait and see where Daniel's negotiations could take them.

Lillian hadn't answered any of Daniel's accusations but had retained her seat at the kitchen table and still stared at the three of them as they stood in front of her. Daniel gestured to Edith that she and Martha should sit down at the table also and he waited while they did so.

"Well, Granny Lillian. What more have you got to say, now that you have our undivided attention?" Daniel was sneering and they all knew it.

"Are you prepared to negotiate then?" Lillian asked. "Are you prepared to consider my proposal if the rewards for it are great enough?"

Daniel glanced across at Edith before he nodded his head once. He was the only one who wasn't sitting down because he knew that Lillian would have to look up at him if she wanted to see the reaction to any of her proposals on his face and, somehow, he knew that this gave him an advantage.

Lillian took his nod to mean that he was prepared to listen and she folded her hands in front of her on the table top. She stared at her clasped hands for a few seconds and then she began to speak.

"I know I have treated you all very badly, especially you, Edith." Lillian began. "If I'm going to explain, I'd better start right back at the beginning so that you all understand why I am like I am. I was never a bonny lass, even when I was small girl but my sister, my baby sister, had a face like an angel. She was also lucky enough to be of a happy nature and her smile came naturally to her, so people always liked her. I was eight years old when she was born; old enough to be able to remember what life was like for me before she was born and old enough to be able to compare those two parts of my life. I was an only child until Emma was born but I desperately wanted to have a baby sister. I thought it would be like having a doll which could walk and talk and I wanted to be able to control that doll's life. Looking back, I can see that I thought she would belong to me. It never crossed my mind that she would be a real person, not a doll and that, once she was old enough to speak for herself, she would want to live her own life. Neither did I expect her arrival to make any difference to the way that my parents treated me."

Lillian stopped for a few seconds, almost as though she was struggling to contain the memories that this story was bringing back to life.

"I was wrong on both counts." Lillian continued. "Once she was born, she made a huge difference to my life, mostly in the way our parents regarded me at first but, later, in how I looked at myself. My parents were utterly besotted with her from the moment that she was born. I no longer got any cuddles and kisses from them because they were both constantly cuddling and kissing Emma, telling me that I was a big girl who didn't need to be treated like a baby. As Emma grew, she proved to be a very beautiful child with blonde hair which curled naturally, big blue eyes and a complexion that was the envy of every other female she met. By contrast, I was as plain as it is possible to be. My mousy-brown hair didn't curl, it just stuck out. My eyes were the same mousy-brown colour as my hair and they were small and piggy-like. Oh, I looked in the mirror often enough, to see if I had changed and become as beautiful as Emma was, but it never happened. I grew bitter at the amount of luck that Emma had and I grew to hate her because my parents stopped loving me and gave her all the affection they had. Then, when we were both older, she began attracting the attention of all the young boys who lived near us. None of them could even see me because they were all blinded by her beauty and her sweet nature. It was to be expected that she would attract the admiration of the best catch of our age group and she fell for him in a big way. Unfortunately for me, he was the one boy I had been attracted to since we had played together on the streets as children and I had carried a torch for him for a long time. I was filled with a jealousy that was so great that I wanted to spoil her beauty and her sweet nature and I wanted to murder her for taking everything that I had, even my one true love."

Edith and Martha were astounded by these revelations and they were both captivated by the tale that Lillian was telling them. Neither of them took their eyes off her while she spoke, but Daniel had prowled up and down the kitchen floor all the time that she had been speaking, only stopping when Lillian spoke those last words.

"I don't believe that the boy was your one true love." Daniel stated baldly, spoiling Edith and Martha's romantic visions of Lillian's tale. "I think you were born without the capacity to love, although I imagine that your jealousy of your sister is a true representation of how you were with her. Tell us what you did to spoil your sister's chance at happiness."

"What makes you think that I would do anything to spoil my sister's chances?" Lillian growled at Daniel.

"Because I've watched you all my life." Daniel replied. "You have never let any small or even imagined slight to go unpunished. You have a sliding scale of punishment for any misdeeds and you always tally your retribution to that scale. How did you punish your sister?"

Lillian shook her head at Daniel but they could all see in her eyes that Daniel's point had struck home. She lifted her chin and continued her explanation of what had happened.

"It was nothing to do with me." Lillian declared. "It was after they had told the family that they were going to get married. I left the room because I couldn't bear to see the happiness in both their faces so I went upstairs to my bedroom and cried over my lost fancies. My parents made it into a party but I didn't go back downstairs to join in. It was the next day when Emma fell ill, vomiting and crying and my mother said it must have been something she had eaten. Then we heard that her sweetheart was ill in the same way. Neither of them recovered so, instead of holding a wedding, we had a joint funeral and I had lost my baby sister."

Lillian put her forehead down onto her hands, as though she were overwhelmed by the emotions that she had stirred up.

"What did you put in the food?" Daniel asked. Edith drew in so sharp a breath at his question that she whistled through her teeth and Lillian's head snapped up so that she could look in his face. They all thought that she would deny Daniel's accusation but, after opening her mouth to speak, Lillian thought again and closed it once more.

"It wasn't in the food." Lillian admitted. "I put arsenic in the bottle of wine which my Dad went and bought for the happy couple. They shared it with a few others but most told them it was especially for them so they had the bulk of it. Some of the other people at the party were poorly too and everyone put it down to something being off. It could have been the ham in the sandwiches or the cream in the trifle. Whatever it was, everyone believed that they had just been unlucky."

"You put some arsenic in the cream and the ham, didn't you?" Daniel asked, but it was more of a statement than a question. "You had to make it look as though it was the food they all shared and not only the wine which they didn't share. Where did you get the arsenic from? Did you enjoy murdering them and getting away with it?"

"We already had some arsenic under the kitchen sink. My Dad bought it because we had caught a rat in the kitchen and he wanted to make sure that there weren't any more. I remembered it was there and I knew that it would kill people as well as rats. I put most of it in the wine, knowing that my sister and her fiancé had never drunk wine before and wouldn't know if it tasted as it should. I put very little in the cream and ham so that it didn't change the taste of the food and so that no-one else would die. I'm not a murderer."

"Oh really." Daniel was even more sarcastic than before. "Killing two people doesn't make you a murderer. Our Mam's right. You are cold and calculating and I don't believe for one instant that you were in love with that chap who wanted to marry your sister. You just couldn't stand to see her happy and you were jealous of her pretty face. So, how did you come to marry dear old Joshua? I notice you haven't topped him yet. Are you waiting for him to die naturally or until you get bored with caring for him? Does he know what you did to your sister?"

Chapter Nine

There was a silence in the kitchen after Daniel had asked his last question. Edith and Martha were spell-bound by Lillian's admissions. Edith was horrified at her mother's confession to having committed two murders although she had a refrain running through her head that kept telling her that she knew her mother was capable of murder. She had been on the wrong end of Lillian's temper so often that she knew how deep that temper went. Oh yes, she was sure that Lillian was speaking the truth and that she had murdered her sister and her fiancé. Martha was less sure although she hadn't had the years of experience of coping with Lillian's tempers and, as a child, she wasn't fully aware of what people could do to other people. Daniel, however, knew exactly what his grandmother was capable of, although he wasn't horrified at what she had done because he knew how deep-seated her malevolence was. Neither was he frightened that Lillian might do the same to him. His thoughts were much clearer than either Edith's or Martha's and his main concern was why his grandmother had chosen to tell them what she had done.

"Why have you told us this?" Daniel asked, still as direct in his questioning and not allowing Lillian to wrong-foot him, no matter what she said. "Are you trying to threaten us, believing that we will do what you want in case you use the arsenic on us? I warn you, I'm capable of more than you think and I'm not so daft that I would attempt to poison you. I would be more likely to use something which wouldn't leave any trace."

Lillian looked up from her contemplation of her hands and stared hard into Daniel's face. She saw, looking back at her, a character who had endured much and come through it. She realised then that she would never be able to bully him again and that co-operation would be her only road from now on.

"Don't worry, Daniel." Lillian answered. "I have no intention of ever murdering another person in my life. The guilt I have felt over the years at what I did has shown me that I don't want to take that road again. I watched my parents shrivel up and die because they had lost their darling daughter through my actions and I couldn't put anyone else through such a torment ever again."

"But it didn't stop you from putting your daughter through hell and you continued to do that for years." Daniel pointed out. "Even though you didn't kill her, you didn't care that her life wasn't worth living and it's only because you are ill and on your own now that you are holding out an olive branch. If Grandad hadn't become ill or if you hadn't got pains in your chest, would you be sitting here now, offering our Mam a wage for the drudgery you call work? I don't think you would. I think you would be acting in the same way that you have done all my life. I think you need to admit that you aren't capable of loving your family and it is pure self-interest that has led you to talk to us today."

Edith hadn't spoken after her initial reaction to her mother's confession but she had listened intently to all that had been said, particularly Daniel's contribution to the conversation. She gazed closely at Lillian, wanting to hear her admit that she was offering Edith a wage purely in order to get her to care for her when she became too ill to work but unable to work out whether she should accept that offer or not. She wanted to discuss the matter with Daniel, without Lillian's presence, but she was still too scared of her mother to ask for this. She also wanted time to assimilate what had been said but she didn't know how to demand that time either. Daniel, who was following his own route through the confession and the offer, spoke again before Lillian had time to answer.

"I think we three need to discuss what you have said and come to our own conclusions. Why don't you go and do what shopping you need while we do that and then we can give you a clearer idea of what we intend to do when you come back?"

It spoke volumes for Daniel's new position in the family that Lillian immediately did what he suggested and went and got her coat and shopping bag.

"I won't be long." Lillian said, before she left the house. "I shall expect you to have come to a decision by the time I get back. I would like to know what my fate is going to be."

Daniel joined his mother and sister at the kitchen table after Lillian had gone out.

"So, what do you think about Granny Lillian's offer?" Daniel asked.

"Offer?" Edith almost choked as she spat the word out. "I have never loved that woman and I've known all my life that she never loved me, but she seems to think that I will quite happily fall in with her plans. When I think of the times I've stood in that backyard while her and my Dad ate their meal in here, I want to scream in her face that I will never lift a finger to help her ever again. I agree with you, Daniel. She's told us about murdering her sister to frighten us into doing what she wants and I've no intentions of hanging around long enough for her to have a go at murdering us. I intend being gone before she comes back from the shops and, if you've got the brains I think you've got, you'll feel the same way as me."

Martha felt that she had been ignored for long enough and chose now to put in her twopennorth.

"Why doesn't she murder Grandad cos he's just a nuisance to her now? If she's that good at bumping people off, I would have thought she would have done for him the day he got poorly."

Daniel looked at his little sister and decided that she had got more upstairs than anyone had ever given her credit for.

"Martha's right. I'm surprised she hasn't got rid of him before now. She didn't tell us why she decided to marry him, if the story about the love of her life falling in love with her sister is true."

"Do you believe it, Daniel?" Edith asked.

Daniel was quiet for a couple of moments while he put his thoughts in order and only when he had did he speak.

"No, I don't believe it. I'm sure that if two people had died after a party, then the authorities would have looked into it and it wouldn't have taken a genius to work out that one of the victims had a very jealous sister. I don't even know if I believe that she had a sister. Do you know anything about the family, Mam?"

Edith paused to think but couldn't remember any mention of a sister.

"Now you come to mention it, I can't remember ever hearing of or seeing any sister, brother, grandparent or aunt or uncle." Edith confessed. "There was never any mention of any relatives apart from Dad's parents, but they both died when I was very young. I can't even remember what they looked like. Unlike other children, I didn't seem to have any relatives when I was a child. I don't think my childhood would have been so strange if there had been other relatives about in the area. Surely an aunt or some relative would have questioned the way my parents made me work and didn't appear to care for me."

"Unless any relative was as strange as Granny Lillian or Grandad Joshua." Daniel remarked. "They wouldn't have seen anything strange in your treatment if they thought and acted in the same way as your parents. But, we need to discuss what we are going to do now. Do we accept wages in exchange for caring for Grandad now and Granny Lillian in the near future? What do you think about it, Mam?"

"My first thought is to get away from this damned house and never come back but on second thoughts, I've invested years of hard work into this business, as well as what you two have done, and it seems a shame to walk away and have to start again somewhere else. If we walk out, we will walk out with nothing to our name and then where will we live? But, I'll be damned if I'll be bullied anymore. I've lived in fear of my parents all my life and I couldn't count the number of times they've beaten me and left me without food. Why should I do anything for them when they've done nothing for me and mine?"

"You've only just found out about Granny Lillian being poorly, so you haven't had time to absorb it and what it will mean." Daniel remarked. "I noticed ages ago that she was taking laudanum every now and again, so I've had time to get used to the idea. I've been wondering for a while when she was going to try and come to some arrangement with us and I've had a good, long hard think about what we should do. Shall I tell you what conclusions I've come to and then you can think it over before you decide one way or another?"

"Hang on." Martha interrupted. "Nobody's bothering to ask me what I think we should do. Just because I'm the youngest, it shouldn't mean that I don't get a say in the matter. It's my life too, you know."

"Don't worry, little sis." Daniel reassured her. "We aren't going to do anything until we all agree on what to do. This is our chance to improve our lives and I don't think we should make any decisions until we are all in agreement. Granny Lillian can't rush us. It means too much to her. Mind you, I'm not advocating that we all roll over and give in to her cos I reckon she's got some making-up to do before she gets her own way, and I don't mean that she gets all her own way. Are we agreed, Mam?"

"We are, Daniel." Edith replied. "I don't know what I would have done without you, son. I haven't got half the brains you have or half the courage in the way you stand up to her."

Daniel smiled at his mother and then got up to put the kettle over the hob. He felt that his mother was going to need a restorative cup of tea if they were going to get through the next step on the road to their new lives. Edith wasn't as adaptable as Daniel and Martha were and she was the one who was going to find the new way of life strange at first.

When they were all settled with mugs of hot tea and Daniel had raided the pantry for biscuits (an opportunity they had never had before), he opened the conversation.

"Since I started school, I have been looking around at how other people live and work. Some people have had apprenticeships and then gone on to earn a decent wage, enough to be able to feed and clothe their families. Some people have labouring jobs which don't earn them as much as tradesmen and the families of general labourers don't live as well as the families of tradesmen. But, the people who get the most money and have the better lives are those who work for themselves, as long as their business brings in plenty of money. Now, this laundry is owned by Granny and Grandad but people don't want to pay a lot for their laundry, so we don't make a great deal of money. I think we should abandon the laundry and do something else which pays more money."

"That's a good idea, pet but how do we persuade your Granny to give up on the laundry? And what do we do instead?" Edith didn't sound very enthusiastic over Daniel's idea. "What other business could we run which would be more profitable and which we wouldn't have to spend years learning how to do it?"

"I've thought about that as well, Mam." Daniel replied. "I think the best way of earning plenty of money is to offer a service like carrying goods around the town. Things like furniture when people are moving house or goods from the railway to the shops. I think that would also give us access to things that people want to sell and then we could set up a shop to sell them. I think they call it second-hand goods."

Daniel paused before he got too carried-away with his ideas and frightened his mother with his enthusiasm. He could see that she was very unsure about his proposal but he knew that she had led such a constricted life that she was afraid of stepping out into the world and grasping Chance by the back of its neck.

"But you can't carry goods around on your back." Edith said, unable to see beyond the practicalities of Daniel's idea.

"I know that, Mam." Daniel replied. "I want to know how much money Granny Lillian has got stashed away because we are going to need some capital to start it off. We'd need to buy a handcart to carry the goods on. Later, we could get a horse and cart for carrying and then we would be able to expand the goods that we carried. I also reckon that we would have to keep the laundry going until I was earning enough to be able to live off my earnings. You and Martha would have to run the laundry until I got enough work to keep us going. So, what do you think? Shall I tell Granny Lillian we will care for her if she gives us the money to start my business?"

Martha and Edith were both silent at this point. Martha was trying to work out how much work she could manage to avoid doing while Edith was battling with thoughts of security for them all. To her, a new business meant taking a huge risk over its possible success and, even though she knew how much toil was needed in the laundry just to keep their financial heads above water, she was frightened of abandoning a business that could at least keep a roof over their heads and food in their bellies. Daniel's new business had no such guarantees, although she did have a great deal of trust in his intelligence. But they couldn't eat intelligence and she had gone hungry too often to want to be in that position again.

"What if Granny Lillian either won't or can't give you some money?" she asked Daniel.

"If you mean you don't think she has got any money stashed away, then don't worry." Daniel answered. "I know she has a stash under her bed, cos I found it months ago, when Grandad had his seizure. She told me to fetch his things from their bedroom when she wanted to put him in the parlour and I took the opportunity to have a good look round. I've been keeping tabs on how much money comes into and goes out of the laundry and so I know for sure that she has it. I look on it as payment for the work we've all done in the laundry over the years that we haven't been paid for, so I'll get it off her. If she won't give it willingly, then I'll take it, but by hook or by crook, I am setting myself up in business."

"Well, I'm for it." Martha put in, before Edith could say anything. "I've done my share of breaking my back for nothing in that laundry. I reckon our Daniel has the right of it. We need a business that pays well cos I'm sick of having nowt. The girls at school get new dresses for the summer and winter and I wear the same old rags all year round. I'm sick of looking as though I live in the workhouse and I'll work hard to help Daniel get his business going."

Edith couldn't think of any other objections to Daniel's idea but she wasn't sure that her mother would look at it in the same way as they were. She had had her eyes opened when Daniel had mentioned the money under Lillian's bed because she had always believed her mother's claims that they all worked hard for a pittance and that every penny had to be accounted for. All her life she had believed that money could only be spent a penny at a time and the ability to spend the same penny twice was the act of an intelligent person. She didn't know how much it would cost to buy a handcart but she was sure that it would amount to a very large sum and her stomach quailed at the idea of demanding such an amount from her mother.

Daniel knew that he had persuaded Edith and he was just about to say so when they heard a noise coming from the parlour. They had all forgotten that Joshua was in his bed in the parlour and the noise made them all jump. Lillian had fed and cleaned him earlier that morning, so he hadn't been abandoned, but Edith wondered if he was trying to shout for a drink. They all trooped through to the parlour together, Edith leading, but they then bumped into each other when Edith stopped dead at the door. Martha and Daniel tried to get round Edith to see why she had stopped so abruptly when there came an almighty scream from inside the parlour. Martha clapped her hands over her ears to try and cut out the sound but the keening wail went on and on. Daniel finally managed to push Edith out of the way and stepped into the parlour but then he too stopped dead. Martha peeped round her mother's skirts, too frightened to enter bodily into the room.

Joshua was on his back on the single bed over near the bay window, but it didn't look as though it was a person who was in it. His heels and the top of his head were the only points of contact between Joshua's body and the bed. The rest of his body was arched so high it seemed to be an impossible feat for a human being. At the same time as he was straining all of his muscles to preserve this position, Joshua was screaming from deep within his chest so that he sounded like a steam train which was fighting its way up an incline to the top of a mountain. It was the most inhuman noise that Edith had ever heard and she had goose pimples rippling up all over her body. The hair on her head and on her arms was standing on end and it felt, to her, as though she had been struck by lightning and her body was sizzling with the electricity of it. Her hands were shaking as she tottered across the room and attempted to push Joshua down until his back made contact with the bed.

Edith didn't have enough strength to be able to force Joshua down and she turned and screamed for the children to come and help her. The screaming which was coming from Joshua went on and on until none of them could hear any other noise above it and they were all frantic to try and get him back onto his bed and to stop the dreadful noise.

Nobody heard Lillian when she entered the house and it was only when she pushed Martha out of the way so that she could reach the bed that they realised that she had returned home. She took charge straightaway and grabbed Joshua's feet and turned him sideways so that his body collapsed without the bed to push against. As soon as this happened, Lillian pushed him down so that he was on his side and unable to push himself upwards again. She stopped the terrible keening noise that he was making by the simple expedient of stuffing a towel into his mouth, so that he couldn't breathe through it and this forced him to stop screaming. Peace fell on the small, dark parlour; a peace which throbbed and reverberated with the memory of the noise that Joshua had been making. Gradually, his breathing became quieter and more even until it slowed so much it stopped altogether. They all stood round the bed and looked down on the man who had frightened them all throughout their lives and who now lay like a baby in a pram, at peace, while the noise of his passing echoed round the whole house.

It was Lillian who put their feelings into words.

"Well, that's it then. The old bugger's gone and good riddance to him, I say. He'll not blackmail me ever again."

"Blackmail?" Daniel echoed her word. "He's been blackmailing you all these years?"

"Too true he has." Lillian barked. "He's blackmailed me to live with him and look after him since I killed my sister. Do you seriously think I would have wanted to live with that apology for a man for any other reason? Grant me some taste, please."

Chapter Ten

No-one moved or spoke after Lillian had made that statement. Daniel was the first, again, to be able to make sense of it and he was the first to put his thoughts into words.

"How did he know that you had murdered your sister and her fiancé? Did you tell him?"

"Tell him!?" Lillian almost screamed at him. "Of course I didn't tell him. At first, I thought he was hanging around this house to get something out of my parents - like money, for example. He was always here, getting in everyone's way and refusing to go home, even when my Dad asked him to. He was like a part of the furniture and, as such, I didn't notice him hanging around when I was putting the arsenic in the drink and the food. More fool me! He swooped as soon as our Emma died, even before she was cold. He would keep my secret if I promised to marry him, he said. I told him to get lost cos I knew he wouldn't go to the police. He had too many skeletons in his closet to start talking to the police but he talked to my Dad instead. Oh, he didn't say anything about me murdering his daughter but he filled my Dad's head with rubbish like how useful he could be in the laundry. Told my Dad he'd been around so much he knew every detail of the laundry and wouldn't he be useful if I married him? He would be able to keep the business going so I wouldn't ruin it after my parents died. Kept digging at my Dad all the time until my Dad came to me and said I should marry him cos he would look after me. That's the sickest joke I ever heard. All he wanted was a slave to cook and clean for him and, in the end, he got me."

Edith had never realised the way her parents' relationship worked but, the more that her mother said about her marriage, the more she could recognise the truth in it.

"So, you slaved for him and we slaved for you both." Edith declared. "Well, that just shows the love in this household. Did either of you ever do anything for the other without expecting some sort of payment for it? You have no idea about loving and giving, have you? No wonder my childhood was so rough, neither of you have the faintest idea about family life or about companionship. It's no wonder I looked elsewhere for love and affection."

"Well, you didn't have to pay for that affection by getting pregnant, you know. Many a set of parents in this town would have thrown you out for getting pregnant without being wed. You should count yourself lucky, girl, that we didn't put you out on the street, especially after you did it a second time."

Edith was spitting feathers now.

"Put us out on the street!" Edith managed to choke out. "That's a laugh, isn't it? What would you have done for slave labour if you hadn't had me and then my two kids to work for you? Would you have got that lazy lump of lard to slave for you like I did? I don't think so. He never did a hand's turn if he could get away with it, but he was always ready to deliver the washing and get the money for it, wasn't he? And how many times did he spend it before he got back home? Too often to count, I would imagine and usually in the nearest public house so that he didn't have to go to bed sober with you."

Daniel was amazed at his mother's venom. He knew how much she hated her parents but he had never heard her speaking the truth as harshly as this before, although he felt it would do his grandmother a lot of good to hear how much she was hated by her family. It made his bargaining position so much better if she was aware how alone in the world she was without them. He didn't say anything about these newest revelations but brought all of them back to the practicalities of the situation.

"Don't you both think that I should go for the doctor to report his death?" Daniel asked. "We don't want the authorities thinking we are trying to hide another death in this house, especially when this one was natural. It would be ironic for the police to want to investigate it."

Lillian saw the truth in what he said as well as the sarcasm and, once again, reminded herself that Daniel was now a force to be reckoned with. If they were to come to any arrangement about her future care, she needed to keep him on her side and she wouldn't do that by raking over the coals of his mother's past life. She needed to learn a lot of new lessons on her dealings with her family if she was going to have any sort of comfortable old age.

"You're right, Daniel, as usual." Lillian spoke in a much more gentle voice than she had been using to Edith. "Would you mind going for the doctor? Edith, would help me to lay him out, please?"

Edith had seen the recognition of her need to change in her mother's face and she did her best to damp down the anger and frustration she was feeling. A spirit of cooperation was new to the household but, if Daniel was sure that they could make a good life for themselves if they followed his advice, she was prepared to put her personal feelings to one side.

"I'll go and get some hot water." Edith replied. "Martha, go and get some towels out of the airing cupboard, please. You don't have to help with the laying out but you can run upstairs for clean towels."

Daniel left the house to go for the doctor. His face was grim as he walked along but his mind was in very fast mode as he went through his plans for his carting business. He was determined that he was going to succeed and equally determined that Lillian was going to part with some of her hoard of coins to help him begin. They were all entering into a new phase of their lives and Lillian could hang onto their coattails if she wanted to, but she was going to have to do her share in future and not leave the donkey work to his mother.

When Daniel reached the doctor's surgery, the doctor was already out on a call. His wife assured Daniel that she would give his message to the doctor immediately upon his return but Daniel was frustrated by the waste of time. He wanted his Grandad passed on to the undertaker so that he could tackle Granny Lillian without any interruptions but this was obviously not going to happen so Daniel made his way back to the laundry on York Street. It was as he crossed Middlesbrough Road that one of their customers hailed him from across the street.

"Tell your Grandad that there's a darts match on in the Station Hotel tonight. I'm sure there'd be a place on the team for him."

Daniel paused, wondering whether he should merely nod his thanks or stop and let the man know that Grandad Joshua was unlikely to be attending. As the man was a customer of the laundry, Daniel felt it was only fair if he apprised him of the day's events, so he crossed the road to speak to him.

"Me Grandad died this morning, Mr Prosser." Daniel informed him. "I'm sure he would have wanted to come to the darts match but he won't be going anywhere now."

Mr Prosser looked down at Daniel from his six feet of height and then rubbed the top of Daniel's head.

"I'm sorry to hear that, lad. Has he been poorly for long then? I haven't heard anything about it."

"He's been off-colour since he had that fit a few months back." Daniel decided it was a good move to be as sociable as possible. Mr Prosser might become a customer of his carrying business, so it was best not to get on the wrong side of him. "We brought his bed down into the parlour so that our Mam and Granny Lillian could look after him but he got worse and then had another fit this morning. I've just been to see if the doctor could come out but he's out at another patient. His wife said that she'll let him know when he comes back."

"I'm sure she will, son." Mr Prosser tried to sound reassuring. "This'll make you the man of the house now, so you'll have to look after your Granny and your Mam."

"Oh, I will, Mr Prosser." Daniel assured him. "I've always looked after our Mam cos she hasn't got a Mr to do it for her."

Mr Prosser stood and watched Daniel as he set off again and shook his head over the little family, so recently bereaved. Like all the folk in South Bank, he had a pretty good idea about the problems that Edith and her children had. He wondered if things would change now that the patriarch was dead, although he didn't have much respect for Granny Lillian and her hard-nosed attitude to her family. He was a friend of Jack Davis who lived next door to the Coleman's laundry and he'd heard many a tale from him of the shenanigans in the Colcman household. He resolved to see if he could do anything to help Edith and her children, starting that night in the Station Hotel.

When Daniel reached home, Martha was in the back yard, stirring the first load of laundry which she had put in the copper.

"Our Mam and Granny are laying Grandad out, although I have no idea what that means." Martha told Daniel as he came in through the gate. "I thought I'd get started on the washing, seeing as how we are going to get paid for all this work now."

"You're a good lass." Daniel smiled, aware of how much Martha hated the laundry work and recognising that she was doing it because of their new relationship with Lillian. She wouldn't have voluntarily stoked and fed the copper the week before. "I'll go and tell Granny about the doctor, then I'll come and help you."

Martha nodded in reply, saving her breath for the arduous task of turning the mangle and Daniel went in through the kitchen. Edith and Lillian were both still in the parlour, although the pile of towels on the floor attested to the fact that they had finished laying Joshua out.

"I'll get rid of these towels and then I'm putting the kettle on." Edith said, as Daniel entered the room. "I'm not starting the washing until after I've had a cup of tea. You're back, honey. Is the doctor coming straight away?"

"No Mam," Daniel answered. "He's out on a call but his wife said he'll be here soon. If we're having a cup of tea, we can continue with our conversation about our offer. We could get it sorted before the doctor comes."

Lillian nodded her agreement and walked away from her husband's body without a backward glance.

"The sooner the doctor's been, the sooner we can get the undertaker to take him away." Lillian said, jerking her head backwards at Joshua's body. "We'll have to go and tell them that we'll be needing a funeral."

"I'll go, after we've got our arrangement sorted." Daniel answered, in a voice which brooked no argument. "I'm not leaving until we've got it sorted in case anyone tries to change their mind."

Both Edith and Lillian knew exactly what he meant. Edith listened to him with pride and no small measure of awe, Lillian listened to him and hoped she was going to come out of the discussion with something for her, because the lad was a tough negotiator. There again, he'd had a hard upbringing which was down to her, so she couldn't expect him to be a rollover.

Martha was called in from the yard when the tea was brewed and they all took their seats around the kitchen table again but, hardly had they sat down when the doctor came striding in, in his usual breezy fashion.

"Did he have another one, then?" Dr MacMillan asked as he dumped his medical bag on the kitchen table, scattering the spoons and two biscuits as he did so. "It often happens that way. They have one large fit and then a second large one later or they have one large fit and then loads of little ones sometimes for years afterwards. To be honest, I think the lucky ones are those who die straightaway, without needing the months of nursing that some patients need. It's a huge strain on any family, not helped by worries about money when it's the breadwinner who has the apoplectic fit and the rest have to nurse them and work more. One day, all these problems will be curable, but not yet, eh? Let's have a look at him so I can write the death certificate."

Lillian showed the doctor through to the parlour where he dropped his loud attitude and quickly but carefully examined Joshua. Then he put the tools of his trade back in his bag and started to write out the certificate, stopping to ask Lillian what time the last fit had occurred. She told him and he scratched some more on the paper in front of him before he looked up at her where she was standing quietly next to the bed.

"You'll miss him, lass but it's the way of the world." Dr MacMillan said, gently. "You've been together a long time but at least you have your family to look after you at this sad time. I feel sorry for those who have to cope alone at times like these, although most people manage it. Will you be carrying on with the laundry without him?"

"Oh yes, Doctor." Lillian answered. "We might even branch out into other things. I've got a very clever grandson who is ready to take the reins and I'm sure he'll make a great success out of everything he turns his hand to."

"Then you are a lucky woman." Dr MacMillan stated as he handed Lillian Joshua's death certificate. "I see a lot of people in a lot of worst states and it's heart-breaking sometimes. Now, keep your strength up with plenty to eat and make sure you get some rest. You'll need it after the work you've put in with Joshua."

Lillian merely nodded; afraid that if she spoke her hatred of her dead husband would show only too clearly and perhaps make the doctor more suspicious about the situation in their household. For the first time in years, she wished that she had made Edith and the children's lives better over the years so that she could be more sure that they would look after her now. The doctor took her silence for grief and patted her arm as he passed her on his way out of the door.

"Keep your chin up, lass. Time's a great healer." He said, thinking he was giving help rather than irritating his patient's wife. Finally, the doctor left the house and the whole family breathed a sigh of relief now that they could finally get down to the serious business of working out their new regime.

"I thought he was never going to go." Lillian breathed as the back door closed after the doctor. "He was of the opinion that I was in a deep depression over the loss of my husband. He couldn't have been more wrong if he had tried. He even told me that time is a great healer, no doubt meaning that I won't be as miserable in a few weeks when I've forgotten him."

Although she was sneering at the doctor and his comments, his words had hit home with her, especially when he had said that she was lucky to have her family around her. Little did he know that there was a possibility that they were just about to walk out on her and she was now waiting for the result of their discussions while she had been out shopping. It was an unusual feeling for her, but she was very insecure at that moment and, if Daniel had but known it, she was ready to give in over a large number of things. Once they were all settled with hot tea (again) Lillian turned naturally to Daniel as the leader of his little pack and asked what the results of their discussions had been. Daniel didn't answer immediately. He had no idea what the doctor had said to his Granny Lillian but he could feel the unease emanating from her and he quickly revised his figures to take advantage of the weakness he knew she was feeling. He wasn't psychic but he could almost hear her heart beating too quickly and this encouraged him to think that she could offer them even more if he played his hand carefully. He took a deep breath because the outcome of these next few minutes was very important to him and then he began.

"Do you own this house that we live in? I'm asking this because you talked about Grandad Joshua coming to this house before you were married and discussing helping you to run the laundry after your parents died."

"Yes, yes I do." Granny Lillian replied. "My father left the house to me in his will and I managed to never give in when Joshua told me to put his name on the deeds. It was an argument between us which raged over the years but, somehow, I kept it in my sole ownership. I needed to keep it in case his violence got too bad and I had to manage without him. Why do you want to know that?"

"I need to have the full picture in my mind." Daniel answered, without going into detail. "Although, now he's dead, anything he owned would naturally have passed to you."

"Take my word for it." Granny growled. "The only possession that lazy pig had was me or a tab at one of the local inns and I have no inclination to pay any of that kind of debt."

"Good." Daniel moved quickly on. "I think I am right in saying that you have some money stashed away. I would like to know how much you have."

Granny Lillian bridled at this blunt question but then thought better of her initial reaction and answered Daniel, although she had to grind her teeth together to stop herself from telling him to mind his own business.

"I have a sum of cash stashed away. You are right in that although I don't know how you know it." Granny tried to keep her voice even. "It amounts to about a hundred pounds but, of course, there is now a funeral to pay for so I will have less than that."

"I understand that you will have to pay for Grandad's funeral." Daniel was quickly adding on to Granny's total because he was sure she was lying in order to keep some of her stash hidden. That didn't matter because he knew he needed about thirty pounds to start his carrier business, so she could keep most of her money. "I would like to have thirty pounds to start my carrier business, which will earn a greater income than the laundry has ever done."

"What?!?" Granny Lillian couldn't believe her ears. "You want to take cash from me to start your own business? What about the laundry? And how do you know what income you will be able to get from it? Huh, you're tilting at windmills, boy, and no mistake."

Daniel listened to Lillian's shock without batting an eyelid. He had expected that she wouldn't be very happy about giving him any money and he knew that she was over-egging the pudding in her reaction to his demand so he let her mutter away about 'his insolence' for a few minutes. Then he spoke again.

"I have done a lot of research into the carrying business." Daniel said, very calmly and quietly. "I know exactly how much work is available for a carrier in South Bank and I also know that there is only one other person doing it. He is an old man and only works when he wants the money so customers are constantly being let down. If I step in and I am hard-working and reliable, I will be able to make a fortune, especially when I buy a horse and cart and expand the goods I will be able to carry. The laundry will carry on with you and our Mam and Martha working in it until I earn enough to do away with it. You have got to admit, it is a lot of hard work for very little reward and there is competition in the town already. Also, now you haven't got Grandad drinking the profits from the laundry, so you'll be able to save more than you used to be able to do. So, will you give me the thirty pounds I've asked for?"

Chapter Eleven

Granny Lillian sat and thought for a while before she answered Daniel's question. She thought that making him wait would strengthen her bargaining position, especially if he thought that she was considering saying no, but Daniel knew how strong a hand he held so Lillian's trick was wasted on him. He took a sip of his tea and then helped himself to a biscuit, looking for all the world as though he didn't care what Lillian's answer was going to be. Lillian knew he was a strong-willed character but she had never appreciated how much he saw and how much he understood of what happened around him nor did she know that he had expected her to prevaricate.

Eventually, Lillian replied to Daniel's question.

"I can let you have thirty pounds from my savings but that will have to be the end of it. Don't forget, I've got your Grandad's funeral to pay for now and I'll bet that will be expensive. And it's not that long since I paid for the new wall on the shed and the piping for the walls, they all cost money you know."

"Yes, I do know." Daniel was quick with his answer. "Now, all we need to decide is how much you are going to pay our Mam and Martha for their work in the laundry. And I expect it to be a sensible offer; no trying to get away with paying them a pittance. Don't forget that we can walk out of here now and leave you to manage on your own."

Daniel knew that his grandmother was fully aware of Edith's desire to walk away from the laundry but he also knew that the laundry didn't make much in the way of a profit, so he wasn't unreasonable in his demands. It took only two offers from Lillian before Daniel was ready to accept, although he turned to Edith and Martha for their opinions before finally agreeing with the amount. Edith couldn't believe that she was finally going to get paid for the work she did and much more than she had ever dreamed of. Martha would have carried on asking for more but she was aware that Edith and Daniel both thought the offer was fair, even though she wanted more, so she gave in, albeit grudgingly. After this had all been agreed, Daniel had one more comment he wanted to make.

"I hope you will come to realise that treating people fairly is the best way of getting good work out of them. Those who carry a grudge against their employer will never work as hard as they could do because they have that grudge on their minds all the time. If you had been fairer with our Mam she would have done so much more for you. I know that you haven't got it in you to be able to have love and affection for your family but you would have had a better life if you had."

Lillian didn't comment on this because she was feeling rather alone at that moment but she was determined to get an agreement out of Daniel before she was finished with the subject.

"I want you to promise that you will all care for me when I am unable to look after myself." she demanded.

"Yes, we'll look after you." Edith replied. "It might not be with a good grace because you have done nothing for me all my life this far, but I will do my duty as a daughter, you need not fear about that."

Lillian was true to her word and paid Edith and Martha at the end of the first week. The funeral was to take place the next day and Edith went out and bought herself a black coat which was smart and would do, not only for the funeral, but also for use in the winter. Martha, not to be outdone even by her mother, also bought herself a coat and looked forward to being able to buy at least one decent skirt for the coming winter. Edith had also bought some wool and spent her evenings sitting next to the fire in the kitchen knitting a jumper for Daniel so that he would have something warm to wear during the coming winter. She congratulated herself on the two sensible children she had managed to rear in the miserable hole that had been their home, although the house was much more comfortable now than it used to be. No-one went cold or hungry and Edith and the children showed their new status in the colour in their cheeks and the cleanliness of their clothes. Daniel, now that he was being fed regularly, was growing at an amazing pace and looked set fair to top six feet in height by the time he reached the age of twenty.

They were all very surprised at the number of people who turned up for Joshua's funeral. Daniel had mentioned the death to Mr Prosser the day that he had met him on his way home from the doctor's and Mr Prosser had determined to do something for the small family. He had always felt sorry for Edith as he had been a contemporary of hers when they were children and he knew that she had been made to work hard in the laundry and very rarely shown her face at school. At one point, in his teens, he had harboured daydreams of taking her away from the laundry and showing her what a decent life could be like but he had been persuaded against it by his mother. He had married their next-door neighbour when he was still a boy of eighteen although his wife had died in childbirth before she had reached her twentieth birthday. Mr Prosser had taken his baby daughter, Grace, home to his mother and had been alone ever since that terrible time, caring only for his child and his mother.

The death of Joshua had rekindled his interest in Edith and he had spread the word of their bereavement to the rest of the town. As a result of this, plenty of people turned up to give Joshua a 'good send-off' even though most of them came because they felt guilty over ignoring Edith and the children's plight over the years. They had a whip-round in the Station Hotel and Mr Prosser presented Daniel with nearly three pounds after the funeral, showing Lillian that the townsfolk were looking to Daniel to lead the family from now on. Daniel didn't want to take the money, but Edith persuaded him that to refuse it would be to upset quite a lot of people, so he acquiesced and told Mr Prosser that it would go towards setting himself up in the carrier business.

That was the best move that Daniel made that day, because Mr Prosser was a self-employed joiner who had a roaring business fitting windows, doors, wardrobes and cupboards and mending broken seats, chairs and furniture, in fact anything that could be made or mended out of wood. His business was so good because he was a very talented joiner, an extremely hard-worker and as honest as the day was long. His reputation in the town was second-to-none and many people followed where he trod. If Mr Prosser used one grocery shop, then other people would begin to use that grocery shop. If Mr Prosser was seen frequenting one of the barbers' shops, then there would be a queue outside the door the next morning. If Mr Prosser had a drink in the Station Hotel, then the Station Hotel would be fit to bursting the next night. And if Mr Prosser was showing an interest in the small Coleman family laundry on York Street, then a lot of people would either begin or go back to using them again.

When Daniel mentioned that the whip-round would be used to help set up his own carting business, then Mr Prosser was all ears. He questioned Daniel closely on his plans for his new business, asking very probing questions and making many remarks which held the germs of new ideas so that Daniel soon had a very clear idea about where he needed to go next. Despite the fact that the gathering of people had been intended to be a funeral for the head of the family, it turned into much more of a social occasion and even Lillian had to admit, by the end of the day, that she had really enjoyed the afternoon. Daniel more than enjoyed the afternoon because Mr Prosser promised him all the carting business that he produced, as soon as Daniel had bought his cart. Word soon went round the gathered throng and Daniel was left holding the contact details for every person there who could possibly need the use of a cart in the next few months. By the time the last of the mourners had left, Daniel was grinning from ear to ear and holding a sheaf of papers with names and addresses on them. Edith was smiling as widely as Daniel and Martha was happy because she had been the centre of attention of a group of old maids and old wives who praised her pretty face and admired her new coat. It could have been that Lillian would have been jealous of the attention her family received or angry that she was being ignored but she very quickly realised that her daughter and her grandchildren were popular with people and that, plus the numbers of people who had promised laundry loads to her, made her as happy as the rest of the family. The only person who could have been in any way disgruntled that day was Joshua and he was far beyond caring.

The promises of loads for the laundry weren't empty promises because the washing started to come in the next day. Most of it was for working single men who didn't have a mother to do it for them but there was also a load of bedding from the Station Hotel, whose manager promised that he would use only their laundry in future. Daniel went and bought a cart and then went round to Mr Prosser's yard and took a delivery of windows to a building site on Queen Street - his first ever business agreement and he made more money that first day than the laundry made in that week.

By the time Joshua had been in his grave for a month, he wouldn't have recognised his old home if he had had the opportunity to walk back into it. Lillian and Martha had cleaned out the parlour and even given it a coat of distemper. It was 'old gold' in colour so not a particularly pleasant shade but it was far better than the dirty brown which the walls had been for years. From then on, although they used the kitchen during the day, they went through into the parlour for the evening, where Edith taught Martha to knit and Daniel made his bills out and made lists of calls he had to make the next day. He had had 'D. Coleman and Family - carters' painted onto the sides of the cart so now word spread about his business every time he stepped out into the streets.

By the end of 1910, the laundry was running well with plenty of customers and Daniel's carting business was busy all day, every day. Life had improved no end for the Coleman family and Lillian often caught herself wishing that she had behaved in the way she did now much earlier in her life. She had missed out on so much, simply because she had carried her grudge about having to marry Joshua around with her for so long and this had made her bad-tempered, unsociable and totally against caring for her daughter and then her grandchildren. She was still worried about her health but the improvement in all their diets had done wonders for her as well as the children, although the major benefit of her new life was that she no longer spent a large part of each day angry with her husband. She had never realised before just how much energy it takes to lose one's temper or to physically fight with another person but she had noticed how relaxed she felt, even after a day's work, and that made her feel better as well.

In the outside world, they had gained a new king that year after the death of King Edward the Seventh had brought his son, George the Fifth, to the throne. It didn't make much difference to the lives of the people in South Bank because London was so far away but they put out their bunting and their patriotic flags and felt they had done their new King proud. The thirteen year old Martha wasn't interested in a new King, who looked like an old man to Martha when she saw a picture of him, and she showed even less interest in the King who had died, who looked like an even older man to her. Edith wasn't at all interested in either King because she was now blooming under the concentrated attention of Mr Prosser, who seemed to need Daniel's services so often that he had to call round to ask for them very regularly. Lillian, who had greatly admired Queen Victoria, saw only two more useless lumps of man-flesh, on a par with her late husband, and wondered what the possibility was of England getting another queen in the not-too-distant- future.

Edith blossomed that winter and, as 1910 moved into 1911, her relationship with Bob Prosser moved on to a more serious level. She was very careful to keep her behaviour at a socially acceptable level because she was determined that no-one would be given the opportunity to sneer at her or tease her about her illegitimate children. So she acted in a very lady-like manner whenever she was with Bob and always dressed in sober colours although the fabric of her skirts and blouses was now a much better quality than she had ever worn before in her life. She had quickly learnt how to sew her own clothes and became adept at turning a length of material into a very attractive blouse and rapidly lost the ragged appearance she had had all her life. With her better nutrition and her new clothes, Edith turned into a very lovely young lady and Martha looked set fair to follow her mother in the looks department.

Martha was still attending school during the week and her behaviour there had improved rapidly once she no longer had need to be jealous of the lives of her classmates. She even managed to make friends with a few of her contemporaries, although each of them could remember when Martha would strike any child who crossed her, so they were careful in their dealings with her. She still did her share of the work in the laundry but, even at home, her temper had improved remarkably so there was a much better atmosphere.

Daniel had finished school when he reached fourteen although he made use of every newspaper or book which came his way in order to assuage the overwhelming thirst that he had for knowledge. If he arrived early at a customer's shop or workroom, he would examine everything that each craftsman made and ask many questions in order to be able to understand the workings of each and every article on display. He enjoyed chatting to the older men, particularly those who were running their own businesses, and never stopped in his search for information and experience. He was given a lot of help simply because he was so openly hungry for what people could impart to him and a lot of people found that trait extremely attractive.

All-in-all, the York Street laundry was a much happier place than it had ever been before, even when Lillian had been a child, and they started to attract visitors who came, not to deliver laundry but to act as friends and neighbours. Lillian found this difficult to cope with at first but, eventually, even she made a friend or two and looked forward to their visits and their chats over a cup of tea. This participation in the life of the community meant that they began to receive invitations to various social functions in the town and, as 1911 drew to a close, they received four such invitations, all on different dates, to attend a tea dance in the Methodist Church Hall; a play to be performed by the Sunday School also in the Methodist Hall; a fund-raising Christmas Fete in St John's Church Hall and a concert which was to be held in the same hall. There was a flurry of fabric-buying from Edith and Martha and then a time when the parlour was taken over by material, cotton and Edith's new joy - her Singer sewing machine. Both Edith and Martha had new dresses finished and ready to wear when they set off to attend the tea dance, escorted by Bob Prosser, who was now extremely eager in his relationship with Edith. Daniel wouldn't give in to any pressure to have a suit made for him but he did wear his best trousers and the jumper his mother had knitted for him. His dark hair and very bright brown eyes made him a target as a partner and he spent the whole of the afternoon escorting various young girls around the dance floor, being eyed-up by plenty of other young girls who wished that the dance was longer so that they could have a turn at dancing with this tall, handsome young man.

Martha was the one who enjoyed the dance the most as she had a line of partners for every dance and saw herself as the belle of the ball. She took very little notice of the other girl whom Bob had brought with him to complete their group that afternoon; his daughter Grace, who was a couple of years older than Martha, although she was younger than Daniel. She had her father's dark brown hair and his blue eyes which made a very pleasing contrast in her face, although she was incredibly shy and only managed to speak a few words to the Coleman family all afternoon. She didn't lack for dance partners either, although she didn't chat to them as Martha did with hers. Even so, it was noticed that she was extremely popular with the young men who seemed to be vying with each other to be the first to make her smile and then laugh out loud.

Edith, who was overwhelmed by being allowed to go to a dance wearing a dress she would have given her eye teeth for in her previous life, had a wonderful afternoon, made especially pleasant by Bob's undivided attention and by the way he clasped her hand whenever he had the opportunity. She was looking forward to the other social engagements which were coming up in this pre-Christmas season, made even more attractive by Bob's presence as her escort and couldn't wait for the opportunity to wear the other dress she had made for herself. Even Lillian had a lovely time, although she didn't dance and hadn't got a new dress to wear. She was dressed in black as befitted her status as a widow and was happy to discover that black suited her complexion now that she was better fed and fitter than she had been for a long time. She, too, was ready to attend the other three social events and had discovered that she fitted-in quite well with the other widows who, together, made a dark area in the hall which was otherwise filled with a riot of colour from the dresses of the assembled ladies.

Bob Prosser, naturally, took his daughter to each event and was pleased to see that Edith and Grace hit it off from the beginning. Edith, who had blossomed so much over the last few months, discovered that she had a talent for drawing the young girl out and took pleasure in listening to her soft-voiced comments. Edith also approved of Grace's obvious attraction to Daniel, even though Daniel hardly noticed the girl as he spent most of his time discussing business with the other men. Neither Edith nor Daniel noticed that Martha's reaction to Grace was different from that of her mother and her brother. At the tea dance, Martha hadn't really noticed the quiet girl but, at the play when Edith was sitting next to Grace, Martha realised that her mother and Grace were very friendly and she didn't like it. They all moved about so much at the Christmas Fete that Martha couldn't tell if Edith was paying Grace any special attention but the matter came to a head at the final social occasion of the season at the concert being held in St John's Church Hall the Friday before Christmas.

Chapter Twelve

It had been a busy day at the laundry for Lillian, Martha and Edith and Daniel had been especially busy with his cart as the old man who was his only competition in the town had decided to retire when the snow began falling. He hadn't given any warning to his regular customers, so Daniel suddenly had a list of customers as long as his arm at this busy Christmas season and it was very late in the day before he got all the goods delivered and paid for.

The concert was to begin at seven pm and the only reason they made it on time was because Martha had spent all afternoon in the bathroom, primping and getting herself ready and so they didn't need to queue to use the bathroom that evening. Even so, it was a mad rush and Daniel was still rather damp about the gills when Bob arrived at York Street, with Grace in tow. Edith welcomed them both warmly. Daniel, yet again, hardly noticed that Grace was there as he was much more interested in what Bob had to say about the joinery work he was completing for the new houses on the far side of town. Martha decided to ignore Grace, hoping that she wouldn't want to accompany her father in future, if her welcome was only lukewarm when she did come with him.

It was just starting to snow again when they stepped out of the door and set off towards the Church Hall. As they walked, they met other people all heading in the same direction and Lillian began to worry that they wouldn't be able to sit together if there were too many people in the hall before them. Edith was talking quietly to Grace at the front of their little cortege; followed by Bob and Daniel who were discussing the problems that the snow would bring to the construction trades; and then Martha and Lillian brought up the rear as the final pair. Lillian had very little to say as she was concentrating on not slipping in the wet snow and Martha couldn't get the pair in front of her to turn round to listen to anything she had to say, so Martha got more and more irritated about being ignored. No-one else in the little company would have said that they were ignoring Martha but that was exactly how Martha saw it after she had tried twice to get Daniel and Bob to turn round and listen to what she was saying. She did try to shout to Edith at the front of the procession, but Edith merely shouted back that she was too far away to hear Martha and continued talking to Grace.

Martha began to seethe internally, although she kept a tight smile on her face for the benefit of the other people they met as they reached the Church Hall. Once inside, Lillian's fears were proved to be groundless as there were notices on the reserved seats and they were seated, together, in the third row from the front. Daniel and Bob stood back to let the women file into the seats first and Martha pushed her way through so that she got the first seat. Lillian followed Martha as both Edith and Grace stood back to let her through and then Edith and Grace took their seats next to Lillian. Bob took the seat next to Grace and Daniel took the final seat. This meant that Martha had Lillian between her and Edith and, as the chairs were all pushed very closely together to get as many bodies as possible into the Hall, it was impossible to lean round Lillian to talk to Edith. Martha could see that Grace only had to turn her head to the left to chat to Edith and to the right to chat to her father. Her inner temperature started to rise and she leaned slightly forward so that she could see out of the corner of her eye, every time that Edith and Grace spoke to each other. She was even more irritated to notice that Bob sat back whenever Grace wanted to say something to Daniel and it wasn't long before she was convinced that she was being deliberately ignored.

The young girl who was sitting in the Church Hall in her fine new dress was only a breath away from the little girl who had lost her temper when the children at school didn't do as she told them and she reacted in exactly the same way as she did when she was six years old. When they all rose for the intermission, Martha pushed her way along the row of seats to the end and then waited for the rest of the party to reach her. In the hubbub amongst so many people, no-one saw Martha put her foot in front of Grace's leg and trip her up. The only thing that saved Grace from falling to the floor was the sheer numbers of people who surrounded her and Martha's attack only served to push Grace into Daniel who caught her and held her upright until she had regained her balance. This irked Martha even more, especially when Daniel smiled his most charming smile at Grace and left his hand around her waist for longer than was necessary to help her back to her feet. Martha glowered inside, but she had to hide her anger as they all went through into the body of the church to partake of the evening's refreshments. Her irritation was calmed by immediately being surrounded by a group of young men who had danced with her the week before and she was all smiles by the time the interval was over and they all moved back into the Hall to take their seats.

Martha wanted to change seats for the second half of the performance but Daniel put his hand on her back and pushed her forward so that she had to enter the row of seats first. Lillian was so close behind her that Martha could feel her breath on the back of her neck, so Martha couldn't even attempt to stop or try to manoeuvre her way into a different seat, but had to accept the same seating plan as the first half of the concert. It didn't suit her that she had been foiled in her attempts to reduce Grace's enjoyment of the concert and she seethed her way through the second half of the performance.

No-one else had the slightest inkling that Martha disliked Grace, or that the attention that Grace received from Edith and Daniel was making Martha jealous and so everyone continued to behave exactly as they had from the beginning of the concert. Martha, sitting right at the end of their small group, continued to seethe internally, ignoring the performers and Lillian who twice attempted to comment on the concert. Lillian could feel the heat coming from Martha but she chose to ignore it, preferring to enjoy the concert than to try and discover what ailed the girl.

The walk home, in heavier snow, was as bad as the walk to the concert and Martha was by now actively sulking. Edith, who once again was walking with Grace, didn't notice her daughter's attitude and Daniel and Bob were in a deep discussion on the value of building during the summer months. Lillian was again concentrating on not slipping in the slushy snow, so Martha's sulking wasn't noticed or commented on. By the time they reached the laundry, Martha was as angry as she had ever been and she blamed it all on Grace.

The tension was dissipated by the fact that Bob decided they should go straight home, rather than pop into the house and join them in a cup of tea and a bite of supper. He was worried that either the snowfall would get even heavier or that the clouds might clear and allow the frost to make skating rinks out of the slushy streets, so they declined the supper invitation. There was a flurry of leave-taking, during which Martha entered the house without saying goodnight to the Prossers, another action which went totally unobserved by the rest of the group. Martha felt as though she had been passed over for the charms of the, to her, insipid Grace and she resolved to get back at the person who, she felt, had ruined all the Christmas entertainment for her. It didn't take her long to decide what to do.

Martha was a clever girl, not quite as clever as her older brother but certainly well-able to hold her own in any company. Since the new regime had begun in the laundry on York Street, Martha hadn't needed to use the malicious side of her character and the rest of the family had forgotten how she had behaved at school in her early years and how she had wreaked revenge on Joshua for hitting her. Martha hadn't lost this unpleasant side to her character, but had felt loved and appreciated enough recently not to have to use it. It now reared its ugly head as she plotted what to do to seek her revenge on Grace.

    She had taken note of what Lillian had told them about the death of her sister, Emma. Daniel and Edith were still not sure that Lillian had spoken the truth, even though Edith had tried to find out from neighbours if her mother had had a sister. It wasn't easy to interrogate other people about her own family without it looking as though she was being disloyal to her mother, so Edith had abandoned her attempts at detecting and had largely forgotten what Lillian had claimed to have done. Daniel wasn't interested enough to bother to try and find out the truth, although he knew that his grandmother was perfectly capable of carrying out such a deed so he stopped thinking about it. That wasn't difficult for him because he had so much going on in his life at that time and he preferred to use his brain for more productive actions.

    Martha hadn't forgotten what Granny Lillian had said. She agreed with Daniel that Lillian was capable of such an action and, privately, had rather admired Lillian's quick wit and decisive actions. Like her grandparents before her, Martha was capable of shutting off the part of her brain which shouted 'inhuman' at such an act and only decried it if the culprit was caught. The day after the concert, Martha's body did her work in the laundry while her brain teemed with ideas of how to gain revenge on Grace for spoiling her enjoyment of the Christmas entertainment.

    Neither Lillian nor Edith noticed that Martha was very quiet and distracted while she worked. Lillian was worrying about her health again, having begun getting pains in her chest again since the weather had got colder over the past couple of weeks. Even the improvement in her diet couldn't stop the damp and the cold getting into Lillian's bones and flesh and the snow of the day before had increased the number of twinges of pain which she was getting. She slipped back into the kitchen and got her bottle of laudanum out of the bread crock in the pantry and swallowed a couple of spoonfuls of it, without benefit of a drink. Martha, who was crossing the yard with another bucket of coal for the copper, noticed what Lillian was doing and a plan began to grow in her mind.

    Edith didn't notice that either of the other two was in any way different to how they normally were. Since the new regime, Edith had blossomed and, for the first time in her life, she lived up to the promise of beauty which had always been there in her face. It was the kind of beauty which is eternal and only improves as the person ages and, if Edith had but known it, showed her resemblance to her mother's dead sister and was the reason why Lillian had been able to hate her daughter from the day she was born. Her relationship with Bob had put a bloom on Edith's visage which made her glow from the inside and the whole town had been amazed at the change in a girl they had all thought of as a slattern, in her rags and with a dirty face and hair. Now, her hair shone with health and her clothes were immaculate and well-made and she cut a very different figure.

    Her mind, that morning, was busy, going over the events of the evening before. She had really enjoyed the concert but had enjoyed even more the fact that Bob had been there. He had treated her like a lady and she could see in his face when he looked at her that he admired her. The thought made her toes tingle and a smile appear on her face and she could do nothing to control either. She had liked Bob from afar ever since they were children, mostly because he had been kind to her on the occasional days that she had spent at school. She had been ostracised by most of her peers because of her dirty clothes and had not been able to make relationships with any of the other children. They called her names, like 'smelly' and 'stinky' which had made her cry and wish that she could be more like them. She used to wish for parents who were loving and kind and who would have made sure that she was clean and well-turned-out. Bob had been the only one who had been kind to her, ignoring the fact that the other boys had laughed at him for bothering about her.

Years later, when Edith was sixteen, she had been delivering clean laundry to the Station Hotel one night when she had been accosted by a group of youths who tried to take the payment for the laundry from her and very nearly succeeded. It had only been Bob's intervention in chasing the lads away that had saved her and the money and she had been extremely grateful to her knight in shining armour who had ridden to her rescue. When the lads had gone, Edith had turned to Bob and thanked him for his help and it was only then that she realised that he must have been drinking. He had sneaked into the bar of the Station Hotel and had managed to swipe a bottle of rum without the landlord realising. He had escaped out of the back door and hidden himself away in a back alley and started to drink the strong spirit. He hadn't drunk a lot of it but it was strong stuff on a young boy's stomach and he was very much the worse for wear when he had espied the youths chasing Edith.

Edith's thanks had been fulsome and Bob hadn't been able to resist the tearful face which had looked up at him as she thanked him. He had bent to kiss her and then, getting more excited than he had ever been in his life before, he had encouraged her to enter the back alley with him. The fumble was quickly over and hadn't properly registered with Bob because he was so drunk, but Edith had been overwhelmed by the idea that he had found her attractive and her loving nature had responded whole-heartedly to her first ever taste of what it could be like to be loved. She had been starved of any affection her whole life and she had responded with her very soul to his fumbling.

Bob, who was so drunk he fell asleep immediately afterwards, there in the alley, couldn't remember the next day what he had done after he had stolen the rum bottle and had no inkling that he had taken her maidenhead that night. Edith, aware that she had committed a deadly sin, kept quiet about the whole thing until she realised that the fumble had born fruit. She had never admitted to anyone who Daniel's father was, despite being soundly beaten by Joshua, but had locked her only experience of love away in her heart until the universe turned and brought her a better life. The fact that Bob had now made her the object of his attentions made her want to laugh and cry at the same time. She had no intention of telling him about that night because she knew he had been too drunk to remember it, so she would never tell him about Daniel being his son, although she felt that the resemblance between them must surely be obvious to everyone. It warmed her heart to see Bob and Daniel getting on so well when they were together, even though neither of them knew their true relationship.

Edith had carried a torch for Bob in her heart ever since that night, so his interest in her now was fulfilling every one of her dreams which had kept her going while her life had been so horrendous. But it meant that she had a lot to think about and therefore she was unaware of her daughter's jealousy and mounting wish for retribution. If she had been aware of Martha's mental state, she would have taken steps to deal with it because she was the only one who knew how strong the blood-link was between Martha and Joshua and, therefore, the only one who knew how dark Martha's soul could be. For Edith's second experience of the relationship between adults hadn't been the starry-eyed encounter that her first had been. Her second had been when she was raped by her father behind the copper in the yard one afternoon when Lillian was out shopping. Joshua had been to deliver some laundry and had then spent the payment in a pub near the dockside, finishing with half a bottle of cheap gin which had come in on one of the boats. He had been barely capable of anything when he had crawled into the backyard, knowing that he was going to suffer his wife's rage when she found out what he had done with the money and already angry at her response, even before he had seen her. In his drunken state, he had thought that Edith was Lillian when he grabbed her from behind and clouted her across the head. She had fallen to the floor, unable to stand as she slipped in and out of consciousness and had only been aware of what he had done to her when he heaved himself off her and stumbled away into the kitchen.

Edith had sobbed out her fear and her hatred of her father into her pillow every night, praying that this coupling wouldn't bear any fruit this time, but her prayers hadn't been answered and Martha had been the result. She had even suffered Joshua's punishment for her transgressions without letting anyone know how her pregnancy had come about because she was so ashamed at having been taken by her own father. It had never ceased to amaze her that she was capable of loving the child of that union but she had adored Martha from the minute she had been born, although she was fully aware of the depths of Martha's soul. If she hadn't been so taken up with thoughts of Bob and their blossoming relationship, she would have noticed that Martha was on a downward path and would have taken steps to make her see the error of her ways, but, unfortunately for Grace, Edith was besotted by Grace's father and unaware of her daughter's machinations.

So Martha was free to concentrate on how she was going to seek revenge from Grace. She had a quick mind and had noticed where Lillian had put the bottle of laudanum after she had taken her medicinal measure from it and she remembered that Lillian had told them she had put arsenic in her sister's drink. She knew that there wasn't any arsenic in the house because she had looked for it after Lillian had made her 'confession' but she also knew that laudanum took away pain and induced sleep when ingested. She was also able to realise that it didn't make Lillian sleepy because she had been taking it regularly for quite some time and her body had got used to it. But she was convinced that meek and mild Grace wouldn't have taken any laudanum in her life and so she would react badly to it. She resolved to put some of the drug into Grace's drink, next time she came to the house with her father, in order to make the girl feel unwell. She had seen Lillian measure two spoonfuls out and decided that she would use only one, as she didn't want to kill the girl, just make her too poorly to stay in their house. Her plan looked as though it had been made by a higher being when she learnt that Bob and Grace were expected to call for tea on Sunday, which also happened to be Christmas Eve. Martha smiled to herself at that thought. It would be a lovely Christmas present for her. She couldn't wait for Sunday to arrive and the opportunity to carry out her plan. Her conscience, never a very strong voice, made no demur at her intentions and Martha was suddenly happy again.

Chapter Thirteen

Sunday dawned bright and clear with little trace of the snow which had dogged the town during the week, although the vestiges of it were still piled around the streets. It hadn't been warm enough to melt it away but it had been mostly covered by a layer of dirt and soot from the many coal fires in the town and the output from the iron and steelworks, so it tended to blend into the background.

Lillian had given way to Edith's urgings and had taken a seat next to the range in the kitchen. She didn't feel ill, just very tired and the cold seemed to eat at her very bones. When Edith suggested that she should bake for their afternoon tea party, Lillian made no demure apart from insisting that Edith make some scones, as these could be dressed with jam and cream and made into a centrepiece for the tea table. Edith agreed and sent Daniel to the dairy on Nelson Street for some fresh cream, aware that the dairy would be open for business because it was Christmas Eve, even though it was a Sunday. Any rules and regulations could be stretched to fit when it came to the business of raking in the money at Christmastime.

Daniel still had a couple of loads to deliver that morning but he promised to collect the cream before he came home, so Edith began measuring ingredients and preparing the tins for her cakes and pastries. Martha had offered to begin washing the last couple of loads of laundry which had been brought to them the day before. Most people managed to organise their lives enough to be able to do without any clean laundry over Christmas but the Station Hotel always needed clean bedding, so they tended to ignore the festive season and had delivered the soiled linens as usual on Friday. Martha sneaked into the pantry while her mother's back was turned and acquired two biscuits and Lillian's bottle of laudanum which she slipped into her pinny pocket before leaving the kitchen. Neither Edith nor Lillian noticed what she was doing and she grinned to herself at her cleverness as she went into the shed.

She soon had the copper going and, while she waited for the water to heat up, she poured a teaspoon of laudanum into a small beef paste jar which she had rescued from the washing-up the day before. She put the jar into her pocket and hid the laudanum bottle behind the copper until she could return it to the pantry. It didn't take her long to get the Station's sheets through the copper and the mangle and she spread them over the drying lines before she finished for the day.

When she got back into the kitchen, Edith was alone because Lillian had 'gone to have a lie down' as she was still feeling very tired. Edith was at the range, putting tins of cakes and scones into the oven to bake before she began to decorate them and was totally taken-up with her tasks so she didn't see Martha put the laudanum bottle back into the pantry behind the bread crock. Martha was feeling very pleased with herself and even asked if Edith needed any help in preparing the tea for that afternoon. Edith was grateful for her help as she was determined to make the tea party as successful as possible so that Bob could appreciate how talented she was. She wanted to wash away any memory he may have of the scruffy, unkempt girl she used to be because she was beginning to have dreams of a more permanent relationship with him, built on the new version of Edith.

When Daniel arrived home, with the fresh cream, Edith and Martha were making sandwiches and cutting the pies and tarts, ready to put out on the table in the parlour. The fire was already lit in there and Edith had scrubbed and polished so that the whole room shone in the firelight. It looked wonderful and the sprigs of holly and ivy which Martha had wound round every mirror and picture made it very festive indeed. Daniel even remembered to remark on it which pleased his mother very much. He went upstairs then to get washed and changed, ready for their guests' arrival.

Edith had changed into a new dress of soft lavender which suited her dark colouring. She had spent many hours making the dress, buoyed up by the thought of Bob seeing her wearing it and she was very satisfied with the end result. She fastened a matching ribbon into her hair and dabbed on the perfume she had bought as her Christmas present to herself. When she was finished, she stood back and looked at herself in the cracked mirror in the bedroom she now shared with Martha and hoped that Bob would appreciate the trouble she had gone to.

It was exactly 3 o'clock when there came a knock on the front door. Daniel let their visitors in and led them into the parlour where Edith was waiting patiently, rather self-conscious in her new finery. She needn't to have worried about Bob's reaction to it, because he was fulsome in his praise, bringing a fresh glow to Edith's cheeks and making her laugh out loud at his complimentary phrases. Lillian was wearing her best black dress, safe in the knowledge that it suited her colouring and made her look like a respectable matron. But the belle of the ball was Martha, who was wearing a bright red dress she had bought in Reed's shop on Nelson Street and which made her white skin look like porcelain. She accepted all compliments with a smile and a laugh, happy in the knowledge that she outshone every other female in the room.

Grace was dressed in a smart brown suit with a cream lace blouse underneath it. It suited her creamy skin and her brown hair, although it wasn't as vibrant as the clothes worn by Edith and Martha. Daniel privately thought that Grace had a more refined taste than his mother and sister, but he wouldn't have said that in front of them and complimented them all equally.

Martha was full of the joys of the season and she insisted on helping them all to sandwiches and cakes, passing plates round and pouring tea as though she had been doing it all her life. She laughed at every joke and shook her dark hair so that it bounced on her shoulders and captured the gleam from the firelight and candlelight, appearing to sparkle in the dimness of the parlour. She swooped from kitchen to parlour and back again, leaving her mother to chat to Bob and encouraging Grace to sit with Lillian so that they could chat together. Daniel felt out of place in this social event, although he did his best to keep Lillian and Grace amused with small talk. He wished that Bob would take his eyes from Edith, if only for a few minutes, so that they could discuss the new development of terraces which were being built over near the railway lines. He desperately wanted to know what Bob thought about property as a source of income, but he didn't want to spoil Edith's enjoyment of the afternoon by taking Bob away from her. As he was at a loose end, it occurred to him to help Martha as she went to make more tea and he walked into the kitchen as she was pouring something from a jar into one of the cups.

The jar looked out of place amongst the cups and saucers and the teapot and his eye was drawn to it almost against his will.

"What are you doing?" he asked, making Martha jump and rattle the tea tray.

"Pouring tea." Martha answered, snappily. "What do you think I am doing?"

"Why have you got a jar in your hand?" Daniel wanted to know. Martha had over-reacted to his question, after she had jumped so guiltily when he had entered the kitchen, making all his senses quiver in suspicion at her actions.

Martha raised her hand and showed him that it was empty of anything. She then pointed to the jar which was now on the table, looking empty and innocent as it sat next to the butter dish and a knife.

"I've been making some more sandwiches." Martha explained. "Beef paste sandwiches, you know, you spread butter on bread and then spread paste over it. It makes a tasty little morsel when people call round for afternoon tea and you run out of cooked ham and cheese."

Daniel could hear the sarcasm in her voice and it almost, although not quite, rang true. He moved closer to the kitchen table, the better to see the items laid out on it.

"But it's empty! How can you make sandwiches out of an empty jar?"

Martha tutted as though he was an irritating fly, hovering and buzzing around her.

"Of course it's empty," she snapped. "I've used the last of it to make the sandwiches I've just taken through to the parlour. When I came back to brew the tea, I rinsed it out with some hot water out of the kettle. You do know that we can take the jars back and get a penny for three of them? But we have to wash them out so that they don't smell while they sit in the pantry; waiting to go back to Jackson's the grocers. Is that ok?"

Martha stared Daniel straight in his eye, daring him to question her further and, because he couldn't justify his suspicion when her explanation had been so clear, he dropped his eyes from hers and stepped aside so that she could carry the tea tray into the parlour. She swept out of the room as though she was a great lady, brushing past the hired help and leaving Daniel standing at the table. After she had gone, he stood for a moment with his head on one side, as though he was considering her answers, then he stepped closer to the table and lifted the jar to his nose. It didn't smell of anything apart from a faint trace of lard, which was to be expected of a jar which had held beef paste. He put it back down on the table and turned to leave. Then he stopped in mid stride and crossed to the pantry. He pulled out the bread crock and reached behind it for the laudanum bottle which he knew Lillian kept hidden there. It was less than half-full but this didn't tell him anything because he had no idea how much should be in it. He unstoppered the bottle and sniffed it, although its odour was very weak. In the background there was a very faint smell of Christmas pudding which had him wrinkling his nose in confusion, until he realised that it was the cloves or cinnamon in a Christmas pudding which he could detect. He knew that their chemist mixed the laudanum with cloves to disguise the bitter taste. He couldn't tell if the paste jar had also had this odour of cloves, so he went back and sniffed it again, but his nose wasn't sensitive enough to be able to give him a definite answer.

Daniel didn't know why he was so suspicious of Martha's actions or who could be the possible target for her hatred, but he resolved to keep a closer eye on her than he had been recently. The visit by her schoolteacher over her bullying behaviour came back to him as he stood and cogitated in the kitchen and this made him consider who the likely target could be. He was sure that Martha had no gripe against their mother, especially as Edith had bent over backwards to help Martha chose clothes and hairstyles since their new status in the household had meant that they could finally get treats for themselves. Granny Lillian could be a target, but her weakened state had reduced her significance as an enemy, although Martha could still be harbouring grudges from earlier times. Daniel finally considered if Grace could be Martha's target, although how could she want to get revenge on a young girl she hardly knew? What could the girl have done to turn Martha back to the belligerent bully she used to be?

The only other candidate for her hatred was Bob, but Daniel couldn't find any reason for that, unless Martha was jealous that her mother had a gentleman friend. Bob was such a pleasant, amusing and interesting person that Daniel could see no flaw in him and he more or less abandoned the thought of Bob being Martha's target.

Daniel couldn't come to any conclusion but he resolved to watch her more closely because he was certain that she was up to her old tricks. He recognised the brittleness of her behaviour, even though he was amazed by her capacity to lie, and the only way to keep a close eye on her was to be in the same room as her whenever he thought that she was tempted to commit one of these acts. He made his way back to the parlour, determined to see if he could detect her target.

Martha was still passing plates around the room, laughing and giggling with each one she served, pretending to be a parlourmaid serving the aristocracy their afternoon tea. Everyone was laughing with her so, on the surface, the atmosphere was happy and benign, but Daniel could see that her laughs were too brittle and her actions were overly-dramatic. He was just in time to see Martha take a cup from the tea tray and pour milk and tea into it. He couldn't be sure, but he thought that there was a movement inside the cup before Martha poured in the milk, as though a small amount of clear liquid was in the bottom of the cup. He glanced at the only other cup on the tray but it was definitely empty. Was he right or had he been mistaken? What did Martha have against Grace because it was Grace who received that cup of tea?

Daniel didn't want to spoil the party by accusing Martha of attempting to drug Grace when he could have made a mistake. He wasn't sure that there had been anything other than milk and tea in the cup and, anyway, what would Bob think of the family if the son accused his sister of such an act? He would think that they weren't the kind of family he wanted to associate with and that would really upset Edith. Daniel sighed to himself, but decided that he couldn't accuse Martha of anything just yet. He would watch and see what happened, although he would have a lot on his conscience if Martha had been up to her old tricks and he hadn't stopped her. He stepped forward to take a cup from Martha and pass it to Lillian, receiving a wink from Martha as he took the cup from her.

Grace didn't keel over and start foaming at the mouth when she had drunk her tea. Daniel felt it was something of an anti-climax when nothing untoward happened and he wondered if he had been doing Martha an injustice by being so suspicious of her. She was still carrying the conversation by chatting about the maid who had brought the Station Hotel's laundry the day before, keeping them all in stitches as she acted the part of the not-very-bright girl who didn't understand the question - 'Do you want us to wash and iron them, or just wash them?' She even rose to her feet and copied the maid's rolling walk as she had left the dairy, which reduced them all to giggles and had Lillian wiping her eyes as she laughed so much.

Daniel felt guilty now, so he joined in and told a few tales of customers he had met on his delivery round and then Bob added a few tales of the strange people he had worked for over the years. The afternoon passed quickly and it was fair to say that they were all enjoying it, apart from Martha. She was performing for them all while, underneath her jolly and jokey front, she was wondering why Grace hadn't shown any reaction to the two teaspoonfuls' of laudanum which Martha had added to her tea. Grace looked as composed as ever, chatting happily to Edith and even smiling at Daniel's anecdotes. Martha couldn't understand why she wasn't reacting to the laudanum and this occasionally made her forget where she had reached in the story that she was telling, gaining her some strange looks from Edith and Daniel.

It was as Bob said that they really should go home as his mother would be back from visiting her ailing sister, that Grace showed the first sign of reacting to the laudanum.

Martha and Daniel had both expected that the person given the drugged tea would fall asleep, as Joshua had always done when Lillian dosed him with it, but Grace was still as wide-awake as ever. What happened was that she didn't seem to be able to control her feet when she attempted to stand when Bob said it was time to go home. She rose from the sofa where she had been sitting next to Bob and made to walk towards Daniel who had brought her coat in from the hall. But her left foot tried to step to the left and her right foot attempted to step to the right, making her do the splits as she tried to cross the room. Naturally, she fell over because she had lost her balance as her feet went walkabout and fell backwards, ending up in a most ungainly and unladylike pose on the hearthrug with her skirts around her thighs.

Martha laughed out loud, unable to keep the merriment within her while Bob and Edith both rushed to rescue her from her embarrassment. Grace was utterly mortified at being seen displaying her undergarments to the world in such a fashion and she promptly burst into tears, hiding her face in her father's arm. Martha pretended all concern and tried to straighten her skirts for her, showing even more of Grace's smalls as she deliberately pulled at the skirt the wrong way. Grace was, by now, in floods of tears, too ashamed to show her face to anyone and demanding that Bob took her home immediately.

Bob didn't know whether to laugh or cry, given that Grace's descent to the floor had been done in such a spectacular fashion, although he felt for his daughter's lost composure and scooped her upright as quickly as he could. Edith bundled her into her coat and then Bob helped her to totter across the floor to the door. He paused there to thank them all for a wonderful afternoon, which brought a fresh paroxysm of tears from Grace, before Daniel opened the front door for them and they stumbled away down the street, rapidly swallowed by the snow which had begun falling again. Daniel watched the couple until they were out of sight and then he slowly closed the front door on the encroaching snow. His brain was working thirteen to the dozen as he strode the length of the hall and re-entered the parlour.

Martha and Edith were clearing the plates and Lillian had dropped into a snooze as she sat in the most comfortable chair in the room. Daniel waited until Edith lifted the wooden tea tray and left the parlour to take the dirty pots to the kitchen. Martha was piling yet more crockery into heaps to put on the tray when Edith returned with it and she avoided looking at Daniel as he stood in the doorway. Daniel took another look at Lillian to confirm that she was asleep and then he crossed the room in two quick strides so that he was at Martha's side.

"You put laudanum in Grace's tea." It was a statement, not a question and Martha bristled as he made it. "I know you did, Martha, so don't lie about it. Why would you do something like that? She's a nice girl and our Mam fancies her dad. Why do you want to spoil it for everyone? Don't you think it would be lovely for our Mam to get married to a good man like Bob? Do you want to spoil her new life for her?"

Daniel ran out of things to say and stood, shaking his head at his sister as she continued to clear the table. Finally, Martha answered at least a couple of his questions.

"Of course I don't want to spoil our Mam's relationship with Bob. He is a nice man and she deserves to have some good luck for a change, but I can't stand that snivelling bore. She simpers at everybody and I'm sick of my family only being concerned with her. Do you know how much I was ignored at the concert or were you too busy making sure that Grace had a good time, like the rest of you?"

Daniel was thunderstruck at Martha's reply. How could she be so spoilt that she only cared about herself? And to take it out on Grace, who hadn't hurt anyone in her life. How low would his sister stoop to get revenge for imagined slights? Daniel was appalled at the evil he could see beneath the pretty exterior in front of him, so much so that he could feel cold fingers of fear walking their way down his back.

Chapter Fourteen

Daniel's mind was spinning as he looked at his sister. At first, he couldn't put any of his feelings into words so he stood and gaped at her, his mouth opening and closing as he tried to speak. Then Edith entered the parlour again and he had to jump to one side to get out of her way as she bustled around him.

"Come on, lad." Edith hugged him as she walked past, so full of happiness that she wanted everyone to share it with her. "You are getting in the way, standing in the middle of the room like that. Grab that teapot and take it through into the back kitchen, if you are in a mind to give us a hand."

"Yes, sorry Mam." Daniel stuttered, forced to drop his gaze from Martha's face. "I'll go and bank the fire up in the kitchen. It's going to be cold tonight with the snow."

"That's a good idea." Martha could still sound normal, even though she knew that Daniel wanted to ask her if she had really put laudanum in Grace's tea. Grace's inability to walk properly when she had stood up had shocked Martha as much as the rest of the family because she hadn't been expecting such a result. If Grace had dozed off on the sofa and snored her way through tea then Martha wouldn't have been shocked because she was expecting it, but for Grace to lose the ability to put one foot in front of the other had shaken Martha more than she wanted to admit. Of course, she wasn't au fait with all the reactions people could have to laudanum but, even so, it had been a shock for Martha and she had had to bite her tongue to stop herself from crying out when it had happened.

It had been obvious to both Daniel and Martha that Grace had very quickly recovered because she had been walking normally again when she and Bob had walked away down the street. It must have meant that Grace would suffer no permanent effects from the substance that had been given to her, for which Daniel was supremely grateful. What would he have done if Grace had been permanently impaired? Would he have admitted that he knew his sister had doctored Grace's cup of tea? To do so would break his mother's commandment which she had drilled into them both since they were small children that they were family and family stick together. 'Family against the rest of the world' had always been Edith's mantra and letting any authority know what his sister had done would break that but, could he really let Martha get away with what she had done? That would be tantamount to agreeing with it and could encourage Martha to go further next time she wanted to get revenge for any other imagined slight. She could kill someone!

Daniel attacked the fire in the kitchen with far more energy than was necessary which resulted in the flames leaping upwards, producing a vast amount of heat which warmed his face as he stared into the flames thinking about Martha. His mind was spinning with his thoughts and he knew that he would get very little sleep that night. It was a good job it was Christmas Day tomorrow and he didn't have to go to work. Daniel's musings were interrupted by Edith who bustled into the kitchen to do the washing up.

"Goodness me, that fire's big enough to set fire to the chimney!" Edith declared as she began putting crockery and dishes into the sink. "I don't think it will be that cold overnight, Daniel. Your Granny is going to bed early cos she's still tired and we'll be in the parlour for the rest of the evening. I thought you were going to bank it down for the night?"

"I was, Mam." Daniel answered, struggling to keep his voice even and as normal as possible. He didn't want to worry his mother when she was so happy about her prospects for the coming year. "I gave it a poke and it flared up like this. It must be good coal that the coalman brought this week."

Edith laughed as she worked over the sink, humming a tune to herself. Daniel couldn't find it in him to spoil her day so he resolved not to mention what Martha had done, deciding that he would keep it to himself this time but, if she tried any of her tricks in the future he would let Edith know what she was doing. But, he was going to give Martha a good talking-to as soon as he could catch her on her own.

　　Edith went up to bed when she had finished returning the kitchen to normal, leaving Daniel and Martha alone in the parlour, so that the opportunity to talk to Martha came sooner than Daniel would have wished. He wanted to concentrate on building his business so that they could stop running the laundry which, he felt, caused too much work for very little return. He had been amazed at the amount of money he could earn with his carting and knew that he stood fair to build up a very successful and lucrative business which would keep them all in a condition which they deserved. He had so many plans for the future and Martha's behaviour was a problem he could do without, but he had to say something while he had the opportunity.

　　When he went back into the parlour, Martha was leafing through a catalogue of ladies' fashion which she had found in Reed's shop, choosing what kind of suit she would like to keep her well-dressed for the rest of the winter. Although Grace's suit had been dark-coloured, Martha had admired the cut of it and wondered if she and Edith could make one for her in a brighter fabric. She didn't want to talk to Daniel because she knew he was going to question her further about Grace and she hated being chastised for her behaviour. Deep down, she had enough of her mother in her to know that she had over-stepped the mark but she usually managed to keep that part of her personality well under control. She hated to feel guilty about anything and she knew that Daniel was going to try to tap into that. As she had expected, Daniel opened the conversation.

　　"Are you going to tell me why you put laudanum into Grace's tea?" Daniel asked, in a very quiet voice.

　　"I've already told you why." Martha snapped. "Everybody ignored me at the concert and fussed over her. She thinks she's God's gift to the world, that one, and I thought she needed bringing down a peg or two. I thought she would fall asleep and perhaps snore so that we could have a laugh at her. I didn't know she was going to go all jelly-legged, did I? Anyway, why are you making such a big thing out of it? It was just a prank."

　　"It wasn't just a prank, Martha, as you very well know. You could have killed her! What if she'd had some sort of reaction to it? For all you knew, she could have been allergic to it in some way and you'd be sitting there with a murder on your hands. Why can't you just ignore her if you don't like her? If anything happens to Grace, Bob would be so upset and it could stop him being so interested in our Mam. Do you want Mam to miss out on a chance of happiness? She's had very little of it up to now and she's worked dammed hard all her life, putting up with Grandad and Granny. Do you know how bad her life has been?"

　　"Of course I know, Daniel. I was brought up in the same way, remember?" Martha was now giving Daniel her whole attention. She dropped the catalogue onto the floor and leant forwards so that she could look into Daniel's eyes. "I had the same upbringing as her, the starving, the cold, the muck and dirt and over all of it, the way Grandad and Granny treated us. I could never understand why our Mam didn't shout back at them or hit them back when they hit her. I watch her now, looking after Granny Lillian as though she was repaying the love she had had from her all her life and I wonder why she's doing it. I would make the miserable old witch pay for the years of misery."

　　"I know you would." Daniel snapped back. "You'd take your pound of flesh out of her hide, if you were given the chance and you'd laugh while you were doing it."

"Don't talk down to me like that." Martha was snarling now, the red light in her eyes giving her the look of a demon in a Christmas pantomime. "Our Mam never once turned on Granny or Grandad no matter what they did to us. He used to beat us both and all Mam ever did was to cry and whinge about it. If she'd had more backbone, they would never have dared to do all that they did. Do you know that other people knew what was going on here and no-one lifted a finger to help us? It didn't matter to anyone what you and I had to endure, the whole world just walked by. Well, I'm never going to live like that ever again and, if I don't like the way someone treats me, then I'll make bloody sure that they know it. I've got nothing more to say to you tonight. I'm going to bed."

Martha flounced out, leaving Daniel sitting staring at the fire and wondering how far Martha was going to go. He thought back to how Grace had looked that afternoon when she and Bob had arrived and he recalled his thought that Grace had more style than either his mother or Martha. He wondered if that was the reason that Martha disliked her so, because she outshone his flashy sister. He sighed deeply and then gave up trying to understand Martha. He went to bed, after checking that the fire in the kitchen was now low enough to be safely left overnight. The fire in the parlour was almost out so he could leave that one without any worries.

Christmas Day dawned fine and crisp. The snow which had been falling on Christmas Eve had stopped and, during the night, a frost had set in, making everything sparkle in the weak sunshine. Edith was still in the very happy mood she had been in the day before, so she rose early and had the fire lit in the kitchen before Daniel and Martha came downstairs for their breakfasts. Daniel didn't want to stay at home with Martha because she was still making him very uneasy so he decided he was going to go to the new shed he had rented which was near the railway lines. There wasn't room in the yard in York Street to store his cart because the laundry shed took up so much space and Daniel had been lucky to get one of the sheds near the allotments for it. He was also looking forward to the future when he would have a horse and cart and he was negotiating to rent part of the spare land there to keep a horse on. He knew it wouldn't be long before he changed to a horse and cart because his business was growing so quickly and now the old chap who had been his only competition had retired, then he expected to be doing much more work. Thinking about work made him happier than thinking about Martha and leaving the house would mean he wouldn't have to look at her.

Edith was frying bacon for their breakfasts, helped by Martha while Daniel went to check on the copper in the yard before he went out. He topped it up with water so that it would be ready when they needed to light it again and was setting the fire underneath when Edith shouted from the kitchen. Daniel put down the newspaper he had been rolling to make the 'bricks' for the next day and ran to the back door. Edith's shout had been very panicky and he wondered what on earth could be the matter. Edith was standing, white-faced, next to the range, holding onto the mantelshelf and looking as though she could faint at any minute.

"What's happened?" Daniel asked, looking from Edith to Martha, who was also very pale and holding onto the kitchen table. The bacon in the pan was sizzling gently but it was obvious that it was just about to catch so Daniel moved it off the range, wondering why the other two were ignoring it.

"What's happened?" Daniel repeated, louder this time.

"It's Granny." Edith managed to say, then her breath caught in her throat and the tears began to roll down her face.

"What about Granny?" Daniel asked, although he thought he already knew.

"She's dead." Martha stated as baldly as though she was answering a request for the time of day. "Dead as a dodo and just as ugly."

"Martha!" Edith exclaimed, appalled at her daughter's lack of taste and sensitivity.

"Well, she is." Martha shot back at her mother. "I'm not going to pretend that I'm mourning her loss when she spent most of my life slapping and starving me. You can pretend that she was a proper mother to you but we all know the truth. The woman was a heartless bitch and I, for one, am glad that she's dead. Good riddance to the old witch. I hope she's in Hell being prodded by the Devil with his pitchfork for all the sins she committed on this earth."

Edith couldn't speak, she was so taken-aback by Martha's words. She slowly sank into the chair next to the range and rubbed her hands together while the tears continued to roll down her face. Daniel crossed the kitchen as quickly as he could and put his arm round Edith's shoulders, but he didn't take his eyes from Martha's face.

"What?" Martha shouted at him. "Do you think I killed her? Is that why you can't take your eyes off me?"

"Martha!" Edith tried to remonstrate but she was too upset and shocked to make it sound meaningful.

"Daniel thinks I'm a wicked person, don't you, my beloved brother? He thinks I gave Grace laudanum yesterday in her tea and that's why she fell over in the parlour. And he's gone straight from that conclusion to decide that I'm now a murderer. Didn't you know that Granny has had a bad heart for years? She'd come to the end of the road and died in her sleep - much more peacefully than she deserved in my opinion but I had nothing to do with it."

"I wasn't accusing you of anything." Daniel said, very quietly. "If you must know, I looked at you to see how you were taking it because our Mam was taking it so badly. Perhaps you have a guilty conscience and that's why you jumped to the conclusion that I was blaming you."

"No, Daniel. I don't have a guilty conscience at all, so stop being so self-righteous."

Martha looked ready to continue the battle of wills but Edith put a stop to it by lifting her hand.

"Please, I've had enough of a shock this morning without you two fighting. You know I believe that family should stick together, not start accusing each other. My mother's heart has given out, after a hard life, and we need to support each other through the coming days. For my sake, will you both promise to stop fighting?"

Edith looked hard at them both and Daniel hung his head, ashamed that he was making things worse for his mother. Martha looked as though she was going to say more but then she thought better of it and nodded at Edith.

"Don't worry, Mam, we won't fight any more." Martha said, in a much more restrained way. "One of us will have to go for the doctor and the undertaker."

"I'll go." Daniel offered. "But, hang on, it's Christmas Day. The undertakers won't be open today and Dr MacMillan might have gone away for the holiday. I'll go round to his house and see if he's there."

"Well, there's no rush, is there?" Edith was down-to-earth enough to realise that this hardly constituted an emergency. There was nothing that anyone on earth could do for Lillian now. "If the doctor isn't at home you will just have to leave a message. It's going to be Tuesday before the undertakers is open, so we can't sort the funeral yet. I'll wait and see if Dr MacMillan comes before I lay her out."

"I'll help you, Mam. We're getting a lot of practise at it recently." Martha offered.

Daniel was relieved to leave the house because he was sure that his feelings about Martha must be showing on his face. He had always had trouble with telling lies, unlike Martha, and getting away from her for a while would give him chance to school his expression into one of innocent neutrality. Heaven knew what Martha would do if she was guilty of something and felt that she was in danger of being unmasked. A walk, even in the frosty air, would give him the opportunity to clear his head and might un-muddle his thoughts about his sister.

Dr MacMillan hadn't left town for the holiday season and he answered the door himself when Daniel knocked. He was fully aware of Lillian's medical history and airily told Daniel that he would call round that afternoon. If Edith wanted to lay Lillian out in the meantime, then that was fine by him, he said. Despite his bluff and breezy exterior, Dr MacMillan knew that Edith and her children hadn't had an easy life thus far and he wondered, before he put aside all thoughts of his patients to concentrate on enjoying his Christmas dinner, how much difference the death of her only parent would make to the Edith's way of life.

Daniel then made his way to George Butcher's premises on Queen Street. George had entered the profession of undertaker only very recently but the Colemans had used them for Joshua's funeral and Daniel saw no need to search out any other undertaker this time. Once again his luck was in and Mr Butcher arranged to collect the body late that afternoon, after the doctor had signed the death certificate, despite it being Christmas Day. Daniel was relieved because it meant that Lillian wouldn't still be in the house with them; a constant reminder of Daniel's suspicions about Martha.

He made his way home, walking past the many families who were on their way to various churches for the Christmas morning services, answering the greetings he received as heartily as he could, under the circumstances. He felt better for the walk and for the distance from Martha and had almost convinced himself, by the time he arrived home, that his suspicions must have all been misjudged. He was calmer than he had been since the day before and hoped that he could now look at the events through a more balanced eye.

He wouldn't have been so happy if he had seen what Martha did after he left the house. She offered to go and light the copper, so that they could have hot water to lay Lillian out and entered the shed with a small smile on her face which stayed as she lit the fire which Daniel had laid the night before. While she waited for the fire to start creating enough heat to warm the water, she removed Granny Lillian's laudanum bottle from her pinny pocket and lifted to the light to see the level inside it. The bottle was less than half full but that obviously didn't bother Martha because she smiled even more. Then she reached round behind the water pipe which ran round the bottom of the shed walls and retrieved a small bottle of gin which she had concealed there two days before. This bottle was also half full, although there was enough in it to catch what light came in through the slightly-open shed door.

Martha opened both bottles and poured some of the gin into the laudanum, shaking the bottle to make sure that the two liquids mixed together fully. Satisfied that they had, she sniffed the laudanum bottle to see if it was possible to detect the aroma of gin, but there was only a very faint tang of it to be discerned over the overwhelming scent of cloves. She put the gin bottle back behind the pipes and slipped the laudanum bottle back into her pinny pocket. Then she stoked the fire and left it to heat the water in the copper, crossing the yard and entering the kitchen. Edith was upstairs with Lillian, so Martha took the bottle from her pocket and hid it behind the bread crock, in its usual place in the pantry and then went to make a cup of tea for them both. Her face bore the innocence of an angel although it was questionable what her soul contained.

Chapter Fifteen

Daniel arrived home as the kettle began to whistle its tune, glad to be out of the cold air and in the warm kitchen. He managed to speak civilly to Martha and, when Edith joined them in the kitchen, he accepted a cup of tea and one of the scones left over from the day before. Edith was looking agitated again, so Daniel had to ask why.

"I was getting our Mam ready to lay her out when I realised that her bed was wet." Edith replied. "Will you give me a hand to lift her so I can put a clean sheet under her?"

"Of course I will, Mam. Don't get yourself upset over it. Granny Lillian doesn't know anything about it now."

Edith sighed and agreed, but she still looked haunted and Daniel decided it must be because she was remembering all that her mother had done to her throughout her life. He finished his scone quickly so that he could help her change the bed and put Edith's mind at rest over one thing at least.

When he entered Lillian's bedroom, Daniel's first thought was that the last time he had been in there was when he had found Lillian's stash of money. His eyes went unbidden to the built-in cupboard where he had found it and it was only when Edith followed him into the room that he actually looked at his grandmother. The sight stopped him in his tracks. Lillian's eyes were still open and she seemed to be staring straight at Daniel, but it was her mouth that grabbed his attention. Her mouth was wide open in a snarl and that, plus her open eyes, made her look like she used to when she was ready to hit out at one of them. The sight took him straight back to his childhood, when Lillian looked like that as she threw them all out into the back yard, to starve and freeze while she and Joshua enjoyed their evening meal.

"My God!" Daniel stuttered. "I would swear that she's still on the warpath. I'm not surprised that you were shocked when you found her."

"I know just what you mean." Edith whispered, as though raising her voice to a normal conversational level would disturb the woman in the bed. "I've tried to close her mouth and eyes but she's so stiff, they won't move. I don't want her looking like that when the doctor comes. He might think that she was trying to call out for help and we've ignored her."

Daniel risked another look at his grandmother.

"I see what you mean, but I don't think she was calling out for help, I think she looks as though she was angry over something. It's almost as though she's died in the middle of berating someone."

"Don't be daft, Daniel. Your imagination is worse than mine. She wouldn't have been angry with anyone. She was alone when her heart gave out."

Daniel wasn't so sure of that so he dropped the subject and went to see if he could move Lillian's mouth and close her eyes. At first, he hesitated about touching her but soon realised that she wasn't going to respond to a gentle touch, he needed to put some force behind it. Swallowing the bile that rose, unbidden, at the thought of man-handling a dead body, Daniel pushed her upper and lower jaws together. There was a slight snap, as though he had broken a sinew, but then the jaws moved together and the anger seemed to fade from the dead face. He then pressed heavily on the eyes and was thankful when he realised that they were going to stay shut. It was only then that he realised that he had been holding his breath all the time he had been touching his granny, as though he thought that the cadaver would breathe noxious fumes into his face as he bent over her. He shivered at the thought and tried to tell himself that he was being silly and childish, but he could still see the lines in Lillian's face that bad-temper rather than old age had put there.

"Oh thank goodness Daniel, you've done it." Edith sounded as though she had been released from under a tremendous pressure and Daniel glanced anxiously across at her.

"I'll lay her out if you don't want to, Mam." Daniel offered. He could see his mother's hands trembling as she rinsed out the flannel she was holding. He didn't know what he was supposed to do but he would do anything to stop his mother being so stressed by the experience.

"No, I can manage now." Edith answered. "It's not so bad now that her eyes are shut. I don't feel that she's watching me and noting where I am going wrong anymore."

Daniel helped Edith lift the dead weight and held it while Edith stripped out the wet sheet and replaced it with a clean one. Then he slowly lowered the body back onto the bed and stepped away from it.

"I'll fetch Martha to help you. You can't do this on your own."

Edith nodded her assent and began washing her mother's body. Daniel went downstairs and asked Martha to go and help upstairs while he went to his shed to check on his cart. Martha gave him an enquiring look but didn't ask why he needed to go out on Christmas Day if he didn't have to. She scooped up a pile of towels from the kitchen table and left Daniel alone. He waited, listening to her footsteps as she mounted the stairs and, when he heard the bedroom door close behind her, he slumped against the range. He forced his brain to stop thinking about what he had seen, threw on his coat and left the house as quickly as he could.

He crossed Middlesbrough Road with his head down, ignoring anyone who passed him, too deep in his own thoughts to hear the greetings tossed across the frosty air towards him. It was only when he unlocked the padlock on the shed door and entered the welcoming darkness within that he allowed his brain to unfreeze and start working normally again.

He was convinced that Lillian had been arguing when the heart attack had claimed her. He was also convinced that the person she was arguing with was none other than his little sister, whose angelic face betrayed no sign of a conscience within. Why would Martha have been in Lillian's bedroom and what did they have to argue about in the dead of night? What could he, what should he, do about it? It was obvious that Edith had no inkling that anything untoward had taken place. She seemed to think that the heart attack had been entirely natural and that it had woken her mother and forced her face into such a grimace at the point of death. He couldn't upset Edith. He didn't want to upset her by accusing Martha of being the reason behind Lillian's death but how could he ignore the warning bells which were ringing so loudly in his head? Daniel placed his forehead against the cold wooden wall of the shed and tried his best to blot out all thoughts of Martha and what she might have done.

It was pointless. He couldn't stop his mind reeling from the shock of realising that Martha could have deliberately engineered her grandmother's death and he didn't know where to turn for help. 'Family sticks together' was jostling in his head with thoughts of Martha arguing with Lillian and he knew that he couldn't take his suspicions to anyone in authority. Edith would be more upset about him breaking the family code than she would be about what Martha might have done. He was in a cleft stick and he couldn't think of any way out of it. All he could do was to stand to one side and let Martha get away with it. But he had to know why she had argued with Lillian, if only to know that Martha hadn't deliberately gone into the bedroom in order to annoy her grandmother enough to make her weak heart fail.

He would have to talk to her again, but he decided to leave it until after Christmas and after Granny Lillian's funeral.

It was with a very heavy heart that he left the shed and made his way home through the now-empty streets to the house where his sister had become a monster, instead of the beautiful child whom he had first met the morning after her birth. His footsteps dragged as he walked and he didn't notice that the frost was lifting and that tiny flakes of snow were floating through the air around him.

When he got home, Edith and Martha were both in the kitchen, peeling potatoes and mixing the batter for the Yorkshire puddings, which would be eaten with gravy on them before the main meal was served. They were both very quiet as they worked and Daniel couldn't think of anything to say. He was sure that if he opened his mouth, his first words would be 'did you argue with Granny until her heart failed her?' That wouldn't improve the atmosphere in any way. While he beat all his brain cells in the hopes of finding a safe topic of conversation, Martha took the need of it away from him.

"Is Bob coming round today?" Martha asked, in a very quiet voice.

"Not until this afternoon." Edith replied. "He said that they were having Christmas dinner with his mother and that he would call round later on this afternoon. I don't think that Grace will come with him, not after having that funny turn yesterday when they were here. She'll probably be far too embarrassed to show her face here for a while."

"I wouldn't bet on that." Martha snarled. "I don't think that will put her off coming round here. I think she's got her eyes on our Daniel, so she won't want to miss an opportunity to be with him. She obviously thinks that it's fun to sit silently watching the love of her life as he goes about his equally-boring life."

Edith looked up from the sink and glanced at Martha.

"I hope you aren't jealous of Grace, Martha." Edith spoke sharply, which Daniel took as a sign of her raised stress levels. "Please don't be awkward with her, at least not until I've, erm, I'm er, you know."

"You mean, not until you've got Bob to propose to you." Martha stated, baldly.

"Martha!" Edith was shocked into almost shouting her name. "I just meant, not until I'm sure that Bob really is interested in me."

"Oh, I think we can take that for granted." Martha laughed. "I've never seen a man more obviously smitten than he is. I reckon he'd walk to London and back if he thought it would make you like him as much as he likes you. Anyway, I'm not jealous of Grace, so you needn't worry that I'll upstage her in any way. It's more likely that she would bore me to death."

Daniel listened to the banter being passed between his mother and his sister and knew that he couldn't do anything to upset the situation that they were now in, not without spoiling things for Edith who was finally being given a chance at happiness. He resolved to have words, again, with Martha, to warn her off from doing anything else which could bring the family to the notice of the authorities, and then he knew he would have to let the matter drop. He could only hope that Martha would behave in the future.

Mr Butcher arrived with his funeral cart early in the afternoon and took Lillian to his new funeral parlour on Queen Street, promising that he would give her a fine funeral which wouldn't cost them an arm and a leg. The atmosphere in the house lightened as Mr Butcher drove away through the now-heavy snowfall, as though all the evil memories of the house were now trapped in the cheap pine coffin and could no longer hurt or upset any of them. Edith relaxed when they went back indoors, feeling that she was finally in charge of her own life and would never be unhappy again.

Bob arrived in the late afternoon and invited Martha and Daniel to leave him alone with Edith in the parlour. Edith's cheeks wore a pink flush which suited her very much and Daniel thought she looked so pretty as he hustled his sister out of the parlour when it seemed that Martha was going to question the need for their expulsion. They went into the kitchen where Daniel pinned Martha against the range and threatened to force laudanum down her throat if she ever hurt anyone ever again, letting her know that he had his suspicions about Lillian's final few minutes on this earth. Martha wouldn't answer this accusation, but did say that she had no intentions of hurting anyone in any way, so he could stop being the bully-boy big brother and concentrate on his own life. By the time Edith and Bob joined them to impart their news, Martha and Daniel were behaving as though everything was normal and they both hugged the newly engaged pair and offered heartfelt congratulations.

"We aren't going to tell anyone else about our engagement, apart from Grace and Bob's mam." Edith told them. "I don't think it would be in good taste to be celebrating when we've got to bury our Mam by the end of the week, so please don't tell anyone else. We are keeping it a secret until after Mam's funeral and then you can tell anyone you want."

The funeral was a small affair, taking place in the quiet time between Christmas and New Year. The snow, which had begun to fall on Christmas Day, delighting the children of the town, stayed to welcome in the New Year, getting heavier and deeper with every day that passed. Daniel had work to do before the New Year holiday and struggled as he toiled his way across the town, slipping and sliding in one place and getting stuck in a snow drift in another place. He decided to go ahead with his plan to buy a horse and cart while he was digging himself and the cart out of a snow drift, expending so much energy that the sweat was running down his face by the time he had extricated the cart from its icy trap and he was moving again.

He managed to secure the small field near the railway lines for his horse, surprised that there was a stable already in place in a corner of it, which saved him having to build one of his own. There was room for the horse and the cart, so Daniel gave up renting the shed as he didn't need it anymore and bought himself a dog which was to share the stable with the horse. He often had items of stock which he would now keep in the stable and the dog would serve as a guard to stop any light-fingered visitors from removing items of value.

Martha and Edith continued to run the laundry between them although it was obvious that they would be able to give it up in the near future because Daniel's business empire was growing at a remarkable pace. He had acquired all of the customers of the old chap who had retired before Christmas and being able to move goods so much more quickly now that he had the horse and cart meant that he could get many more, and bigger, loads done in a day. During his travels around the town and into Middlesbrough, he often came across items of furniture which he was asked to dispose of and he kept anything which he considered to be of good quality and in good condition. He would then sell these on, if he came across someone wanting such an article of furniture and it wasn't long before he was looking for some bigger premises to store his stock. The house on York Street had no spare space for storage and his stable was bursting at the seams when he heard that there was a small shop up for rent on the corner of Pearl Street and Station Road.

The shop had been empty for a couple of years, ever since the old lady who owned it had become too old and ill to work in the confectionary shop she had built up from nothing. She had sold it to a chap from Middlesbrough who had thought his wife might like to run a sweet shop until she had informed him, in no uncertain terms, that she had no intentions of flogging herself to death selling sweets to all the riff-raff of the town. Daniel swooped upon it and negotiated a rent which the man from Middlesbrough who owned it thought was fair for a small shop in a back street in the town. Daniel took possession of the small house and shop, thrilled that he was moving up in the world and expanding his business much more quickly than he had ever imagined. It wasn't long before the shop was also groaning at the seams with the amount of stock which Daniel had garnered in his travels and he was filling up the two small bedrooms upstairs. He had an eye for a pretty piece of furniture as well as the more mundane but usual articles like settees and tables but he felt he was taking the right road when he brought home a huge wardrobe which a family in Middlesbrough couldn't fit into their tiny two-up, two-down house in one of the terraces in the town.

When he got the wardrobe back to his shop, he struggled to get it in through the shop door and only succeeded when a passer-by stopped to give him a hand. The man was a fitter down the docks and Daniel knew him vaguely from seeing him around the town.

"By heck, you've got some stuff in here, mate." The man said when they had finally managed to squeeze the wardrobe into a space near the shop door. "What are you keeping it all for?"

"I'm not keeping it." Daniel answered. "I just store it in here until I hear of anyone wanting to buy it. But I seem to be gathering quite a lot of stock."

"Quite a lot! It looks like at least ten housefuls to me. Why don't you open the shop door and sell it? I mean, this is a shop, isn't it?"

Daniel was thunderstruck. It had never crossed his mind to open a shop to sell the furniture he was collecting. He usually got the articles for peanuts, considering the amount of wood which had gone into making each item but they were usually excess to the requirements of the people he bought them from and they were glad to get rid of them. If he doubled the price of each one he would make a tidy bit of money if they sold. He thanked the man who had helped him, locked the shop up and mounted his cart once again, his mind whirring with plans.

When he got home, Edith and Martha were both still in the laundry shed, slaving over the most recent deliveries of dirty laundry and feeling the cold, despite the hot water pipes which ran round the bottom of the shed. They still had to go outside to the tap in the yard to get the water to fill the copper and this was a dangerous business in frosty weather when they had spilt water on the ground. Twice that day, Edith had slipped on the now-frozen spills and the second time she had bruised her leg badly. Hearing their complaints, Daniel was sure that this was the ideal time to pass on his new ideas about his next business.

"You know I've been renting that little shop on Pearl Street for the furniture I pick up when I'm out on my rounds?"

"Yes Daniel, but do you mind if we talk about it later?" Edith's leg was hurting, her hands were icy cold and she could only concentrate on getting the washing through so that she could sit down next to the warm range in the kitchen.

"Well, I'm thinking about opening the shop to sell the furniture." Daniel wasn't giving in just yet. He wanted them both to listen to him. "How do you feel about working in my shop instead of flogging yourselves to death doing other people's dirty washing?"

He now had their undivided attention. Martha looked at the dirty towels she was holding and threw them on the ground.

"Do you mean we can both work in a warm shop, selling tables and chairs to customers?" Martha asked, the delight in her voice obvious to all. "We will be inside all the time and collecting money from people? We won't have to lug water about and scald ourselves in the process? No more scrubbing sheets with soap that lifts the skin from your hands? Daniel, lead me to the shop. I'm your first member of staff!"

"Well, Mam, what do you think? Would you rather carry on washing other people's dirty clothes, or will you come and work for me?"

Edith stared at her son while the meaning of what he had said sank gently into her mind. Then she took off her pinny and threw it onto the ground next to the towels that Martha had dropped.

"Lead me to your shop, Danny boy." Edith said. "I've just closed this bloody awful laundry."

Chapter Sixteen

Martha crossed the yard in two strides and flung her arms round Daniel's neck.

"Me too? Am I going to work in your shop? Please say yes, please say yes."

Daniel untangled himself from Martha's arms which were threatening to cut off his air supply and nodded at her.

"Yes, you too Martha. I'll need two of you in there to be able to open it six days a week." Daniel said. "There's a kitchen behind the shop and two small bedrooms upstairs, so there will still be room to store stock and you'll be able to light the fire and have a warm kitchen to sit in when it's not busy. If anyone wants their furniture delivering, just let me know and I'll deliver it for free. So, are you both ready and willing to start work in the morning?"

"Are you going to open it that quickly, Daniel?" Edith was concerned. "Wouldn't it be better if we went and gave the whole place a good clean and polished up all the furniture you have got in it? The whole place would look better and you'll get more customers that way."

"Yes, I suppose you are right." Daniel admitted. "Now I come to think of it, a lot of the furniture I have picked up needs a proper clean and I don't suppose the shop has been cleaned for a while."

"If it's the one on the corner of Pearl Street and Station Road, I wouldn't go in there to buy sweets cos the place was filthy. The old woman who ran it was too old and nearly blind. She won't have given it a clean since Adam was a lad so I should imagine the muck has been breeding in there for years."

"Oh Mam, what a thing to say! I don't know whether I want to go and work in it now, if it's that mucky!" Martha was horrified by the image her mother's words had conjured up in her mind.

"By heck lass, you've got a short memory." Edith was pretty scathing in answering Martha. "It's not that long since this place grew the biggest germs in the whole of South Bank. Granny Lillian was never one for hygiene."

"My memory must be as bad, Mam." Daniel remarked, making his sister give him a happy smile in thanks for siding with her. "I must admit I never noticed the dirt either here or in the shop. I suppose we are all so used to it that we don't notice it."

"Well, it's time you both learnt what keeping a clean house is all about, so we'll start with this little shop of yours. Our lives are so different now from how they used to be. I, for one, want to forget all those years and concentrate on how we live now."

"Are you sure you don't mind giving up the laundry, Mam?" Daniel asked. "I know it'll be a big change for you."

"Mind?!! I've never been happier in my life. If you knew the number of times I nearly walked out of this place. The only thing that kept me here was you two, but look where we are now!"

It took Edith and Martha three days to scrub the little shop and house from floor to ceiling. It would have been better to have done it in springtime when the lighter days and warmer weather made airing and drying things so much easier but they made the best job of it that they could. In reality, by the time they had cleaned the house and then polished all the furniture which Daniel had stocked inside it, the whole place looked and smelled so much better and more welcoming. Daniel was convinced that customers wouldn't be able to resist coming inside and buying the now-pristine furniture. A number of the pieces had been damaged in places or lost handles or feet, but Bob came round and mended everything that he could, and showed both Daniel and Martha how to make the repairs. Martha turned out to have the best hands for mending furniture and she had a knack of choosing the right accessories when an article of furniture had lost all its fittings. She was also very good at re-polishing furniture, taking great delight in turning a scuffed and dirty chest of drawers into a smart chest which would look good in any room.

They opened the shop on a Tuesday morning. Daniel and Martha had covered the town in posters announcing the opening which promised free tea and biscuits to all who came, a promise which brought very high numbers to Pearl Street corner that morning. Daniel made the most of having a crowd of people turn up by asking them all if they had items of furniture they wanted to sell as well as trying to sell as many items to the members of the crowd as was possible. He soon had a long list of contacts who wanted him to look at and offer for furniture and other household items, which he promised to do as soon as he possibly could. By the end of the first day, they had sold a number of items of furniture and the till was nicely heavy when Daniel picked it up to take it home with him that night. All in all, it had been a very successful day and all three of them went to bed, very tired but satisfied with their new business venture.

Edith and Daniel went to sleep almost as soon as their heads touched their pillows but Martha had carried a candle upstairs with her because she had no intentions of falling asleep straight away. While they had been preparing the shop for its grand opening, she had repaired the lock on a bureau which they had found in the back room of the shop when Daniel had first rented it. Daniel could only presume that it had been owned by the old lady who had run the sweetshop and that the owner of the house hadn't wanted to bother with it when his wife had turned her nose up at the prospect of being a sweet shop proprietor. Whatever the reasons, it had been abandoned in the back room and Martha was the first person to touch it for years.

Martha's interest in it had been roused by the picture which had been painted on the back of the bureau, as though someone had used the expanse of wood as a canvas on which to paint their masterpiece. It was entirely normal as a bureau until it was moved away from the wall, which then revealed the landscape on the rear panel. It was a woodland scene, at twilight, with the full moon rising above the trees and sending light into many dark places within the forest. It had taken Martha's breath away when she had first seen it and, after cleaning the whole bureau and repairing the lock on the front, she had put it back up against the wall in the back room. When she saw Daniel that night, she told him she wanted to own the bureau and offered him ten shillings for it. He had laughed at her and then told her to keep her money. She could have the bureau for nothing and he would even cart it back to the house in York Street for her. He had brought it that afternoon, in case a customer managed to catch sight of it and wanted to buy it and so Martha wanted to spend some time in admiring the painting before she slept that night.

She knew she should sleep but the call of the bureau was too strong and she ran her hands over the polished surface of the front of it before she pulled it away from the wall. In the candlelight, the woodland scene seemed almost as though it was waiting for a group of fairies or angels to come along and start to play amongst the trees. Martha smiled at her own silliness as she thought this but the idea was stuck in her head now. She called the painting 'The Enchanted Forest' in her mind. She ran her hands over the picture, noticing how smooth the wooden surface was. Whoever had painted it had sanded the surface until it was incredibly smooth. After the last few days working on wooden furniture, Martha could appreciate the amount of work which had gone into making the surface as smooth as was and it increased her admiration of the piece.

Then, in the top right-hand corner of the back, her stroking fingers touched a raised section which was impossible to see by the light of a candle, try as she might to do so. She stroked it over and over again and then moved her position to see if the section cast a shadow from the candle light. As she moved, her hand pressed harder onto the wood and there was a sudden click, as though she had pressed a button. She sat back from the bureau but couldn't see that the click had made any difference to the painting so she ran her hands over it again. There was a quieter click when she pressed in the right place and then another, louder click when she pressed it again. She moved the bureau slightly to one side, but there was still nothing to see on the back, apart from the painting. She stood up and crossed the room to get the candlestick from the windowsill where she had placed it. She turned back to move it closer to the bureau and, this time, she noticed something different. Pressing the section on the back of the bureau had altered the front of it, which she hadn't been able to see from where she had been crouching behind it. Now she could see a small wedge of wood which was sticking out from the front of the bureau.

Excitedly, she pressed the section on the back of the bureau and, this time, she watched the wedge of wood disappear into the front of it. Pressing the section again made the wedge reappear. She moved the candle until it was shining onto the front of the bureau and touched the wedge. It tilted as she touched it and a very shallow shelf of wood slid out of the front of the bureau. She fiddled with it and discovered that tilting the wedge the other way made the shallow shelf slide back into its housing. She immediately tilted it again because she had seen that the shelf contained a number of sheets of paper and she was sure that they must be something of great importance to be hidden so well inside the rather ordinary bureau (ordinary apart from the painting). She lifted them out and closed the shelf, returning the wedge to its hidden position and then pressing the section on the back of the bureau which locked the shelf in its hidden position.

She carried the candle over to her bedside table and sat down on her bed to see what the sheets of paper contained. The thought that it could lead to hidden treasure was uppermost in her mind and she squinted at the writing on the paper which was very faded and difficult to read by candle light. It took her a while, repeatedly holding the paper to let the candlelight shine onto it before she managed to read the crabbed and faded letters on the page. Her initial reaction was to throw the papers onto her bed as worthless, but then she picked them back up and held them under the candle again.

They didn't contain a treasure map with riches marked by an x on the paper, but were a collection of hundreds of short phrases and sentences which seemed to be itemising the actions of certain people from the town. Martha recognised a number of the names which appeared on the first page and was very interested to read the comments which were appended to these names.

'Robert Leigh, postmaster of this parish, seen entering the house of Olivia Westcott, widow of a retired butcher, where he stayed for two and a half hours.'

'Michael Lewinson, architect, seen entering the house of Harriet Winters, dressmaker, where he stayed for four hours.'

Martha sat back on her bed and thought about the various entries she had read and changed her mind about the papers being worthless. They were a goldmine of information about many of the town's worthy residents, itemising their relationships with other worthy residents - not necessarily people they should have been having a relationship with. She smiled hungrily as she thought about the worth of these papers and the information they contained. They were the secrets of some outwardly upright citizens who seemed to have feet of clay. Martha wondered who had written down all this information and if the writer had personally witnessed these events as they happened. She flicked through the rest of the pages and noted that they were all laid out in the same way as the first two pages. In other words, she had in her hand the peccadillos of about half the town's population, mostly people who wouldn't want their actions to be discussed in public and who could be persuaded to pay to keep their secrets just that - secret.

When she turned to the last page, Martha noticed that this one was set out differently from all the others. There were no names on this sheet, just a short paragraph which seemed to have been added to the end of the collection as an explanation of the previous pages. It was written by the same hand but in a better and darker ink and Martha had no difficulty in reading every word.

They all think I'm blind, the people in this town, and I let them think that I am. I pretend I have to feel my way around and, if someone speaks to me, I make sure I look in the wrong direction when I answer them. My sight isn't as good as it was when I was young, not good enough to make the fancy sweets and cakes that I used to make, but I can still tell who is walking past me. I just pretend that I can't. When I lost enough of my sight to stop me from being the wonderful confectioner I used to be, nobody cared. They turned their noses up at what I produced and went elsewhere to buy their fancy goods for weddings and parties. They didn't think about me at all. They didn't care that I wasn't earning a living anymore. It made me bitter but I decided to make my living another way. I used to hide in back alleys and watch those who moved around at night for nefarious purposes. I didn't realise, at first, that I would see 'upright' citizens going places that upright citizens shouldn't visit and doing things that they shouldn't but a few weeks of walking the streets in the dark showed me a whole other world. My mind turned to a way of profiting from learning these secrets, so I wrote notes to those who I had seen breaking into places or stealing from sheds and back yards. I told them I would go to the police unless they put a tenth of the profit they had made from breaking the law into a shed I own near the railway lines. I would collect the money in the middle of the night when no-one was about. I grew very good at telling if there was anyone else watching me and I was never discovered retrieving my payment. If I thought anyone was watching for me, I left it until another night. People are so stupid; they deserve to lose their money. But then I realised that I could get more if I wrote notes to the ones who were cheating on their wives or their business partners. I didn't ask them for a tenth of their profits, I asked them for a specific amount, letting them know that I would make public what they were doing if they didn't pay me. The money rolled in! I let the petty thieves go about their business without bothering them because I could get so much more from those who were cheating on their wives. I'm a very rich woman now but I have no-one to leave it to, so I've hidden it. All the money that I have gathered over the last few years is hidden somewhere and I've put these papers in the bureau. If a clever person comes along and finds them, they have only to read them through and work out where I would hide money. Then they can have it, with my blessings. So, if you are reading this, work out where I would hide the money and enjoy yourself with it. Just remember, no-one cares about other people so look after yourself. With money you can pay for people who HAVE to care for you.

Martha dropped her hands into her lap and stared at the far wall of her room. It was treasure, hidden where a clever person could find it and she was, most definitely, a clever person. This was now her secret and she wouldn't rest until she had found the treasure. In the meantime, she could do a bit of blackmailing herself. There was a huge amount of information about local people in these pages and she didn't have a guilty conscience to stop her using that information. But she would have to check that the immoral townsfolk were still committing their deadly sins, otherwise she wouldn't make anything out of it.

Martha hid the papers back in their shallow home. She didn't want either her mother or Daniel finding them in her bedroom and possibly destroying them. Daniel, she felt, would be full of righteous indignation that someone had spied on the activities of certain people and he certainly wouldn't have thought of blackmailing those mentioned. But Martha was thinking long and hard about blackmail as she blew out the candle and got into bed. Her dreams, when sleep claimed her, were filled with pictures of piles of coins and people tip-toing around the town in the dark, entering houses which weren't their own.

The next morning, Martha woke up feeling happier than she had ever done in her life before. At first, she couldn't remember what it was that was making her feel so happy but then visions of the close-written sheets of paper flooded into her mind and she smiled with the sheer joy of the future which was opening up in front of her. She bounced out of bed and dressed as quickly as she could, forcing the smile off her face before she went downstairs. Daniel had already left the house because he had a load to pick up from Grangetown which needed to be delivered to a shop in Middlesbrough before it opened that morning. Edith had made toast for breakfast and she gave Martha her share as she entered the kitchen.

"Hurry up, pet, or we'll be late opening the shop." Edith gently scolded but Martha threw her arms round her mother and gave her a huge cuddle.

"What's up with you?" Edith asked. "You aren't usually this happy first thing in the morning."

"Nothing, Mam." Martha smiled at Edith. "Isn't it wonderful that we can work in a warm shop now and not have to scrub our fingers off in that horrible laundry?"

"It is, Miss, but you need to get a move on. We can't sit here all day or Daniel won't make any money from the shop and then we'll have to re-open that horrible laundry."

"Oh I don't think so." Martha replied, swinging her mother round by her arm. "I've got a good feeling that this shop is going to make us a fortune."

Edith couldn't help smiling with her daughter. She agreed with her that the shop was going to make them a good living, going on the amount that they had bought and sold since it opened and she was happy that, very soon, she was going to become Mrs Prosser. Life was good for all of them now, since her parents had died. Edith refused to let the tiny voice of her conscience whisper in her ear that she was being ruthless and cruel wanting to forget her parents and her earlier life. She'd already paid in hard work and starvation for any of the good luck which came to her now and she deserved to be as happy as Martha was.

When Martha had eaten, they banked down the kitchen fire and got their shawls from the peg on the back of the pantry door. The washing up could wait until they came home after they had closed the shop, then Edith knew that Bob was coming round that night. Yes, life was good.

Chapter Seventeen

It was a fairly quiet morning and so Martha offered to spend some time in the back bedroom of the house, sorting through a collection of furniture which Daniel had picked up from a house in Middlesbrough the day before. He wasn't sure if any of it was worth keeping and he had asked Martha to have a look at it when she got chance. She was genuinely interested in the furniture which came through their doors. Although she wouldn't have admitted it to anyone, she loved the feel of the wood under her hands and the different grains which showed up so beautifully when she polished it. She had even begun to appreciate her own skill at matching stains and polishes to furniture she had repaired, making it look as though it had never been broken or shabby. Because of this new-found love, she was gathering skills which she would never have thought about, let alone attempted in her life before and the world was opening up for her. But, now she had found the confectioner's blackmailing notes, her mind turned in again to causing pain to other people.

While she had been reading the notes the evening before, she had noticed one name which jumped off the page at her, despite the faded writing and the lack of light. Mrs Lucy Renwick worked in Reeds clothing shop where, recently, Martha had been buying both dresses and fabric for Edith to make into dresses or skirts for them both. Mrs Renwick was a lady in her mid-forties, a very elegant lady who made the most of her slender figure and her pretty face. Edith was convinced that she used some kind of false colouring to make her face appear so smooth and flawless and Martha had often wondered if she applied some sort of colour to her lips. This was frowned upon by most people but Mrs Renwick seemed to get away with it, if she did wear it, because she was every inch a lady in her manner.

However, her manner changed when she was dealing with Martha. Although Martha had only recently begun spending money in Reeds, Mrs Renwick knew who she was and she treated her as though she was a nasty smell which lingered under her nose. It didn't seem to matter that Martha was now a good customer who frequently bought very expensive materials and trimmings, Mrs Renwick still insisted on speaking to her as though she was still the ragged-arsed child she had been before and Martha bridled at every meeting with the woman. Martha had regularly wondered who Mrs Renwick thought she was, to look down her nose at her, but Mrs Renwick had the capacity to appear as though she was being perfectly polite as she spoke to Martha but sounded as though she was sneering at her with every sentence which left her mouth. Martha had come to hate her, much more than she hated Grace, who now disappeared into the background as far as she was concerned.

Seeing her name in the confectioner's blackmail notes had given Martha a tool with which to pay back every real and imagined slight which Mrs Renwick had inflicted on her and Martha had already resolved to make Mrs Renwick her first blackmail target. Martha knew that Mrs Renwick lived in Redcar Road East with her husband who was a boiler man in the steel works, an occupation which meant that he worked shifts and could be out at work over night. According to the notes that Martha had found, Mrs Renwick was regularly visited overnight by Mr Dundas who was the town clerk. Martha also knew that David Dundas was a married man with several children and a rather pathetic-looking wife who constantly seemed as though she was about to collapse under the pressure of looking after these children. It was strange that the children always seemed to be remarkably well-behaved whenever they were seen outside the house and many folk wondered why Mrs Dundas was always so stressed. Martha couldn't have cared less about any stress that Mrs

Dundas may have been under, but she was extremely interested in Mrs Renwick and Mr Dundas together. Mrs Renwick had never had any children, so Martha surmised that her house was an ideal place for her and Mr Dundas to conduct their sordid little affair.

Martha smiled to herself as she gave the new articles of furniture a good examination, looking for any cracks or dents and, after her discoveries in the bureau, any hidden drawers or doors. It was fairly plain furniture without any ornamentation and she quickly rated it as plain but cheap. Her mind continued to formulate a plan for finding out if the Renwick/Dundas relationship was still ongoing and she nearly missed the little stool which was hiding behind a frankly horrendous chest of drawers. She had been about to leave the little bedroom when she spied it nestling behind the chest and had to spin on one foot to face it. It was made from a very dark wood, or the wood had been stained with a very dark stain and it looked totally out of place next to its neighbours.

It was very finely made, with turned legs which had a barleysugar twist to them and a patterned seat which had been worked by hand from very soft wool. Martha picked it up and was surprised to find how heavy it was, considering the narrow legs and ledges which meant it didn't have a huge amount of wood in its construction. It was only when she turned it upside down to have a look at how the top was attached to the legs that she saw the catch. It was made out of the same wood as the stool and had been stained to match it exactly, which was why she had almost missed it with a cursory look. Moving the catch made the top of the stool swing out to the side and revealed a space which was nearly as deep as the edging of the top. Inside this space were six metal tins which Martha thought looked to be old tobacco tins, although any advertising had been sanded off them. They accounted for the extra weight in the stool and Martha couldn't wait to see what was inside them.

Her first thought was that they may contain jewellery or coins but, even before she opened the first one, she knew that she was wrong. The tins made no noise as she lifted them out of their home and shaking them didn't produce a rattle. The first tin that she tried was very difficult to open and Martha realised that they were covered in rust. Whoever's house they had been in had obviously been very damp and the tins had rusted. Her new-found skills made her next move easy as she ran downstairs for a jug of hot water from the range in the kitchen. No-one would consider it odd that she wanted hot water while dealing with the second-hand furniture; everyone now knew that Bob had instructed her in many little tricks for making life easier when repairing old furniture.

When she got back into the bedroom, she tipped one of the tins upside down and dipped it into the hot water until the lid was completely submerged. Listening closely, she heard a faint click as the metal lid reacted to the heat from the water. She lifted it out, dried it quickly on her pinny and then released the lid with ease.

Having to wait to find out what was in the tins had made her impatient, but curbing her impatience eventually brought its reward when the lid came away in her hand. Inside, the tin was filled to the brim with white fabric. Martha wrinkled her brow in puzzlement, wondering why anyone would fill half a dozen tins with material. She scooped the fabric out and the puzzle was solved. Wrapped inside the fabric, so that it didn't make any sound, was a block of metal. It was roughly three inches long, two inches wide and about an inch thick, very smooth to the touch and a dull yellow colour. She knew what it was but her brain seemed unable to comprehend the truth of it and she stared and stared at the piece as it lay in her hand.

Suddenly she was galvanised into action and she quickly released the lids on the other five tins. All of them contained a small but heavy ingot of metal, just like the first tin. When she had unwrapped all six of them she spread them out on the bare floorboards and continued to stare at them while her mind reeled in shock. Not even the sound of Edith making her way upstairs made Martha move so, when Edith entered the room, she found Martha sitting on the floor with the six ingots laid out in front of her.

"I've closed the shop so we can have some dinner." Edith began but then she saw the ingots on the floor. "What are those? Where did you get them?"

Martha lifted a bemused face to her mother.

"I found them in the top of this stool. I wondered why it was so heavy and why it was different from the other furniture which Daniel had picked up. When I turned the stool upside down, I saw a catch and moved it. The top of the stool opened and I found all these old tobacco tins, and they were inside the tins."

"What are they? Is it,.. is it,.. really?" Edith couldn't put a sentence together, so shocked was she by the sight of what looked, to her, like gold.

"Yes, it is." Martha said, dreamily. "Its pure gold, all six of them, there on our floor."

"But how did it come to be in the top of that stool? Who does it belong to? What should we do with it?" Edith had more questions but she realised that Martha didn't know the answers to any of them, any more than she did. They were both saved from saying any more when they heard Daniel enter the kitchen downstairs. They heard him moving about and then his heavy tread on the stairs.

"This is nice." Daniel was saying. "I ask my mother and sister to run a shop for me and when I come home, I find that they've closed it early for dinner and they are nowhere in sight. What are you both doing in here?"

Daniel stopped talking as he reached the bedroom and saw what was on the floor.

"Good God! What are they?"

Martha looked at him and smiled.

"They are what they look like, Danny boy." Martha answered. "You've brought home our futures in that furniture you got in Middlesbrough."

"Where in Middlesbrough did you get that furniture, Daniel?" Edith asked. "Who does it belong to?"

"I don't know, Mam." Daniel replied, still staring at the gold on the floor. "It was a chap called Greaves who stopped me and said he had a house of furniture he wanted to get rid of and would I take it off him. The family in the house had done a moonlight flit, owing him rent and so he wanted to get some of his money back by selling their furniture. It was cheap rubbish and I told him so, but he agreed with me and said he would be happy to get anything for it so that it wasn't a complete loss for him. Where did you find those bars?"

"They were in the top of that stool." Martha pointed to it. "I found a catch under the rim and when I moved it the whole lid slid over and the tins were packed into it."

"I thought that stool was different from the rest of the furniture. It was heavy, so it had to be good wood." Daniel agreed.

"It was heavy cos there was a fortune in gold bars hidden inside it." Martha remarked. "So, we don't know who the family was. They obviously didn't know that there was gold inside the stool cos they would have taken it with them when they ran off. This Greaves bloke didn't know about it either, or he would have taken it, so it looks like it belongs to you, Daniel. You bought the furniture."

"Don't you think we should try and find the family it belonged to?" Edith asked. "It belongs to them, even though they didn't know the gold was in the stool."

"Hardly." Martha said. "The furniture belongs to Daniel, fair and square, which means the gold belongs to him too. I can't see a problem in that."

"I don't think we would be able to find them." Daniel said, haltingly. "If Greaves didn't know where they had gone, I doubt we would be able to find them. He's never been one to miss a trick, that Greaves."

"Well, that settles it." Martha got up off the floor and shook her skirt. "Our Daniel is suddenly a very rich man. Grace will definitely want to marry you now, Daniel. You are so much more attractive with gold in the bank."

Daniel pulled a face but didn't reply. His mind was too taken up with thoughts of the gold and what he could do with it. He picked up one of the bars and gave it to Martha.

"For you. I wouldn't have it if it wasn't for you finding it, so you deserve a share in the profits."

Martha smiled and thanked him, putting the bar into her pinny pocket where it nestled against her stomach. She closed her hands over the top of it and dreamt what she would do with the money. Daniel handed one of the bars to Edith.

"You should get one, too. You've spent far too much of your life with nothing. You will never be in that position again."

Edith smiled back at him and closed her hand round the smooth bar of metal. She had lost any inhibitions she may have had about keeping the gold once she got hold of one of the bars.

"I'm going to invest some of it into my business." Daniel said. "The rest of it I will keep for a rainy day. You never know when you may need some money."

"Well said and well done." Edith stroked Daniel's cheek. "My children have grown up into responsible adults now. I'm so proud of you both."

Martha smiled but she knew that Edith wouldn't be proud of her if she knew that she intended blackmailing people. But Martha had never been bothered by a conscience, so this thought didn't upset her in the least. What Edith didn't know wouldn't hurt her.

Martha had made no move to hide the gold from either her mother or Daniel. She had known that Daniel was as straight as a die and would share his bounty with the whole family because that was his nature, so she hadn't tried to hide the gold and keep it all for herself. She was far more interested in the confectioner's papers than she was in the gold because she was far more interested in manipulating other people than in money. Besides, she knew that she was going to make plenty of money out of blackmailing transgressors and sinners and wouldn't need the money that the gold ingot could be sold for. Being open about the gold made Daniel and Edith think that she was as honest as they were and that suited Martha down to the ground. They wouldn't be looking out for any sins on Martha's part when she had so openly shared the gold.

She declined Daniel's offer of hiding her gold ingot in the space under the loose tile of the kitchen floor where he and Edith were going to hide theirs and chose to put hers in the bottom of the built-in cupboard in her bedroom. She had a removable floorboard in her room which Lillian had used to hide her money before her and Martha was going to use this as her place of safety for her gains from her blackmailing pursuits, when she began earning money from it. She decided to move her bed so that it stood over this loose floorboard, to make her stash even more safe from prying eyes and sticky fingers. She fully intended that this empty space would be filled very soon, but she needed to plan how she was going to utilise her ill-gotten knowledge of the misdemeanours of her neighbours.

She had gathered, from the notes which the confectioner had left, that she had watched the houses of her victims from a number of different hiding places spread around the town. As this had worked for the confectioner, Martha was sure that it would work for her and she began making plans for her first foray into night-time surveillance of the

Renwick/Dundas couple and of another cheating couple called Robert Leigh and Olivia Westcott. Leigh was the town postmaster with a wife who could flatten a whole street of terraced houses with one bellow from her capacious lungs and Westcott was the widow of a butcher called Dennis Westcott. Olivia Westcott also lived on Redcar Road East, like Lucy Renwick, so Martha decided to spy on both women to see if they were still engaged in their nefarious, night-time wanderings.

The confectioner had indicated that she had watched both couples from behind the conveniently-placed low wall which surrounded the Baptist Chapel, even though it was unpleasant to have to crouch amongst the dirt which had blown, gathered, and been deposited there. Both houses were on the same side of the street as the Baptist Chapel, but both were on the Grangetown side of the Chapel so that any caller to either house had to pass the Chapel on the way. To Martha, this seemed like the perfect position from which to watch passers-by as it would completely hide the fact that she was in position there. The confectioner's notes had mentioned that Robert Leigh called on Mrs Westcott every Tuesday and Friday and that David Dundas made his way to Lucy Renwick's house every Monday and Tuesday. Tuesday was therefore the day (or rather, the night) to be in position so that Martha could look out for both men as they arrived at their respective ladies' abodes. She shook her head over the regularity of these illicit affairs and wondered if it was possible to conduct an affair if one's mind wasn't as pedantic as the two couples she had chosen to watch.

So Martha decided that the following Tuesday would be the night she got into position behind the Chapel wall in order to find out if both couples were still enjoying their illicit meetings. She had other items to prepare for her first surveillance, namely some dark clothing so that she could flit from house to house without the danger of being seen by anyone else. She didn't want to risk becoming the subject of gossip around the town, especially as she wasn't the one who was having questionable relationships with men who weren't her husband. Her normal day-to-day skirt would suffice for her nocturnal rambles as it was a sensible shade of black and, if she wrapped a black shawl across her shoulders and fastened it in place, it would hide the brightness of her white blouse. She drew the line at putting ash on her skin to stop any light reflecting from her forehead and cheeks but she did get out her black gloves to darken her hands. She decided she could put her hand across her face if she thought there was anyone about who might see her.

Neither Daniel nor Edith noticed that Martha was unusually quiet that week. Daniel was planning his next foray into the world of business and was deciding whether or not to invest some of the gold into buying a motor wagon to replace his horse and cart. He was sure that motor transport was going to be the way forward and he didn't want to be overtaken by anyone moving into his area with a truck which would be faster and carry more than his horse and cart. Every time he saw a motor car, he was struck by the speed of the new form of transport and he itched to try his hand at driving it. He was sure that a motor truck would be better than sending goods on a train which then had to finish their journey on the back of a cart. He could pick up and deliver goods door-to-door if he had one of the new trucks. The possibilities of that kept his mind busy and he didn't notice any change in Martha.

Edith was far too busy dreaming about getting married to Bob to notice that her daughter was often distracted and rarely took a turn in any conversation. She had dreamed of being a married woman for so long that she could hardly believe that it was going to happen and she kept reliving the moment that Bob had proposed to her, shivering with excitement every time that she did so. This all left Martha free to pursue her own dreams, free of any maternal or fraternal interruption.

Chapter Eighteen

Tuesday came round too slowly for Martha but it did, eventually, creep into being and Martha spent the whole day shivering with nervous anticipation, sure that she was going to find that both couples had returned to the straight and narrow path of marital honesty in the interim and that her surveillance was going to be in vain. It was still winter and Martha knew that she would have to be wearing plenty of layers of clothing while she was out, otherwise she would get very cold while she waited and watched. It was no problem for her to sit in the kitchen after teatime and wait for Daniel and Edith to indicate how they were preparing to spend their evening.

Daniel intended going to bed early that night as he had a delivery to make the next day to a farm in one of the outlying villages. A crate of household goods had been unloaded at the docks that night, destined for the farmer from his sister who had emigrated to Canada during Victoria's reign and had now died alone. As the farmer couldn't afford to leave his farm to tend to his sister's house and goods, he had asked the solicitor who had informed him of her death to sell the house and send any useful furniture to him, which the solicitor had done, for a fee. Daniel needed to be out early to get to the farm and back before they lost the daylight the following day, working on the principle that it was best to be travelling on roads he was familiar with when it was dark, so he needed his sleep that night.

Edith and Bob were going to see a house on Normanby Road the next day which, if it was suitable, was going to be their new family home. Bob intended selling his house and moving his daughter and his mother to the new house immediately and Edith would join him after their wedding, leaving the house in York Street for Daniel and Martha. This suited them all, especially as it left the possibility of selling the house in York Street if Daniel and Martha wanted to live with Edith and Bob in the near future. It also meant that they were crossing yet another new threshold into a different life and they all hoped that their futures would be even better than their lives had been recently. They all looked back on their early lives with horror and loathing and wondered why they had waited so long to rebel against the regime of slavery which had cowed them all.

Edith went to bed early also because, although she didn't want to go to sleep, she wanted to have the time to dream about her new life and her new house. It was impossible to daydream successfully downstairs because there was always a noise or someone wanting to talk and, just as she reached the point where Bob swept her off her feet to carry her over the threshold, someone would say 'Mam' and spoil the whole dream. She would then have to start again at the beginning, only to be interrupted again before Bob carried her into their new home, so she went to bed to dream the whole dream uninterrupted.

Martha said she wanted another cup of tea, so she was putting the kettle on the range to boil as the other two went upstairs to bed. She promised to bank down the fire before she went to bed and picked up a fashion catalogue to show she didn't want to chat anymore. She listened to their footsteps as they went upstairs, hearing the tenth stair creak in its usual fashion as they stepped on it. The creaking of the landing floorboards let her visualise their entries into their rooms and, after a few bangs and bumps, all went quiet upstairs.

Martha sat with her cup of tea, waiting for Daniel and Edith to fall asleep so that they wouldn't hear her opening and closing the back door. Conveniently, both Daniel and Edith slept in the front bedrooms which made it even less likely that they would be woken by the opening and closing of the back door, especially if Martha closed it very gently. The catalogue worked its usual magic on her and it wasn't long before she was reading it with her usual concentration and it was only when the coal shifted in the fire that she looked up and realised that it was nearly midnight. She closed the catalogue quietly and went into the back kitchen to get her thick shawl from its peg. The shawl had originally been black but repeated washing had dulled it to a dark grey colour which blended into the darkness of the back kitchen very nicely. Martha wrapped it round her shoulders, appreciating its weight and warmth as she left the heat of the kitchen. Quietly, she slipped on her new gloves and checked that the fire was banked down before she left the house, closing the back door so silently that even she couldn't hear it.

Outside, the night was cold and clear with a promise of a frost, once the last of the wispy clouds had disappeared. The cold didn't bother Martha overmuch. She had grown up spending so much time in the back yard in all weathers that she was immured to the bite of the wind and could tolerate more cold than most people. She crossed the end of York Street and headed for Normanby Road crossing to the far side when she reached it. It wasn't far to Redcar Road East and she didn't see a soul as she walked the streets. It was only at this point that she hoped that no-one would see her making her way to her surveillance position. 'Walking the streets' at night was a pointer to loose behaviour and she didn't want anyone to see her abroad in the dark of the night and think that she had changed her occupation. The thought made her smile, especially as she was out at night to gather gossip on other people's lewd behaviour.

Redcar Road was deserted, like the rest of the town, when she reached it. The dark mass of the Baptist Chapel loomed up out of the darkness as she approached it and she scanned the area to make sure that she wasn't being observed. If anyone was watching her, she couldn't see them. It was a risk that she had to take in order to carry out her plan. She slipped through the wrought iron gate in the low wall around the chapel and carefully made her way to the corner where the two walls met. She had a very good view of both of the houses she was intent on watching that night so she settled herself against the wall, as comfortably as possible in the circumstances and began her wait.

She had been expecting that she would have to wait for a long time but she was surprised by the arrival of David Dundas less than a minute after she had stopped moving. Her breath caught in her throat as she heard his footsteps on the pavement. He was making no attempt to approach the house carefully or quietly and she marvelled at his brass neck in being so open about his destination. She wondered how long he had had to wait until his wife and children were all asleep before he left their house, no doubt creeping out as quietly as she had done from her home.

The footsteps stopped as he reached the house just two doors away from the Chapel and halted on the step. In seconds, he had the door open and slipped inside it with practised ease, proving to Martha that he had his own key to the door which did away with the need to knock on it and possibly rouse any light-sleeping neighbours. It made his entry into another man's house very quick and very quiet. Martha smiled grimly at the man's organisation of his hidden life. It was going to give her so much pleasure to have him dangling on a string, worried that his secrets might be revealed to the whole town. She knew, however, that she was going to get so much more pleasure from making Lucy Renwick worry that she was going to be unmasked as a hussy instead of the superior being which she considered herself to be. Perhaps, once she had squeezed the pair of them dry, she might just spread the word about her nocturnal habits because she would love to see that snooty nose dragged through the dirt. The idea had a certain allure for Martha, even if it meant that it would bring an end to one of her sources of income. It would be worth losing a few bob to see Mrs High and Mighty laid low.

No sooner had this thought crossed her mind but she heard footsteps approaching once again and she hugged the low wall to make sure that she wouldn't be seen. A man went past her hiding place, making much less noise than David Dundas had done and walking further along the street than Dundas had reached. Martha had to stick her head out over the wall in order to be able to see where the man stopped this time and she was acutely conscious that he would see her if he turned his head towards Normanby Road. To Martha's great relief the man didn't turn his head but raised his hand to knock on the front door he had stopped at. This was obviously less well-organised than the previous couple, or Olivia Westcott had no intentions of allowing anybody easy access to her house. That thought needed some quiet reflection but that would have to wait until Martha got home and could reflect without the possibility of being discovered hiding behind a wall.

Olivia Westcott opened her front door and then glanced up and down the street to make sure that no-one was watching them before she grabbed Robert Leigh by his coat front and dragged him inside the house. Martha froze as she saw Olivia glancing along the street but she must have been too far away to be seen because Olivia didn't hesitate about getting her man inside her house. Martha almost giggled out loud at Olivia's unseemly haste, although she appreciated that Olivia had been a widow for quite some time and was having difficulty coping with some aspects of it. No doubt she would have many similar feelings if she was in the same position as Olivia.

Martha decided to wait a while before she left her hiding place. She wanted to make sure that neither of the men did an about-turn and left the houses as rapidly as they had arrived. Although it was a strange time to be calling at a house for any reason, Martha didn't want her plans scuppered by failing to check that the men both stayed in the houses for the right amount of time. She didn't mind waiting in her hidey-hole, despite the smell of rotting leaves (or worse) which was beginning to percolate the air she was breathing. She placed her gloved hand over her mouth and nose as a filter in case the obnoxious smell got inside her and made her ill and continued to lean against the wall. The town was very quiet now, seeming more so since she had heard Dundas' heavy tread along the pavement and she realised how still the night was. Not a breath of wind could be felt, only the cold which was now beginning to sink into her bones. Through the cold night air, she heard the clock on St. Peter's Church chime the hour and was amazed to realise that it was one o' clock in the morning. She hadn't noticed how quickly the time was passing.

There came a low rumble in the distance and soon Martha could see a glow in the night sky which was coming from the distant iron works. The whole town wasn't asleep. She should have remembered that the iron works were in production twenty four hours a day and that there would be men who were toiling in there. The docks would also be alive, even at this time of the night because they worked by the tides not the clock. She was aware that she should make her way home before anyone else decided to wander the streets and who might see where she had been.

Martha stepped out onto the pavement after checking that the street was deserted and turned for home. Out of the shelter of the Chapel, she felt much colder than before and was glad that she hadn't waited any longer to walk home. The frost had settled on the ground and the air had that sharp tang which frost brought to it, nipping at her nose and cheeks as she walked along. She heard a train approaching the station and was glad that she would be home before any late travellers on it managed to reach her, although she didn't imagine that there would be many people on that train. She had never realised before just how busy the town was in the middle of the night and she was happy to reach their back yard and slide silently through the door into the kitchen.

It felt warm in the kitchen, compared to the cold outside and Martha divested herself of her outer garments and poked the fire to get more heat out of it. It was strange, trying to poke a fire quietly and she grinned to herself at the thought, happy that she had succeeded in her task for that night. She was going to have a great deal of fun with the information she had garnered from her hiding place next to the Chapel, but that would have to wait until the next day. Her eyes were beginning to close of their own accord, now that she had warmed through and so she made her way to bed before she fell asleep in the kitchen. That would excite comments from Edith and Daniel, if they found her fully-dressed, asleep in the kitchen.

The next day was busy in the little shop. Daniel had acquired the whole contents of an empty house the week before and Martha hadn't had time to work her magic on the broken catches and lifted veneers of the stock that he had brought home. It seemed a good opportunity to disappear upstairs and pretend to work on the broken furniture while, in reality, she composed her blackmail notes to send to Mrs Lucy Renwick and Mrs Olivia Westcott. She had decided to write, in the first instance, to the female halves of the illicit couples, purely because she was so desperate to make Lucy Renwick pay for the dirty looks and sneering comments she had made about Martha, although she knew that she would get more money out of the male partners. She wasn't doing it for the money, although she had to admit that it made her revenge all the sweeter, but to punish Lucy for being so uppity, as she called it. It didn't take her long to dash off a few sentences in two letters, describing their 'crime' and explaining just how she would release that information to their families. What needed a lot of concentration and thought was how she was going to successfully achieve the hand-over of the money without revealing her identity.

She decided to have another look at the notes that the confectioner had made, describing her forays into blackmail. The old woman had had plenty of time to consider ways and means and the fact that she had made a very good living out of it proved that she knew what she was doing. How had she managed the transfers of money? Martha hadn't brought the confectioner's notes with her to the shop, so she had to curb her patience until she finished work and they closed the shop for the day.

When she got home, Martha helped with making the tea and, after everything was eaten and all cleared away, she pronounced her intention of having an early night. In reality, she was tired because she had been out so late the night before, but what she really wanted to do was to work out a way for her victims to hand over the money she was demanding. If she couldn't find a way of achieving that successfully and without her identity being revealed, then her blackmailing career would be over before it had begun. She needed to be able to add the last couple of lines to both letters before she dropped them into the post office for delivery to her victims.

Martha had forgotten that it was very cold outside and it wasn't long before she was feeling the low temperature in her bedroom. She didn't want to sit with Daniel and Edith in the warm parlour and she knew that the kitchen fire would have been banked down for the night and wouldn't be throwing much heat out, but where could she sit to think about places for her victims to leave their money? She didn't know if it was lack of sleep from the night before or simply that there was no answer to her dilemma, but getting frustrated about it wasn't conducive to insightful thoughts. She kicked out at her nightstand as the frustration mounted and then wished that she hadn't when Edith called up the stairs.

"Are you all right? Have you fallen, Martha?"

No, no, I'm fine." Martha shouted back. "I dropped the book I was reading."

"It's because you are so tired, pet. Go to sleep now and you can read tomorrow. I hope you aren't coming down with anything."

Martha reassured her mother that she wasn't about to succumb to any disease which might be rampant at that moment and then got into bed. It was much warmer in there and her frozen brain began to work again as soon as she had thawed out. She was on the verge of sleep when the view from the bedroom window above the shop where she had been working that day, popped into her head and brought the answer to her dilemma. There were allotment gardens on the other side of Station Road and the front bedroom window of the shop looked out over these allotments. While she had been working on the furniture and composing her blackmail letters, she had watched so many people going to the allotments either to work on their patches of land or to buy vegetables from the allotment owners. It would be a perfect place for her victims to put their money because she could watch for them from the bedroom window. She was prepared to bet that the confectioner had directed her victims to the allotments and that she had watched as they had complied. She would also have been able to make sure that her victims had left the area before she went across the road to collect the money.

Martha was ecstatic that she had solved her problem and decided to explore the allotments the next day to find a hidden area to which she could direct her victims. She was sure, now that she had worked out how the confectioner had done it, that she had hit upon the best answer to her problem and she had no difficulty in giving in to her body's craving for sleep. She closed her eyes and didn't stir until the next morning when Daniel dropped one of his boots on the stairs which bounced, very noisily, all the way down to the bottom stair.

"Sorry, I was trying to be quiet." Daniel said when she stomped into the kitchen a couple of minutes later.

"Try and be noisy next time then." Martha growled. "You might be more successful if you try the opposite." Then she remembered that her plans were coming to fruition and she couldn't stop herself from grinning at him. How could she be bad-tempered when she was about to bring snooty Lucy Renwick to her knees?

Daniel grinned back, even though he had detected the trace of satisfaction in her smile and his mind was racing trying to work out what was making his sister so happy. He would have bet the money for his new motor wagon that she was up to something, but he couldn't work out what it was. He didn't want her to know that he had his suspicions about her because he had nothing concrete to go on, so he pretended to thump her arm as he passed her and she laughed and clipped his ear because he was too slow in passing her.

Chapter Nineteen

Martha didn't have a clue that Daniel suspected anything about her so she went off to the shop as happy as a mudlark that morning, ready to work hard on the rest of the houseful of furniture that Daniel had brought in and to spend some time looking through the bedroom window for a convenient hiding place in the allotments over the road.

The furniture was exceptionally boring, having no ornamentation or fancy accessories which made renovation such an enjoyable task for Martha. She secretly wondered why Daniel had agreed to pay for and remove the furniture from the house but she was also well-aware that they would make much more than Daniel had paid for it when they sold each item separately. She couldn't expect to find hidden hoards every day or enjoy the satisfaction that she got when she renovated a particularly fine piece of furniture, so she worked through the articles which still waited her expertise with as much grace as she could muster. Edith brought her a cup of tea half-way through the morning and watched, fascinated, as Martha worked on a chest of drawers, not knowing that her mother was there.

Edith stood in the doorway with the cup in her hand and watched Martha as she rounded the edges of the chest with some fine sandpaper and then dusted away the debris. Not for the first time, Edith wished that her parents could come back and see how successful the family was now that they had the opportunity to use all of their strengths and capabilities. She knew that her parents would still have found something to moan about but Edith took strength from their success, glad to have managed to produce two children who were so well-motivated and talented. Martha looked up and smiled into her mother's face.

"Have you come to check up on me?" Martha asked, still in the same happy mood she had been all morning.

"No, pet. I've brought you some tea. You deserve a break."

"Thanks, Mam. I'll have it in a minute when I've finished this sanding down. It only needs a coat of polish and it'll be as good as new."

"You are very clever, Martha." Edith was never unstinting in her praise of her children. She knew only too well how much a few words of encouragement meant to everyone.

"Tell me that when we make a fortune selling the furniture." Martha laughed as she wiped the duster over the small amount of debris on the surface of the chest.

Martha took the proffered cup from Edith and squeezed behind the drawers to place it on the windowsill so that it would have a firm base to rest on. She knew that if she put it on the chest of drawers she would be likely to knock and spill it as she finished the last rub down of the chest. Edith went back downstairs rapidly because the shop bell rang as Martha put the cup down so Martha was once again alone. As she turned back to the chest, she saw a movement out of the corner of her eye. A small child, not old enough for school, had climbed onto a large wooden hutch which formed part of the end fence of one of the allotments, butting onto Station Road. He kicked back with his heel and Martha saw one plank of the wood which made its construction move as his heel collided with it. The child didn't notice the movement of the plank because he was sitting above it but it's movement had caused him to lose his balance and he fell, nose first, onto the pavement. His cries were loud enough to wake the dead and his distraught mother rushed to gather him to her chest.

His cries were heard by many passers-by and, in seconds, there was a small crowd gathered around mother and son, all anxiously trying to stem the flow of blood from his nose and reassure him that he hadn't done himself any permanent damage. The mother was adding her cries for help to the child's screams and the noise level rose as the crowd all tried to make themselves heard above mother and son. The baby in the pram, which the mother had abandoned to attend to her older child, now added his or her screams to the melee and Martha smiled at the number of people who were all making the crying children their main concern. She waited with a great deal of patience until the bleeding stopped and peace was restored to the street and, eventually, the people moved on and the mother and children resumed their walk.

That gave her the opportunity to look at the large hutch in more detail and she was convinced that the loose board was only loose at one end. She was sure that the nails were still in place in the other end of the plank because neither the wind nor the passage of people made it move. It had only moved when the boy had kicked his heel into it. It would be perfect as a drop-off point for her victims to place her reward for finding out their dirty little secrets. It seemed very apt, that an abandoned hutch on a weed-strewn allotment next to the railway line could become a repository for a fortune. Martha smiled even more at her thoughts and resolved to visit the hutch before she went home that night. It would be dark at six o'clock, so it would be perfect to check it out then, when most people would be at home.

She spent the rest of the day in that small bedroom, constantly looking out of the window at the people passing in the street and always checking that the allotment on which the hutch resided didn't have an eager owner, keen to repair and possibly replace the hutch. It seemed unlikely, because the whole allotment was a lumpy mass of weeds and puddles. It didn't look as though it had been touched in over a year, although it could be that the owner was unwell and may have been unable to work on it for a while. Martha knew that nature could cover any eyesore in a matter of weeks so it was possible that the owner had had a break and might come back at any time. He could possibly return at any day but Martha knew that she was going to have to take that risk because the hutch's location was perfect for her needs. She could watch from the bedroom window without fear of being seen when she had instructed her victims to place their money in the hutch and she could also wait until her victims left the scene before she went to collect her dues. It was perfect. It did cross her mind that the confectioner could have chosen the same drop-off point for exactly the same reasons that Martha had chosen it and that thought warmed her as she realised that she was now thinking in the same way as the confectioner. If that was the case, then she stood more chance of being able to find the place where she had hidden all of her ill-gotten gains when she was too ill to continue with her blackmailing. The thought of finding the treasure made Martha smile all the more.

That night, Daniel was even more concerned about his sister. She was far too happy for his peace of mind and the fact that she also seemed distracted worried him even more than her smiles. She was plotting something, he was sure of it, and that worried him a lot. For some reason, he didn't think that Grace was her target this time. It seemed to him that she now had much bigger fish to fry and bigger fish meant bigger trouble, at least in Daniel's estimation. But he was stumped over what her plan could actually be, so he couldn't say anything, either to Martha or Edith.

Daniel wanted to think about his new motor wagon, which he had ordered from a supplier in Middlesbrough. He had taken one of his gold bars to a jeweller in Newcastle, mainly because he normally didn't travel to Newcastle at all and nobody there would know him, and collected cash in return for the bar. He was staggered at the amount of cash which one gold bar had brought him and he suffered another crisis of conscience at not having made more effort to trace the family who had done a moonlight flit from the house in Middlesbrough, leaving the furniture behind. They couldn't have known that the bars were in the stool, otherwise they wouldn't have been parted from it, nor would they have been in the dire financial straits which they were so clearly in. It followed, therefore, that they hadn't known about the stool, so had it been part of the house when they moved in and belonged to the person who had lived there before them? Should he try to find out who those people were? But why had they left the stool with the gold bars in? Had it belonged to a family who had lived in the house years ago? Daniel got ever more frustrated and tried to push the thoughts away although they simmered in the back of his mind all the time. He didn't like the heavy feelings of guilt which dogged him but he didn't mention his feeling to his mother or his sister. He knew that neither of them had the same capacity for introspection as he had, trying to explain to them would only frustrate them all, although he was surprised that his mother could disregard the facts so easily. He could believe it of Martha because she was totally without a conscience but he had thought his mother did have one, even if it wasn't as vociferous as his own. So, Daniel kept his worries to himself and tried to concentrate on how much more money he would be able to earn with a motor wagon which could deliver any load at greater speed than any horse and cart.

Martha spent that evening putting the finishing touches to her blackmail letters, describing the location of the hutch in great detail so that neither of her victims would be able to miss the place, before she sealed the envelopes. She would post them in the morning on her way to the shop. She had told her victims that they were to place the money in the hutch on Friday night, late enough for the streets to be empty and the possibility of discovery to be very small. She had instructed Lucy Renwick to put the money in the hutch at eleven o'clock and instructed Olivia Westcott to put hers in the hutch at eleven thirty because she didn't want the two women to meet anywhere near the allotment. The blackmail letters were short and to the point as Martha thought it wasn't necessary to stick to any social conventions of letter-writing when one was writing a blackmail note. She could hardly wait for Friday, so excited was she at the prospect of taking the wind out of Lucy Renwick's sails. She didn't have a personal axe to grind against Olivia Westcott as she hardly knew the woman, but she was getting a great deal of satisfaction out of blackmailing her as well as Lucy Renwick, so she didn't let little considerations like that stop her from enjoying herself.

The week passed very slowly for Martha, only enlivened by going through the confectioner's notes and making a list of the people she would blackmail next. There was certainly no shortage of candidates for blackmailing and she had trouble in whittling down the number of people on her list. She also wanted to re-read all the confectioner's notes to see if she could solve the conundrum of where she had hidden all her treasure before she had died. It also gave her an opportunity to put a name to the confectioner as she hadn't taken any notice when she had first got access to the papers. Thinking about her as 'the confectioner' irritated Martha and she was pleased to see that she had signed her name at the end of the notes - Sarah Salton. So now Martha had a name for her contact to the world of blackmailing and she could stop thinking about her as the confectioner.

Friday came eventually, as most Fridays usually do, and Martha was on hot coals all day because of her expectations for that night. Edith couldn't understand why her daughter was so jumpy that day but questioning Martha only got her a smile and 'I'm fine' so she abandoned her attempt to get to the bottom of it, especially as Bob was taking her to choose her wedding ring the next day and she wanted to float on a world of bliss, not find out why her daughter jumped every time the shop bell went.

Daniel had left for work before Martha had got out of bed that morning but he was at home when Edith and Martha got home from the shop and he noticed Martha's heightened reactions as soon as she walked in the door. He was immediately suspicious but watching her closely through tea and afterwards didn't give him any clues as to the reason for her nerviness and, as he was going to Middlesbrough the next day to collect his new wagon, he too soon forgot Martha and her strange behaviour.

Perhaps, if Edith and Daniel hadn't been so wrapped up in their own concerns, one of them may have watched Martha more closely but that didn't happen. They might have been able to stop Martha's descent into blackmail before she got started at it, but that wasn't to be. Martha took the next step in her life with a heart full of happiness and satisfaction, not realising just how addictive blackmail was or how dangerous it could be.

The evening dragged for Martha as she pretended to be perusing a book she had bought the day before. Edith was desperately trying to finish a new shawl she was making because she wanted to wear it the next day when she and Bob went to choose her wedding ring. This meant that Edith was prepared to sit up until the small hours in order to finish making the shawl, which would scupper Martha's plan to exit the house at half past ten in order to go to the shop and watch the hutch from the upstairs bedroom window. Daniel took himself off to bed quite early as he wanted to be well-rested for his first attempt at driving a motor wagon the next day so Edith was the only fly in the ointment. Martha watched as Edith finished knitting yet another row and asked how much more she had still to do before the shawl was finished. Edith thought she was showing an interest in what she was doing and lowered her knitting needles so that she could explain the pattern more easily. Martha could have screamed in frustration but she couldn't say anything without making it obvious that she wanted Edith to go to bed, so she bit her tongue and managed to smile through her gritted teeth.

It was over forty minutes later that Edith put down her knitting needles and declared the shawl finished. Martha gave her a smile and clapped her hands, trying to appear relaxed and interested. It crossed her mind that she should change profession and take up a career on the stage, given that Edith didn't seem to realise that Martha was willing her to go to bed and leave her to her own devices. If she could fool her mother as to her mental state, surely she would be able to pretend to be a great actress. She reckoned she could make a fortune on the stage but she decided to leave that thought until she had perfected being a blackmailer.

Eventually, Edith mounted the stairs to bed, reminding Martha that she needed to be up early in the morning as she would be the only member of staff in the shop. Martha managed to hold on to her smile until Edith closed the door and then she pulled a face that would have frightened any child as a way of releasing her pent-up frustrations. But, even then, she had to wait while she made sure that Edith had actually gone to bed and that she was safe to leave the house and make her way to the shop.

The church clock was chiming the half-hour as Martha slipped her key into the lock and took one last look around to make sure that there were no loiterers hanging about the street. The street was deserted and the town was very quiet, making the night ideal for what Martha wanted to do. She quickly mounted the stairs, not needing a light to move around the small house and shop so that no-one would know that she was in there. From the bedroom window, the street still looked to be deserted and Martha took up a position standing behind the old curtains which still hung at the window.

She waited and waited. It was beginning to seem that she had waited a lifetime when she heard the church clock strike the quarter hour. It must be quarter past eleven! Martha started to panic. Wasn't Lucy going to submit to being blackmailed? Had she decided that she wasn't going to turn up? How dare she? Martha's anger was starting to mount and her agile brain was considering ways of leaning even more heavily on Lucy's neck when she heard footsteps coming along the street outside. She peeped out from behind the curtain and was surprised to see not only Lucy but also David Dundas. They were walking along the street together, side by side but not holding hands or touching in any way. They stopped when they reached the hutch which was looking enormous in the moonlight and David knelt down and pushed against the plank of wood which Martha had marked with a piece of silver paper taken from a children's sweet. David put his hand inside and then withdrew it hurriedly. He got to his feet and then they both turned and followed their own footsteps back towards Lucy's house.

From where Martha was standing, almost hidden behind the curtains, she could see a long way along the street. When they reached approximately the middle of the street, they stopped walking and looked back towards the allotments. Martha stiffened as she watched them. What were they intending doing next? Did they think she would appear and collect the money while they were still standing and watching her? Surely, they would realise that a blackmailer didn't collect his money in full view of the victim he/she was blackmailing. Martha was irritated even more by their actions. If they stayed in the street much longer then Olivia would meet them as she came to deliver her money and that would never do. Martha had deliberately made a full half hour in between the two drops, expressly to prevent the two victims meeting at the allotments. She couldn't stand still, she was so irritated and concerned by their actions, but she couldn't stop watching out of the window. She had to let her frustrations out by lifting each leg in turn and marching on the spot where she stood.

Five minutes slipped slowly by and Lucy and David were still standing in the same position. Martha was hot and cold all at the same time and seemed to be able to hear a clock ticking the minutes away in her head. She jumped when she heard the church clock start to strike, expecting it to strike the half hour for half past eleven but it didn't. It struck eleven o' clock and Martha realised that she had been way out in her estimation of the time. Lucy and David had been early with their delivery which was all to the good but Martha was still anxious for them to be gone. If they waited a few minutes longer and Olivia was early for her appointment, then there was a good chance that they would meet in the street outside. Martha didn't want that to happen, not only because it might encourage them all to wait for the blackmailer, but also because she didn't want her victims joining together and becoming a team who might decide to root out the blackmailer and punish him. She didn't want to give any power to the victims.

Time dragged slowly by and when the church clock struck quarter past the hour, Martha really began to panic. It wouldn't be long before Olivia arrived now. To try and take her mind off the possibility of a concerted fight-back by Lucy and Olivia, Martha began to plan what she would do with the money she got that night. Buying a watch could be a good move, she decided, especially as it would stop her from making mistakes, as she had that evening. Martha was getting very cold now, having had to stand in the same position for so long. The windows were old and badly fitted and the cold was seeping round the edges and into her very bones. When her nose started to run with the cold, Martha was seriously considering giving up blackmail as a way of making a living. It was producing far too many problems, but then she heard footsteps outside.

At first, Martha couldn't see who was walking along the street but then she realised that the steps were coming from the opposite direction to where Lucy and David were standing. They had also heard the footsteps and she saw them stiffen and then walk away as quickly and as quietly as they could. Thank goodness for small mercies! The approach of someone else had dissipated their resolve to find out the identity of the blackmailer and they disappeared from the street without making a sound.

 Martha turned to look the other way along the street and saw Olivia, on her own, walking as quickly as she could, with her head down and her shawl wrapped tightly around her. Martha laughed to herself. The shawl wasn't going to stop her from being attacked, if that was why she was afraid of walking the streets alone at this time. Martha surmised that Olivia, unlike Lucy, hadn't alerted her partner in sin of the blackmail letter. Was she afraid that Robert Leigh would decide that it was too dangerous to continue with their liaison if he knew that a blackmailer was watching them? Martha didn't know the answer to that one but she was sure that Olivia would drop the money in the hutch and then disappear as quickly as possible. She was oozing fear as she walked along and would want to deposit the money in the hutch and then get back home as quickly as possible.

 Martha was right. Olivia stopped at the hutch, pushed the plank and shoved the paper-wrapped bundle she was carrying into the space behind the plank so quickly that Martha would have missed it if she had blinked. Then she rose and almost ran back the way she had come. Martha stayed where she was. She was determined to make sure that the other two had gone home and weren't still waiting to see if they could catch the blackmailer at the hutch. She wasn't going to fall for that trick. She was inside a house which, although it was admittedly cold, she was sheltered from the worst of the weather. The other two were out in the open air and would be suffering far more than she was.

Chapter Twenty

Martha waited until the church clock had struck not only the half hour but also had chimed midnight before she finally left her position at the bedroom window. She was stiff with cold and she couldn't tell if her nose was still running or not because the tip of it was almost frozen, but she wasn't going to give in to the desire to collect the money and go home. She hadn't planned all this and spent such a long time waiting in that cold bedroom to be caught as she collected her reward. She wouldn't make that mistake.

Martha went downstairs as quietly as she could. She knew that the house next door to the shop was occupied and she didn't want to wake the householder and have a hue and cry after her when she collected her money from the hutch. She crept through the kitchen and checked that all was in order in the shop before she decided she really had to go back upstairs and look out of the window once again. What if Lucy and David had hidden while Olivia was leaving her money and were now waiting for her to make an appearance? The street was still deserted when she looked out of the window again and she leant her cheek against the window frame as she pondered what to do. Was the coast clear or not? How would she ever know if she didn't go back outside? She kicked the wall below the window in frustration and lumps of plaster fell out and crashed to the floor.

Martha winced at the noise she had made, all her senses alert to see if she had disturbed the neighbours but when the silence continued she slumped against the wall with relief. She couldn't stay here any longer because she was now exhausted and knew that she would soon fall asleep, despite the bitter cold. Then her brain began to work sluggishly again and she realised that she had to collect the money as quickly as possible before anyone else found it. She couldn't leave it to collect the next morning. She checked out of the window again and the street was deserted so she grabbed her courage in both hands and crept downstairs and let herself out of the shop door. It was a matter of moments to cross the street, push her hand through the swinging plank, grab the packets of money and dash back into the shop again. She went straight upstairs to check out of the window again but there was no-one outside. She leaned against the wall next to the window and waited while her breathing returned to normal.

She obviously hadn't been seen collecting the money because the street was as peaceful as it had been all the time she had waited, but she did wonder if Lucy and David were waiting in hiding further along the street to catch her as she walked past. Then it struck her that she didn't have to exit through the shop door and walk along the street where they may still be hiding. She could leave by the backyard gate and walk along the back alley until she came to Nelson Street. That would avoid having to walk along Pearl Street or Station Road and, if Lucy and David were still lying in wait for her, they would miss her.

She grinned as she realised she could outmanoeuvre them and then slipped back down the stairs, through the kitchen and into the backyard as quietly as a mouse. The latch on the gate was rusty and didn't lift easily but she managed to move it without making any more noise and stuck her head out to look up and down the back alley. It was deserted and so she stepped out into the alley, making a mental note to deal with the rust on the back gate the next morning. She was home in a matter of minutes without meeting anyone else in the streets. By the time she reached the back gate at York Street she was hoping that Lucy and David were still waiting to ambush the blackmailer and she smiled at the thought of how cold they must be by now. She opened the back door and slipped into the kitchen, grateful for the warmth which enveloped her as soon as she was inside. She couldn't resist taking her 'earnings' out of her pocket and counting the money. A wave of happiness washed over her as she looked at the money on the table and she began calculating how many names there were in Sarah's blackmail notes. She could be a rich woman in a very short space of time. Adrenalin poured through her system, making her want to jump up and down with joy but she knew she had to keep quiet and not disturb the rest of the house.

She began gathering the money together and decided to put it all in one bag before she hid it in the space underneath the loose floorboard in her bedroom. As she opened the bag to receive its precious load, her fingers touched a piece of paper which she hadn't noticed before. She pulled it out and anger shot through her as she read the words written on it. It was from Lucy Renwick and it said - 'I may have given in to your blackmailing this time but don't ever try it again. If I receive any more demands for money from you, I will spread the word around the whole town that we have a cowardly blackmailer in our midst, so that people will be looking out for you and you will be caught. I hope you understand me - no more!!!'

Martha was furious that the woman dared to threaten her but her anger cooled pretty quickly. At first, she wanted to confront Lucy but a moment's thought convinced her that it would be a mistake to allow her rage to rule her head so she bent her mind to punishing Lucy in another way. A moment's quiet thought gave her an idea and she decided to reflect on it the next day before she took any course of action. Anyway, she was utterly exhausted and she knew that she had to be up early the next day, looking as though she had had a full night's rest so she battened down her wrath, gathered up the bags and climbed the stairs to bed as quietly as she could.

She was asleep before her head hit the pillow but she hadn't been as quiet as she had thought because Daniel had heard her moving about in the kitchen. He knew that he was collecting his new wagon the next day and he needed to be as alert as possible, so he didn't go downstairs to see where Martha had been, but he couldn't stop his active brain from trying to work out why Martha should have been out on her own in the middle of the night. He didn't know why, but he had a terrible feeling that she was up to no good and that worried him immensely. He decided to wait until the next evening before he tackled her, but tackle her he must. He and his mother were slowly building up a reputation for good, honest business and he couldn't have Martha upsetting the apple cart. If she was doing something illegal, it could have endless repercussions on his businesses. And let's face it, anyone going out in the middle of the night had to be doing something illegal unless they were a shift worker which Martha most definitely was not.

It never crossed Daniel's mind that Martha may have been having a romantic meeting with a young man. He knew that Martha only got excited when she was winning at something, usually by doing someone else down and her behaviour recently had had all the hallmarks of Martha 'getting one over' on someone she disliked. He was sure she wasn't still acting against Grace, but he couldn't rule it out completely so he resolved to keep a wary eye out for Grace's safety, as well as trying to find out who was the target for Martha's ire at the moment.

Daniel was up and out the next morning as soon as it got light. Edith was up early to see him off and also because it was the day that she was to choose her wedding ring, so she had awakened before dawn. Martha was the only one who wanted to sleep late but Edith got her out of bed because she was desperate to make sure that the day was going to be perfect and Martha not opening the shop would spoil that. Edith was so wrapped up in her own thoughts and dreams that she didn't notice that Martha looked as though she had hardly slept all night, so Martha didn't have to answer any awkward questions. Daniel had already left the house with his mind full of his expectations about his new wagon, and so he didn't see how tired Martha was.

Martha left the house and walked briskly to the shop, revelling in the bright day which had only a hint of frost. It wouldn't be long before spring came, a thought which made Martha reflect on her blackmailing activities because spring would bring lighter nights. She would have to arrange for her victims to leave her money after night had fallen if she was going to carry on with her new career. That could mean a lot of very late nights for her and she groaned inwardly at the thought. But she was determined that black thoughts weren't going to spoil her first day as a (moderately) rich woman and, in any case, she needed to plan how she was going to get revenge for Lucy Renwick's note. It didn't take long for an idea to pop into her mind and she spent the rest of the morning mulling over in her mind how she could best achieve her desired result - to ruin Lucy Renwick's reputation, once and for all.

It was a quiet day for selling second-hand furniture, so she had plenty of time for thinking. It was impossible for her to leave the shop and go upstairs to do any of her restoration work but she made good use of her time by estimating how many names there were in the notes that Sarah Salton had left. When she had read the list through the first time, Lucy Renwick's name had jumped out at her because she disliked the woman and was glad to find out that she had feet of clay. She had then arbitrarily chosen her second victim but she knew that there were more than forty other names in the notes. She could afford to lose Lucy as a victim and still make her fortune from the other people she could blackmail. Satisfied that the loss of Lucy wouldn't spoil the outcome of her new career, Martha considered how she was going to achieve her ends.

Martha closed the shop at lunchtime, as she was working on her own, and ate a sandwich which she had brought from home that morning. She couldn't see the point in going home to York Street when they had a fire in the kitchen at the shop and she could boil a kettle for a cup of tea as easily there as at home. She was surprised by Edith's return just after lunch, wondering if Bob and Edith had had a row and hadn't bought the wedding ring, but Edith assured her that the purchase had been made and the wedding was still on. Edith's arrival released Martha so that she could mount the stairs and get on with the restoration of a large mirror on a wooden stand which she was sure would sell well after she had mended the broken base and polished out the marks in the wood.

Her mind worked overtime as her hands polished the mirror. She needed someone who would repeat the gossip she was going to provide into the right ears so that the rumours spread as far and as quickly as possible. The drawback was that she wanted her confidant to accept the information without asking how Martha was in possession of it and who wouldn't reveal that it was Martha who had revealed this secret. Put bluntly, Martha needed someone who wasn't sharp-witted enough to ask any questions but who would repeat what Martha told her as though it was gospel. After a couple of minute's rumination, Martha hit on the perfect candidate. Prudence Golightly had been in Martha's class at school, a large, unwieldy girl with very protuberant front teeth, very little in the way of a brain and the worst bully the school had ever seen. She had tried to bully Martha during her first week at school and had been brought up short when Martha had knocked her down the outside steps to the lavatories, following that up with tying her plaits to the railings around the steps and leaving her to cry and wet herself before someone had come along to rescue her. She hadn't ever tried to bully Martha again but had followed her around like a puppy, desperate for Martha to take notice of her. She was the ideal candidate for Martha's needs at that moment

- willing and eager to do anything to make Martha like her and close-mouthed enough to keep her informant's name out of the gossip she would pass on.

This satisfied Martha's problem about passing out information about Lucy but she then turned her mind to the question of the legacy that Sarah Salton had left. The notes had said that Sarah had hidden the money and that, once the reader got into the way Sarah's mind worked, then they should find it pretty easy to locate the hiding place of the treasure. Martha had never been known for her empathy. It was the reason that she had always been able to hurt other people either physically or emotionally without feeling one jot of remorse for what she had done. She didn't know it, but she had inherited this trait from her father/grandfather, who had never cared how much he hurt other people. With such a double whammy in her paternal line, it would have been a miracle if she hadn't turned out as she did.

Martha was sure that Sarah had used the hutch as her collection point but she hadn't reached this conclusion by copying how Sarah's mind had worked. She had reached the conclusion by concentrating on what she needed to find, close to the shop. Is that how she could find Sarah's treasure? If she inspected every inch of the shop and house, would she come across some likely hiding places which she could then investigate one at a time? Martha decided that it was worth trying and it was a better plan than just sitting back and waiting for the hiding place to be revealed to her. What she needed now was the opportunity to search the building without having to explain what she was doing to either Edith or Daniel. She didn't want either of them to learn that she had a list of people ripe for blackmail or that she had already begun her new blackmailing career. Daniel would be bound to want to destroy the notes so that no-one could ever use them and she wasn't patient with his morality.

Daniel had picked up his new motor wagon that morning, grateful that the salesman was also the company's trainer and had taken him for a ride round Middlesbrough before letting the eager new owner loose on the roads. Driving the wagon was much more complicated than Daniel had expected it to be but he soon learnt how to ignore the terrible grinding noise when he crunched the gears together and the whine of the engine as he gathered speed, forgetting to change gear. Most people jumped out of the way when they heard the wagon approaching but Daniel could manage the steering particularly well, especially because it was very similar to keeping a horse and cart on a road. It was different holding a steering wheel rather than holding the reins for a horse but not so dissimilar that he couldn't carry over the techniques needed.

The salesman privately thought that Daniel was one of the better drivers it had been his luck to come across and he was sure that, given a little practise, Daniel would make a very good driver. He wasn't as worried about waving Daniel off on his own as he had been about some of his other customers, especially as his commission for selling the wagon would ensure that his family ate well the following week. The salesman knew only too well the financial problems he had when he didn't manage to sell one of the new generation of transport, so every sale was a bonus for him.

Daniel made the trip from Middlesbrough to South Bank in minutes and he blessed the day he had decided to invest in one of these new methods of transport. He was going to be able to cover so much more ground than he had before and he would be able to carry larger loads as well, because the back of the wagon was so big. It even had a tarpaulin which could be stretched over the top of any items to keep them from the vagaries of the weather. He stopped at the shop to show Martha his new investment and then headed for the railway station to collect some goods which were waiting for him to collect to take to a shop in

Eston. Martha's reaction had been everything that he wanted and, in his joy and pleasure at showing-off his new toy, he had completely forgotten that he was suspicious of her actions. It was only as he pulled up at the railway station that he remembered about Martha's midnight wanderings and he could have kicked himself for forgetting to question her, especially as Edith's absence would have made it the perfect opportunity. He would find another time to question her, he promised himself as he strutted into the station, swinging his new keys round his hand. He revelled in the admiring glances he received from the men who passed the wagon and he couldn't help swinging the starting handle with an extra stroke of panache as he noticed that many people had stopped to watch him.

Martha watched her brother negotiate the bend in the road as he drove away and she smiled outwardly at Daniel's obvious great delight in his new acquisition. She was grinning hugely inside at her own success at blackmail and already had the names picked out for those whom she was going to torment next but she needed to finish her business with Lucy Renwick before she could properly concentrate on her next victims and on her search for Sarah Salton's treasure. She knew that Prudence worked in the kitchen of the Station Hotel, washing up dirty pots and cutting up vegetables for the meals of the hotel's guests and any other passing trade, but Martha didn't want to have to walk into the Station without an escort, or even with one, but how was she going to get her message to Prudence? She had no idea where Prudence lived, so she couldn't call round to see her and she didn't know if she was still friends with the other girls from school. In the end, Martha decided that visiting the Station Hotel was the only way she was going to get to see Prudence, so how could she get in without being stared at by the male clientele? Then it struck her, in the same way that she used to get in when she was delivering clean laundry - through the kitchen door in the back yard. How stupid was she being, worrying about getting into the Station? She had been inside it loads of times. All she needed to do was to barge straight in and she could talk to Prudence.

Martha made her way to the Station Hotel as soon as her lunchtime came round and she could leave Edith in the shop alone. Edith thought that Martha was going to look for a new outfit for her and Bob's wedding, so she was happy that Martha was showing herself to be interested in it and insisted she would be happy on her own for an hour. Martha didn't disabuse her mother of her idea and left the shop as quickly as she could. Once she reached the Station, it was a simple matter to slip into the backyard and then open the kitchen door. Prudence was at the sink, scrubbing potatoes for the main meal of the day. It was a simple matter to persuade her to join Martha outside so that Martha could speak to her in private without the boot boy listening in to their conversation.

Chapter Twenty One

Prudence was flattered beyond Martha's expectations by this visit from the only girl she had ever admired and was ready to agree to anything in order to please Martha. It crossed Martha's mind that she could use Prudence in a more concrete way in the future but she stored that thought away in her head and concentrated on the task she wanted Prudence to perform for her at the present moment. Prudence listened in awe to the information which Martha now shared with her, amazed at how Martha had found out about Lucy Renwick's slip from grace (although Martha didn't enlighten her as to the source of her information) and how Martha wanted to use the gossip. Prudence would have done anything for Martha, short of murder, so passing on gossip about a local resident was not only acceptable to her but was also extremely enjoyable. Martha impressed on her that the source of this gossip had to remain totally anonymous but that only increased Prudence's pleasure in the task. She was honoured that Martha had chosen her to do it and incredibly flattered that Martha should seek her out in order to make her request.

With a final admonishment that she must keep Martha's identity secret, Prudence was allowed to return to the kitchen and her duties and Martha decided to use the rest of her lunch hour to see if Reed's had an outfit she could wear for her mother's wedding. It would give her the opportunity to see if Lucy was in any way cowed by the blackmail letter or irritated by having lost so much money. What made it all the sweeter was the fact that Martha would be spending the money she had got from Lucy to buy the outfit and it would give her so much pleasure to hand the money over in payment.

Reed's shop was busy when Martha entered through the main door. It wouldn't be long before spring arrived and Martha wasn't the only woman in South Bank who was looking for some new finery in which to welcome the new season. Martha waited until Lucy had finished dealing with Mrs Oxley from Station Road, who was attempting to squeeze her ample girth into a dress made for a slight young thing much more like Martha and who wouldn't listen to Lucy's urging to try something more fitting. Martha could see that Lucy wasn't in the best of tempers and even though Mrs Oxley had as much money as she had extra inches, Lucy was finding it very difficult to keep her temper with her and respond to her comments with any civility. She turned as Martha entered the shop and Martha saw the contempt in her face when she saw who her next customer would be.

For the first time since Martha had begun buying clothes from Reed's, she wasn't annoyed by the look on Lucy's face when she realised that she would have to serve Martha. Even this day, when she was obviously still irritated and annoyed by having been blackmailed, she still lifted her nose as she looked at Martha and sneered openly at her wish to buy clothing in the shop. Martha felt a touch of her usual irritation at the woman's attitude but it was overwhelmed by her joy at her knowledge of what had happened to Lucy in the last week and she couldn't resist making her decision about an outfit take as long as possible. By the time she had looked at and tried on at least ten garments, Martha went back to the beginning and chose the first outfit Lucy had shown her when she had declared that she wanted a dress for her mother's wedding.

Lucy was grinding her teeth quite audibly by the time Martha made her choice and her responses to Martha's questions and comments had been reduced to a strangled 'yes' or 'no', depending on the comment made. Martha had never fluttered from one item to another in such a way as she did that day and she could hardly contain her glee when Lucy finally only managed to grunt in reply to Martha's question as to whether she could return the outfit if her mother didn't like it when she got it home. Martha had to finally pay, with Lucy's own money, and leave the shop at this point because she was sure that she couldn't keep her merriment in for any longer and was likely to laugh out loud right in Lucy's face if she didn't leave.

She hurried back to their own shop, hugging the memory of Lucy's behaviour to her as though it were a cuddly animal to keep her warm. Edith loved the outfit and laughed when Martha told her that Lucy Renwick had been in a terrible mood. Edith had suffered incivility from Lucy as well as Martha and she joined in with her daughter's laughter at Lucy's mood and actions, commenting that perhaps someone had finally put Lucy in her place. Martha forbore to tell her that 'someone' had done just that, in a way that would make her bad temper so much worse, saving that for when Prudence began to spread the word of Lucy's fall from grace in the arms of the town clerk.

It wasn't long before word of the scandalous behaviour of the woman who acted like the queen of one of the town's drapery establishments began to filter through to Martha, who had to applaud Prudence's success at the task she had been given. Nobody knew where the information came from, but everybody believed what was being spread through the town, especially as the bare information of Lucy and David's relationship had been embroidered by Prudence's over-active imagination with regard to exactly what they did and where. Even Martha was shocked by some of the gossip that she heard but she was aware that Prudence had merely 'set the scene' and that further gossips had added their own tasty titbits so that Lucy's relationship with David was beginning to sound like a chapter from the story of Sodom and Gomorrah.

Martha had concentrated on Lucy and her attitude so much that she had totally forgotten about David Dundas' part in the relationship and she was pulled up short by the revelation that his meek and mild wife had utterly changed character once her husband's relationship with the Jezebel of Reed's had been made public. Instead of keeping herself to herself, cleaning her house until it shone and producing beautiful children who were always clean and well-mannered, Mrs Dundas had visited Reed's one afternoon and poured the contents of her sink, which she carried there in a bucket, over the always-elegant Mrs Renwick as she was helping a customer to choose some summer underwear for the coming season. Not only did Mrs Dundas soak her love rival in dirty dishwater, but she also ruined a drawer full of silk 'smalls' at the same time which Mr Reed insisted was paid for by his errant shop assistant.

Mr Reed had heard the rumours circulating about Lucy and was rather worried about his shop's reputation. He didn't want to appear as having a very lax approach about his staff and was concerned that he might lose customers who could refuse to be served by a lady of dubious reputation. Even though he had owned the shop for a number of years and had always traded fairly and honestly, he knew that it took only one wrong move and he could lose the reputation he had built up. He wasn't prepared to run that risk and, the day after Mrs Dundas soaked his staff and his stock, he informed Lucy that she was 'no longer required' to work in his shop. Lucy was devastated by losing her job. It had been a pleasant place to work and she had always considered herself to be above the level of those who worked in grocers or an ironmongers. She heartily wished that she hadn't written the note and put it in with the money she had paid the blackmailer now that her world had collapsed around her. Her secret had come out, she had lost money and now she had lost her job. She knew who to blame. It was the scum of the earth who had spread the tales about her, ignoring the fact that it was her own behaviour which had drawn the attention of the blackmailer. When her husband arrived home from work after hearing the rumours about his wife, and declared their marriage over, Lucy reached a decision - she would have to find out who the blackmailer was and take her revenge.

Martha didn't know that Lucy had lost her job, nor did she know that Lucy's husband had left the family home and gone back to live with his mother, but she did hear that Mr Dundas had publicly apologised to his wife for his behaviour and had sworn on oath that he would never go near Lucy ever again. His wife decided that she liked the public sympathy she had received and was happy that David didn't intend ever visiting Lucy again and was prepared to allow him to stay with her 'for the sake of the children'. It gave her the upper hand in their relationship and she found thousands of little ways of reminding him of his errant behaviour, a situation which he bore with gritted teeth and which his wife enjoyed immensely. She had never had the upper hand in their relationship before as David Dundas belonged to the old school who thought wives should be meek and mild, keep house and look after the children their menfolk had bestowed on them and never have a thought of their own.

Martha, meanwhile, had retrieved her list of wrong-doers from under her bedroom floorboard and was planning her next venture into blackmail. She was totally ignorant of Lucy Renwick's campaign to find the blackmailer who had ruined her life and had no qualms about spreading more unhappiness in her wake.

The next couple on her list were Harriet Winters and Michael Lewinson. Michael was an architect who had a fine sense of his own importance amongst the population of a town who nearly all worked in the iron and steel industry or down the docks, using their hands to wring a livelihood out of these huge industries while he used his brain to conjure up marvellous buildings, never dirtying his hands with anything more rough than pen and ink. He enjoyed being the social superior of everyone he met and was too fastidious to choose a mistress who worked in a shop. His mistress was a dressmaker, who worked from her home, making elegant gowns for the few members of the upper echelons of society who formed the social backbone of the Middlesbrough area. Harriet was quietly-spoken, reasonably well-educated and alone in the world since her parents had both died in an influenza epidemic while the last Queen had been on the throne. Harriet had nursed them both but had been unable to save either of them and, after their deaths, had sold the large house they had owned in Middlesbrough, bought herself a tiny terraced house in South Bank and invested the rest of the money in bonds so that she would have a small income for the rest of her life. She supplemented her pension by making clothes for the women who had been her friends when her parents were still alive and they assuaged the guilt they felt at by-passing her socially by paying through the nose for the garments they received. It worked for them all.

When Michael Lewinson had first noticed Harriet at a tea party given by the Mayor's wife, years before, he had been drawn to her self-possessed demeanour and her quiet humour. He enjoyed their conversations which were always leavened by her ability to see the comical in any situation and he admired her determination to provide for herself without the need for any man. She was so unlike the rather grasping young ladies who inhabited his social circle that he sought her out whenever she appeared at any event he attended, although he couldn't persuade her to walk out with him. Harriet hadn't felt secure either financially or emotionally since her parents had died and, although she didn't have money to throw around, she could at least afford to feed and clothe herself. She had no intention of ever getting married because that would mean she would become dependent on someone else and that someone else may let her down.

Michael finally married the daughter of his partner in the architectural firm they had both set up when the old Queen was on the throne but he still hankered after Harriet's company. Harriet, who enjoyed being with Michael even more, now that he was unlikely to propose marriage to her again, allowed him to visit her on dark evenings so that they could chat together without raising any eyebrows at their close relationship. Theirs was a purely platonic relationship, a meeting of minds and an enjoyment of each other's company without any of the complicated romantic problems associated with other relationships. When Sarah Salton had seen Michael tapping at Harriet's door one dark night and gaining entry, she had immediately assumed that it was because they were in the throes of an illicit relationship and when she had then seen that their meetings were a regular occurrence, this conclusion had been reinforced. This was the one and only time that Sarah had made a mistake but she had never gotten round to actually blackmailing the pair, so she hadn't taken them off her list.

Martha, like Sarah, was incapable of believing that a man and a woman would meet purely to talk, so she fell into the same mistake as Sarah and now had them picked out as her next targets. This time, she decided to spread her efforts more widely and scanned Sarah's papers for at least another two couples who could be relieved of some money. She had decided that she didn't need to waste her time in watching her chosen candidates for blackmail, not when she had a very willing accomplice who would be more than happy to spend a cold evening hiding in the dark and watching to verify that the couples named in the list did actually meet. It was a very short step for Martha to reconsider her decision of choosing just three couples to make into her targets and finally giving Prudence a list of six couples and their addresses so that she could spend a couple of evenings checking that these chosen ones were still enjoying their illicit trysts. Greed and the need for power had begun to worm their way into Martha's soul, finding in there a well-prepared and very fertile bed for them to set their seeds and begin growing.

Prudence swore on all that was holy to her that she would never reveal what she had been asked to do nor who had asked her to do it. She was grateful for the notice that Martha paid her and would have spied on these couples for free just because Martha wanted her to. Having been a bully at school, she missed the companionship of her peers because nobody wanted to be her friend now that they had all grown up and, apart from the boot boy and the irascible chef who ran the kitchen where she worked, she didn't have any companions anymore. She wasn't even interested in the money which Martha had said that she would pay her because she didn't go anywhere to spend it but would have done what Martha asked purely for the pleasure of thinking that she had a friend.

Their joint venture into blackmail worked very well and Martha's nest egg grew even bigger. It no longer fitted in the space under the floorboard in her bedroom and she began to look about her for another hiding place which would be big enough for her stash of coins. It suited her to search the house above their shop for a hiding place because it meant that she was also searching for Sarah's hidden loot at the same time and she was convinced that it wouldn't take her long to find where the old woman had hidden her ill-gotten gains.

Martha's second foray into the world of the blackmailer was almost as successful as her first. This time, because she had targeted six couples, the amount of money she received was staggering, even for her new ambitions and she resolved that she would use the six again later on in the year. She had no knowledge of the reactions that her blackmail letters had had on the six couples concerned and didn't particularly care if she had upset them. She was only concerned with the amount of money she received and the huge sense of power which it gave her. She paid Prudence a tidy sum for her time and for her silence although

Prudence's portion was only tiny when compared with the massive amount of money which Martha received. Prudence had no idea what was in the letters which she had posted to the couples and so had even less idea how much money they produced, although Martha did tell her who was carrying on with whom when she handed the letters over for posting.

Prudence cared as little as Martha that these people were losing money. If they could afford to live in a house of their own, not shared with other members of their families, then Prudence reckoned that they were well-off in comparison to her family where three generations were all squashed together in a tiny house with very few amenities. Even if the blackmail victims were renting their houses from a landlord, then Prudence still considered that they were comfortable because they had a house to live in. Her older sister, her sister's husband and their two children occupied the second bedroom of Prudence's family home, while her aged grandmother had her bed in the parlour. Prudence had the choice of either sharing with her granny or sleeping on the floor of her parent's bedroom, neither of which were attractive options. She longed for a room to call her own and, in her more imaginative moments, wondered what it would be like to have a whole room given over to a bath.

Martha had no idea that Michael and Harriet's relationship was a purely platonic one. If she had thought about them as a couple she would have confirmed that they were definitely having an affair because Harriet had paid the amount demanded of her although Martha didn't know that she had done it without telling Michael that she was being blackmailed. Harriet had paid up because she was terrified that her name would be spread around the area as being that of a loose woman. She had a business to run and couldn't afford to lose customers who, she was sure, would disappear in their droves if they thought that she was acting like a 'lady of the night' with a respected architect. Harriet wasn't happy about paying out her hard-won money to stop someone gossiping about her but she couldn't think what else she could do. She had no idea who the blackmailer was or where the blackmailer had got the information about Harriet's and Michael's meetings. She only knew that she had to stop her name being bruited abroad and the only way to confirm that was to pay what the blackmailer asked for. It didn't suit Harriet at all and she put her mind to working out a way of finding out who the blackmailer was.

Thus it was that Martha had made, unknown to her, two dangerous enemies in her first two forays into the world of blackmail. Lucy was the more open opponent as she was the more likely to challenge whoever she believed was responsible for her fall from grace but Harriet, although small and quiet as a person, was the more likely to put her rather clever brain to the task of tracing her blackmailer and seeking the revenge she needed from her.

Life in the house on York Street moved on towards the beginning of summer, swept up in the preparations for Bob and Edith's wedding. Daniel was finding that his haulage business was expanding at a tremendous rate and he always had more customers than he had the time to do the work they wanted of him. He was beginning to think that he would have to buy another wagon and employ a man to drive it for him and this thought pleased him and terrified him in equal measure. His brain would dance when he thought about being a proper employer as he was reaching this goal far earlier than he had expected and he was worried about over-reaching himself and losing all that he had worked so hard to achieve.

Chapter Twenty Two

With the onset of summer came weather the like of which no-one could ever remember. The sun shone every day and the heat was enough to make babies and old folk spend a lot of their day asleep. There was no let-up from the heat of the sun which rose every morning adding to the already-high temperature and set every night without bringing any relief from the heat. Even the air was as dry as dust and those Englishmen and women who had lived in this northern outpost of the land all their lives weren't used to these levels of temperature. It was as if the whole country had loosed itself from the shackles which tied it to the North Sea and had drifted down towards the equator, getting hotter and drier the further south it travelled.

Bob and Edith's wedding was a great success and Daniel finally achieved his ambition of joining in with a street party when the wedding feast was taken out into the fresh air and spread on trestle tables nearly the full length of the street. Neighbours who hadn't been invited to the wedding didn't hesitate to join the party and Edith watched them, happy that she was finally accepted and liked by those who surrounded her. Her only wish was that these people hadn't ignored her plight for all those years that she had been a downtrodden slave for her own parents, when their good wishes might have made such a difference to her and her children's lives.

The summer stretched out in front of them all - hot, dry and incredibly unusual. The shops and public houses did a roaring trade in soft drinks and ale, although some men found it more difficult to get drunk in the hot weather. Children, especially, clamoured for drinks and those women who made lemonade were suddenly the centre of everyone's attention.

Daniel worked even harder, despite the stifling weather and the dust which rose around his wagon in clouds every time that he put his foot to the accelerator. He was constantly covered in a layer of this dust and his throat was permanently parched, so much so that he broke his own rules and called in at the Station Hotel one night after a late run to Middlesbrough. He was surprised to be accosted by Prudence Golightly when she entered the bar to bring a tray of clean glasses. He had hardly ever spoken to her in his life, although he was well-aware of her reputation as a bully at school. To his surprise, she stopped next to him and greeted him by name, making a big show of being friendly with him as though she had been one of his childhood friends. He was polite and answered her comments as best as he could but he was uncomfortable in engaging her in conversation, especially as one man shouted across the bar, asking if Daniel had got himself a lady friend.

Daniel blushed at the innuendo in the comment and cursed himself for not being able to stop the blush. His reaction made him look guilty of the man's accusation and Daniel found himself shaking his head and repeating 'no' several times. Prudence wasn't at all put out by this and her flirting grew in response to the men's jests, to the point where Daniel threw his drink down his neck and left the bar to the accompanying cheers from the men. He was even hotter and more uncomfortable when he got outside than he had been before he went in and also irritated at Prudence, at his own reaction and at his inability to stay at the bar where some of the men had been discussing the rumours of a war coming. He was desperate to hear if the rumours were true but he had no intentions of entering the Station again that night and so had to go home without picking up the information he wanted.

Home was very different now that Edith and Bob were married. They had moved into the house on Normanby Road as soon as they got married, sharing it with Grace and Bob's mother, Louisa and leaving Daniel and Martha in the house in York Street. The house was often cold to get home to because neither Martha nor Daniel were at home during the day to keep the kitchen fire going, although at that time the lack of a fire was a blessing in the continued heat of the summer. Martha was showing a side to her character that Daniel had never seen before as she was doing her best to produce a cooked meal for them every night. She had taken to leaving Edith to close the shop and was getting home early enough to prepare a meal for them both. Daniel was very grateful because he was eternally hungry, a matter he put down to his childhood when he regularly didn't have enough to eat. At times, he thought he would never feel as though he had had enough to eat and that it would stay with him for the rest of his life but Martha was doing all she could to alleviate it.

That night, the meal was ready as he walked into the kitchen where the smell of the cooked pork was enough to start his mouth watering before he had washed his hands. He sat down at the place Martha had set for him and she took her seat and then began to ladle the pork stew onto their plates. Martha also felt twinges of hunger more often than most other people and even the heat of the day wasn't enough to put her off the plateful of food which was in front of her. There was silence while they both took the edge off their hunger but Daniel was soon ready to talk.

"I called into the Station for a pint on the way home tonight." Daniel said. "It has been so hot today and my wagon churns up so much dust that I thought my throat had closed up."

Martha smiled at this and nodded her agreement.

"That lass who was in your class at school was working in there." Daniel continued, watching his plate rather than Martha's face as he spoke. "You know the one I mean. The lass you pushed down the toilet steps and then tied her pigtails to the railings."

Martha stopped eating long enough to glance at Daniel's face. It was bland as he concentrated on his food and Martha couldn't detect any suspicion showing so she tried to answer as normally as she could, although she was sure her guilt must show in her face.

"You mean Prudence Golightly. She was a typical bully and stopped if anyone stood up to her. What did she say to you?"

"She was flirting with me and the other customers saw it and began to take the mickey out of me. I'd only gone in because my throat was so dry with all the dust my wagon throws up at the moment. It won't be so bad once we get some rain but I needed a drink tonight. The customers were all talking about the possibility of a war and I wanted to listen to what they had to say but then she stopped right next to me and started acting as though I was her best friend. I had to drink up and leave so I didn't get to hear all that was being said."

Martha was watching him like a hawk now but she was sure that he had no idea about her recent contacts with Prudence so she could ignore it and concentrate on his news. She made a mental note to tell Prudence to keep away from Daniel in future so that she didn't make him suspicious and then let out a small sigh of relief before responding to his comments.

"What do you mean about a war? Who with? Aren't we friends with France now?"

"It isn't France that's the problem, it's Germany." Daniel was still eating and paused while he chewed the mouthful of food. "It seems that their Kaiser is causing worries amongst the other countries in Europe and there's been a lot of talk of war. I wanted to find out if there had been any new developments but Prudence put the kybosh on that cos all the men were more interested in what she was doing. It really irritated me. I think I'll have to buy a newspaper in the morning and see if there is any truth in the rumours."

"Do you think we could go to war?" Martha asked, all thoughts of her blackmailing efforts forgotten for the moment. "Would you have to go and fight?"

"I hope not." Daniel's answer came very swiftly. "I've got plans for the business but they'd all be thrown out if the country went to war. A war with anyone could set us back by years and it was all going so well. I was thinking of getting another motor wagon seeing that this one has been such a success. I've got customers throwing themselves at me because I can move goods and materials so quickly and I've jumped in at the start of a new world in transport. So many of the older firms are frightened of getting a motor wagon and I wanted to cream as much business off as I could before anyone else followed me."

Martha could see that Daniel was genuinely concerned about the idea of a war and tried to put his mind at rest.

"Well, if there's a war against Germany, won't it be fought in Germany? And we have the British Army. Why would it bother us here at home? We didn't see any of the fighting during the Boer War so why would this be any different? Don't start worrying about something that might never happen."

"That's what I want to find out." Daniel finished eating and rose from his chair. "I'm not going to wait for the morning. I'm going to the newsagent's to get any papers that they have left. I've got a terrible feeling about this, Martha. I'm sure that it's going to happen and that it will affect us in ways that we have never dreamed of before. Why can't people concentrate on making life better for everybody instead of wanting to start fighting with each other?"

Daniel stormed out of the kitchen, leaving Martha still at the table. She put down her knife and fork, overcome with a feeling of impending doom, and stared out of the kitchen window at the gate in the backyard which Daniel had forgotten to close in his haste to get a newspaper. It swung in the slight wind and she watched it as it moved back and forth but her eyes weren't seeing the gate. In her mind, she could see a small hill with a cluster of three trees on its summit. Suddenly, soldiers carrying rifles came over the top of the hill and streamed around the trees, making for some target which she couldn't see. A sound like summer thunder came from overhead and several of the running soldiers fell to the ground. She expected them to rise and continue running towards their target but they didn't. Those of the soldiers who fell to the ground stayed on the ground and she realised that they had been shot and that they were dead.

Her blood ran cold as this realisation hit her and then the scene faded from her view and she was left staring at a swinging yard gate. She shook her head to clear it of the horrendous pictures in her mind but she couldn't clear the sense of impending doom which filled her head and she groaned with the horror of it all. When Daniel returned with a newspaper, she was still sitting in her place at the table with her meal forgotten in front of her. Daniel's face was as bleak as hers when he raised the newspaper to show her the headlines on its front page.

"It's going to come, Martha. The papers are full of some problem in a place called Sarajevo. Some Duke has been assassinated and Germany is mobilising its army. We won't be able to escape it now. You can bet your last farthing that Britain will be at war soon."

Still shaken by what she had seen in her mind, Martha stared across the table at Daniel, her face drained of all colour and her hands shaking.

"Oh this is going to be so bad, Danny." Martha whispered. "I can see it - it's going to be a blood bath and we are going to join it. Oh my God what should we do?"

The news in the papers had shaken Daniel to the core but Martha's behaviour frightened him out of his wits and, by the time he had managed to get her to tell him what she had seen in her mind, he was as distraught as she was. What frightened him the most was that Martha was so down-to-earth and practical but she totally believed that she had seen a snippet of the future; a future that was as bleak as a future could possibly be. Could it be true? Had she seen a view on a battlefield or was it just an over-active imagination? Daniel threw that idea out of the window immediately. Martha didn't possess an imagination unless money came into it so it was unlikely to be a fancy. She genuinely thought she had seen a scene from the near future and this worried Daniel immensely. He tried to reassure Martha about her vision, telling her that she must have fallen asleep at the table as a result of the heat and had had a dream but her ashen face belied his words.

"If war comes, life will be very different." Martha said. "I think we should start stocking up the larder with items which will keep. Do you know, I found out last week that a lot of our flour comes from America? If Europe goes to war perhaps America's ships, which bring the grain, won't get to us. We could starve!"

"I think it's a good idea to replenish the larder but don't panic overmuch." Daniel said soothingly. "It might all blow over and then we'll have worried for nothing."

Martha nodded in reply just to convince Daniel she believed him but she couldn't get the scene of a battlefield out of her head and she knew it wasn't a dream. She didn't believe in dreams but what she had seen had been as real as the scene in their kitchen at this moment. She forbore to speak about it again so that Daniel didn't worry about her but she began making plans in her mind to make sure that they wouldn't have to do without if war brought changes to their lives. She also determined to carry out one last, huge blackmail before war came, as she was convinced now that it would.

Daniel didn't try to reassure Martha anymore. He had been so struck by her face while she had told him what she had seen that his own panic was rising within him and he couldn't keep it down. He would have to make sure that he had some stocks of fuel for his wagon, in case it became scarce because what use was a wagon if he couldn't get it to run? Damn! Why did there have to be a war, just when he was starting to realise his dreams? He lifted his chin as he forced his active brain to work harder than it ever had before. He needed some fuel and a place to store it. He needed some land to grow food in case there were shortages. He needed a new cart in case the fuel ran out and he had to go back to using a cart. Thank God he hadn't got rid of the old horse which had pulled his cart before he got his motor wagon, so that wouldn't be a problem. The idea of going back to the very beginning and pulling a handcart himself ate at his soul, making him see just how transitory life was. And he thought he had come so far!

Thinking of the old horse brought some sort of answer to his problems. The horse had its stable on the allotments near the railway lines, opposite their shop at the end of Pearl Street. He was sure that the next door plot to the stable was overgrown and hadn't been tended for a long while. He would look at that tomorrow and then go and make sure that he got possession of it before anyone else had the same idea. He seemed to remember a huge hutch which backed onto the road on that allotment. He could soon get rid of that so that he could use the whole plot for growing food. He felt better now that he had some plans in place and he turned to Martha to share his thoughts so far.

"I'll have to get another cart, just in case we get to the point where we can't get any fuel for the wagon. Thank goodness I kept Arthur in his stable on the allotments so that, if fuel does run out, I'll be able to still move goods around. This is rather like planning for those sieges that we learned about at school, where castles came under fire from rivals to the throne. I'll go and see if I can get that allotment opposite the shop so that we can grow food. You know which one I mean? The one with that wooden hutch backing onto the street?"

Martha couldn't remember the lessons about sieges at school because it had never interested her but her ears pricked up when Daniel mentioned the allotment and the hutch.

She didn't want to lose that hutch. It was central to her blackmailing business so she needed it. Where on earth would she find another place that was so close to the shop with its uninterrupted view over the allotments? Mind you, second thoughts told her that it was better that it became their allotment than someone else got it and knocked down the hutch. Where else was there a place that she could she make into her drop-off point for her victims? She'd never find anything else as useful as that hutch.

She realised that Daniel was waiting for her to answer his questions and she shook her head to force her thoughts away from blackmail.

"Yes, I know which one you mean. I'm sorry, I can still see those soldiers dying and it's frightening me."

Daniel was appalled that he had moved on with his thoughts without stopping to see if Martha had recovered from her experience. He put his arm around her shoulder and hugged her to him.

"I'm sorry, chick, that I've ignored what happened to you. You must be horrified by what you saw, even if it was a dream. Don't worry. Nothing like that is going to happen, so there's no need for you to worry about it. Now, come on, we've got to get our plans in order in case a war does happen and I need your sensible suggestions to make sure that we don't miss anything."

Daniel hugged Martha one last time and then sat down at the kitchen table, pulling a small notebook out of his pocket. He took the pencil from behind his ear (a permanent position for it) and began making lists of what needed to be done and what other actions they needed to take.

Martha was grateful for his concern and slightly guilty that he took her worry about her blackmail business as shock at the sight she had experienced, so she hugged him back and then tried to force her brain to come up with suggestions for items they needed to buy before the whole town began buying them and supplies ran out. She concentrated on items needed for the home and left Daniel to work out answers to his problems over fuel and other items connected to his work. Eventually, they had a list of commodities which they needed to buy and actions they needed to take in order to set themselves up to withstand a war, although they both were well-aware that this war was going to be very different from any that had been fought in the past.

"It may all come to nothing." Daniel remarked as they cleared up the kitchen ready for bedtime. "But I don't think there's anything wrong in being prepared for what we might have to face before this year is over. I just wish we had more idea of where and how it'll be fought and how many of us might have to join the army."

"Do you think that ordinary men will have to join up?" Martha asked. "Haven't we got an army to fight for us? Why would they need untrained men to join them?"

"According to what I read in the paper, Germany has got an army of thousands of men, all ready to fight for the fatherland. We have a very small army in comparison, so it will need civilians to join up and expand it, after some training of course."

"So they will be looking for volunteers to join up?"

Daniel nodded grimly before he spoke.

"Unless they bring back the press gangs to force men into the army and navy. We might not have enough men who would want to volunteer, so they may have to be forced to do it and that means that I would have to go and fight too. I don't want that, not because I'm a coward, but because I have two businesses to run and I had such plans for expansion. Dear God, I don't want a war, not now."

Chapter Twenty Three

Martha didn't want to think of a time when men would be forced to enter the armed forces in order to defend their country. It horrified and frightened her and she wanted to blot it out of her mind but couldn't manage to do that. She could still see those soldiers coming over the hill and being shot down as they tried to run away from whomever it was who was chasing them. She tried to clear her mind but that picture had now been replaced by a view of Nelson Street and hundreds of young men marching towards the railway station, followed by crowds of children and women who were waving flags and singing as they all marched along.

Martha wasn't a sensitive soul, not by any stretch of the imagination, and she wasn't in any way fey, so these 'visions' disturbed her mightily. She had little in the way of empathy and rarely looked at any situation from another person's point of view so seeing these scenes and being able to feel the panic in the first vision and the excitement in the second vision gave her an outlook she had never experienced before. She didn't like any of it- not the views nor the emotions - and she did her best to try and banish them from her mind. That wasn't particularly successful as they dominated her mind when she went to bed so sleep didn't seem to be an option for her that night.

The next day, Daniel rushed straight off to get more fuel for his wagon and to buy a cart for the horse to pull for when his stock of fuel ran out. He visited the allotment authorities and slipped easily into taking the tenancy of the allotment opposite their shop, so, by lunchtime, he was pleased with the progress of his day's tasks and hoped that he had done enough to stop his business collapsing if war broke out.

There was much more talk on the streets about the prospect of war. It seemed that the world and his wife needed to talk about their fears, with even strangers discussing the possibility of the government declaring war and the social order collapsing around them. The hot weather meant that people could stand on the streets and chat to others without having to get inside to get away from rain or a biting wind, although it was necessary to find a sheltered spot out of the direct sunlight for those who wanted to discuss the possibilities of a war to a great degree. Daniel was amazed at the number of people who had been gripped by a surge of patriotism and the number who were desperate for war to be declared so that they could join the colours and go and fight for King and Country. Daniel soon realised that he had to keep his misgivings to himself so that he didn't become a target for those who jeered at the anti-war lobby. He had a business to run and couldn't afford to alienate any customers who held different views to him.

Martha, still suffering from the visions she had seen, threw herself into preparing the household for war with what she thought would be its attendant shortages. Their kitchen overflowed with any commodity which would remain usable for any length of time and she even had the foresight to buy fabric for summer and winter clothes, expecting that the woollen and cotton mills of Yorkshire would soon be working round the clock to provide uniforms for those thousands and thousands of men who seemed determined to throw their lives away by signing up for the army. She, too, learnt to keep her opinions on the possible war to herself so that she didn't alienate their customers in the furniture shop although it was a difficult task for her because she was so used to announcing her opinions and expecting others to follow where she led.

Martha had decided, the night that she had the two visions, that she would make a final journey into her world of blackmail. If all the menfolk went off to war their paramours wouldn't have the opportunity to partake in any sinful behaviour which would leave Martha without any victims to terrorise. It could be her last ever foray into the world of blackmail so she decided that she would go out in a haze of glory and blackmail as many people at the same time as was humanly possible. She wanted to use the hutch again because her 'customers' were used to putting their money into there, before Daniel removed it from his allotment in order to increase the land he had on which to grow vegetables.

She went through Sarah's list one last time and picked out every name she had used before. It was a substantial list and she had to be very careful about her timings for her victims to drop off her money, so that she didn't end up with a queue of people waiting to put an envelope or bag into the hutch. In the end, she realised that she would have to be at the shop well into the night as the last drop was going to be in the early hours of the morning. She briefed Prudence, explaining that this was going to be their last attempt at blackmail for a considerable time to come, not realising that she was removing Prudence's one and only enjoyable hobby.

Prudence hadn't been happy about the way in which Martha had forbidden her to speak to Daniel or the way in which she blamed Prudence for Daniel's supposed interest in Martha's exploits, so the news that this was the final escapade didn't sit well on Prudence at all. She became very sulky, hoping that Martha would ask why she was upset but Martha was so wrapped up in writing blackmail letters and stocking their house for a possible war that she didn't notice Prudence's bad mood. That increased Prudence's temper and she began to work out a way of paying Martha back for treating her as a slave without feelings. It didn't help Prudence's mood that she had actually formed a romantic attachment for Daniel and being told to avoid him didn't suit her plans at all. She had laboured under the misapprehension that Daniel would be bound to find her attractive and only needed a little encouragement in order to fall head over heels in love with her. The fact that he hadn't was, in Prudence's mind, all the fault of Martha, that high-handed bitch who now wanted her to take all the risks in this blackmail palaver, delivering the letters and collecting the money out of the hutch. If any victim chose to hang about in the dead of night, it would be Prudence they would see, not Martha. Prudence was now annoyed at being made the scapegoat for any comeback and even more annoyed that she was only being paid a pittance for taking all of Martha's risks.

The latent bully in Prudence lifted its head and roared with her indignation, anger and thwarted love life and Prudence determined that she was going to get more out of this last foray into blackmail than she had out of the previous attempts. Martha was going to be made to pay dearly for using Prudence as an unfeeling skivvy.

Martha was totally unaware that she had roused such emotion in Prudence and continued with her plans, unworried by her new, brusque and short-tempered ally. She was more concerned about Daniel's desire to begin altering the layout of the allotment in order to be able to wrest the maximum growing space from it because he was still intending to remove the hutch which, he said, was in the way of what would be a long row of potatoes. Martha brought the date of the blackmail drop forward so much that she nearly didn't have enough time to deliver all the letters, making Prudence moan even more when she realised that she would have two late nights together: one for delivering the letters and the next for the collection of the money.

So, Monday night saw Prudence delivering the last of the blackmail letters, all of which had messages which demanded the money to be left in the hutch on Tuesday night, beginning at a quarter to eleven. It was early August and, although the nights were starting to draw out again after the midsummer solstice, it was still light until late in the evening. Martha didn't want either her or Prudence to be seen collecting the money from the hutch so she had planned a later start than earlier in the year. It also meant that the last drop was to be well after midnight with the last collection at one in the morning.

Prudence made her way to the furniture shop on Pearl Street after she had delivered the last letter and knocked softly on the back door. Martha was waiting and pulled Prudence into the shop's kitchen as soon as she heard Prudence's scratching on the back door.

"Did you deliver them all?" Martha hissed, closing the door as quietly as she could. She didn't want any of the neighbours thinking that the shop was occupied after closing time.

"Yes, I did." Prudence's reply was as quiet as Martha's question but Martha could make out the sulky tone to it, even though she couldn't properly see the girl's face in the dark kitchen. She pulled Prudence through to the passage between the shop and the kitchen where she could light a candle without any sign of it showing either at the front or the back of the property. Prudence's lip was sticking out as far as Martha had ever seen it and she knew that Prudence wasn't happy about something.

"What is it? Were you seen delivering one of the letters?"

"No." Prudence replied. "I'm sick of being the one taking all the risks in this game and I don't reckon I'm getting enough for doing it. I'll be the one carted off by the police if I'm seen delivering the letters or collecting the money and I don't reckon that the police will believe me if I tell them that it's all your idea."

Martha doubted very much that the police would believe that Prudence had the brains to be able to hatch a plot of this magnitude but she didn't put this point across to Prudence. She didn't want Prudence ducking out now because it needed two of them for the money collection. Prudence went to the hutch and removed the money and Martha stood guard in the bedroom window of the shop, checking that nobody lurked further along the street, watching to see who collected it. If Prudence cried off, then Martha would have to collect it and that made her vulnerable to being caught. There was no way that Martha was going to abandon this, their last foray into blackmail. If war came then her career as a blackmailer was over and she wouldn't be able to amass this amount of money ever again, or, at least until she found Sarah's treasure hoard. Martha did a quick calculation in her head.

"All right. I'll pay you more for your trouble." Martha needed to keep Prudence onside and mute about Martha's criminal activities. "I'll give you five pounds for the two nights work. That's more than you'd earn in the Station for months."

Prudence was well-aware that five pounds was a princely sum. She had never even seen that much money, never mind possessed it and she stopped sulking immediately.

"Really? You'll give me that much money?"

"I will, I promise, but if you ever mention my name in connection to any of this, I will spread it around town that you've been fiddling in the Station ever since you started working there and that you steal food to take home. I'll say that your Mam told you to do it so they'll arrest your Mam as well as you. Do you understand? Try and pass this off on me and I'll see that your whole family ends up in prison. I could prove that your Dad has stolen furniture from this shop and sold it on, so he'd go down as well as your Mam. Do you want that?"

Prudence was nearly in tears with Martha's threats. She was sure that Martha was clever enough to prove anything and she knew that the police were more likely to believe a shop owner than they were to believe a kitchen slut like her. Life wasn't fair but it never had been fair. Her Dad regularly moaned about the rich people who had got rich on the backs of poor people like them, so distrust and dislike of any authority was ingrained in her. She wouldn't even dare to speak to a policeman, never mind try to lie to one. She knew that she wouldn't betray Martha because she had too much to lose herself and if Martha got wind that Prudence had even mentioned this to anyone, she had no doubt that Martha would carry out her threats and her parents could both end up in prison. She was stuck with it. She might as well carry it through to the end and be the proud possessor of a five pound note! Prudence's back shivered in delight at the thought of that five pounds. She could buy herself a posh dress which would make Daniel notice her. She could buy perfume so that he swooned when she walked by. She could have her hair cut by a proper hairdresser instead of doing it herself. That five pound note was the doorway to a new world and Prudence wanted desperately to belong in it.

Prudence was trapped by Martha's threats and by her own ambitions and, even in the dimly-lit hallway, Martha knew that she had won that tussle of wits by the greed showing on Prudence's face. She smiled to herself at the ease with which she could manipulate Prudence, while promising retribution for these last-minute wobbles by her lapdog. Next time she produced a money-making idea, she would make sure that she wouldn't need any help. She didn't like being open to threats from any quarter, especially one who had the intelligence of a fly. Martha had more brain power in her little finger than Prudence had in her whole body, yet she had nearly scuppered Martha's greatest plan. From now on, Martha would work alone, so this would be her final attempt at blackmail. Her next plan would be to find Sarah's treasure trove and see how big it was. But she was going to go out with a huge bang, of that she was sure.

Tuesday dawned as sunny and warm as the previous weeks. Martha was alive with excitement, so much so that her fingers and toes sparked with it and her hair flew around her head as though a breeze was lifting it. She was so excited that she sang as she prepared her breakfast, glad that Daniel had left home early to collect a shipment from the docks. Her eyes shone and her face was pink with the thoughts of the money she was going to collect that evening. If Daniel had been at home, he would have been very suspicious of this overflowing of emotion from Martha, but she dressed and got ready for work without any witnesses to her delight. It was as she left the back yard that she came face-to-face with Daniel, who screeched his wagon to a halt outside the back gate and then jumped down to grasp Martha's arm as she exited the yard.

"What's the matter?" Martha cried, seeing the wild look on Daniel's face. "Let go. You're hurting me!"

Daniel seemed to come to the realisation that he was squeezing Martha's arm hard enough to bruise her and he released his fingers' stiff hold. His face and eyes were still wild and he was having difficulty in speaking sensibly.

"They've gone and done it." Daniel spoke through clenched teeth, not daring to open his mouth properly in case he screamed his frustration to the four winds.

"They've gone and done it!" He repeated as Martha could only stare at him in shock. She had never seen him so out of control and the sight of his staring eyes frightened the very core of her being.

"Who has gone and done what, Daniel?" Martha almost screamed back at him. "What do you mean? Please, stop it, you're really frightening me now."

Daniel took one long shuddering breath and then his eyes came back into focus and he looked straight into Martha's face.

"They've declared war. We're at war with the Hun. Oh my God, they've really gone and done it now."

Martha's arms fell to her sides as the full import of what her brother had just said hit her square in the stomach. She tottered back from him and leaned against the back gate so that her legs didn't have to bear the whole of her weight. She felt as though the ground had moved beneath her feet and, for the first time in her life, her senses swam and a blackness gathered around her. Daniel's voice seemed to be coming from a great distance and she wasn't sure where her body was. She felt as though she was floating and her panic level rose as she wondered how much it would hurt when she fell. Then, Daniel took hold of her arm again (much more gently this time) and his touch gave her back her feet and her head stopped spinning.

"Sorry, I should have found a kinder way to tell you." Daniel was appalled at his own thoughtlessness and aghast at the fright that he'd given his sister. Her face was drained of all colour, even her lips were only one shade darker than her skin, making her look like a cadaver on a table in a morgue. He had never seen anyone as deathly-looking as this before and he wished that he had held his tongue. But the damage was done and now Martha had to come to terms with what he had told her. Slowly, the colour began to ripple across her cheeks and her eyes focused on his face.

"Tell me that you are joking, Daniel." Martha spoke in a quiet whisper, unable as yet to find the strength to speak normally.

"He's not, pet."

The voice came from next door where Mr Davis had just stepped out of his back yard gate.

"I've heard it too. The news is all over Middlesbrough Road and Nelson Street cos one of the solicitors down there got a telegram from his London office. He rushed out into the street and started telling everyone. We're at war with Germany and they are already asking for volunteers to join the army. Thank God I'm too old to go and fight for my country but you'll be a prime candidate for the army, Daniel."

"I hope not." Daniel's voice was brusque and sharp. "I've got a business to run here. I haven't got the time or the desire to go off to war. Who's going to drive my wagon if I bugger off to Germany? Sorry, Mr Davis. I didn't mean to swear at you."

"That's all right, lad. I'd be swearing myself if I thought I might have to go and fight. I couldn't care less about that Archduke something in some foreign place getting shot. I didn't know him and I aren't going to miss him, even if they shot him ten times over. But there are a lot of lads who can't wait to get into a smart uniform with a gun and start showing off to all the lasses about the place."

"Well this lass won't be impressed by a bunch of little boys dressing up and playing soldiers." Martha spat out. "Lads should be out working and earning money for their families, not running away to play armies in some foreign country."

"I agree with you, Martha." Mr Davis said. "If I had my way, none of it would happen but I reckon you should keep your feelings close to your chest at the moment. The whole country is up in arms over what has happened and the bulk of them are all for going to fight. There's a group of them on Nelson Street all gathering together and singing the National Anthem at this moment. I saw them on my way home this morning after I'd finished my night shift and I couldn't believe my eyes. I reckon we're a small group, those of us who don't want to go to war, and we'd best keep our mouths closed so we don't start any fights amongst the patriotic majority of our fellow townsmen and women. Take heed you two if you don't want to become targets for some unruly mob."

"I think you've given us some very good advice there, Mr Davis." Daniel was quick to respond to their neighbour. "I'm not telling anyone how I feel about the prospect of a war. It's my business and it doesn't need to be shouted abroad"

"Oh, I'll keep my mouth shut." Martha added her twopennorth. "I don't believe in letting anyone know what I think about anything."

Chapter Twenty Four

It was devastating news for both of them but they had to agree that Mr Davis had the right idea about keeping their mouths shut over their own opinions of the war. Martha had hardly opened the shop before customers began coming in and they all were of the opinion that it was going to be a landmark in Great British history. Martha lost count of the number of people who told her that the war wouldn't last five minutes, not once their army got to the battlegrounds and began showing the Hun how to fight a battle. Mark my words, they all said, it'll all be over before Christmas. Martha smiled and nodded her agreement but didn't reply to their comments. She knew that she couldn't say she believed them, not without it showing on her face that she thought they were stupid and that wasn't the way to keep customers.

The only thing that kept Martha going that first day of the war was to think about the money that she was going to amass that night. It didn't cross her mind that any of her victims would refuse to pay nor had she thought about her strategy if the unthinkable happened and one of them did refuse. She daydreamed all morning of the heaviness of the bag that she would pick up that night to the extent that Edith had to shout at her four times to get her to hear her question. At that, Martha tried to put everything out of her mind in order to concentrate on work but, just before lunchtime, the shop bell went and Martha looked up to see Prudence standing in the doorway.

Martha shot out from behind their small counter and was next to Prudence in less time than it takes to say hello.

"What are doing here, you fool?" Every nerve ending which Martha possessed was crackling inside her body. "You fool, you know you aren't supposed to come here." Her voice was hardly above a whisper but Prudence winced at the venom in it.

"I only came to check that you still want me to come tonight." Prudence whispered back. "I didn't know if you were going to cancel it, what with the war and everything."

"Don't be ridiculous. Can you see anyone fighting in the streets here? Get out and don't come back until ten o'clock tonight." Martha gave her a shove towards the door to emphasise her haste and annoyance. Prudence didn't answer but sidled out of the shop door without even making the bell ring because she was hugging herself in so closely, she only took up two inches of space.

Martha went back behind the counter, thankful that Edith had been in the kitchen when Prudence had come in, so she didn't have to answer any questions about the girl's presence in the shop. It was time that she got rid of Prudence before she opened her mouth about their exploits. The girl didn't have a brain to speak of! But she would have to be careful how she did it, because she had already seen the light of rebellion in Prudence's eyes and bullies didn't change their behaviour. She could turn on Martha and cause her a lot of problems.

Martha spent the rest of the afternoon trying to put Edith's fears to rest about all the men going off to war; trying to fend off anyone who wanted her opinion of the war and trying to think up ways of getting rid of Prudence which didn't involve dropping her down the nearest well with a stone tied to her legs. If she got Martha into any bother with the police, she didn't think she would be able to stop herself from doing Prudence some serious damage.

Daniel was out all day and had a run to Scarborough that evening where he was going to stay in a lodging house and then call in at Whitby on his way back to pick up some fish for the wet-fish man on King Street who was using Daniel's transport in a bid to reduce his costs by cutting out the middle man between the fishermen and himself. It made it the perfect evening for Martha's blackmailing as there would be no witness to say that she had left the house and she would be able to carry her money back into the house and hide it while the house was empty. She had a few seconds panic when Edith asked if she wanted to come round to their house for supper, but she managed to avoid that by pleading fatigue. It was an excuse but, in truth, Martha did feel tired as her brain had never stopped working overtime all day and the heat from the sun added to her weariness. Edith was easily placated and Martha locked the shop door behind them with an enormous sense of relief that the day was over.

Martha wasn't the only person in the town that night to be thinking of the coming evening. Prudence had gone home after she had left the furniture shop, thrown herself on her bed and sulked all afternoon at the way that Martha had spoken to her. It was a good job, she decided, that Martha was paying her extra for this last night of blackmail or she might have taken her complaints to the police. She sighed at this point in her musings, knowing that she wouldn't dare go anywhere near a policeman because Martha was right when she had said that the police would believe her not Prudence or her family. Only the day before, Prudence's older brother, George, had been arrested for drunken behaviour after he had spent the afternoon (and his lodge money) in the nearest public house, downing pints and bragging of how he was going to enlist and get away from the rat hole he lived in. He had taken exception to the way the barman had made him wait for his drink and had climbed over the bar to convey his thoughts to the barman through his fists.

George had been three sheets to the wind before he had attempted to take retribution from the barman and that hadn't helped his balance, so that his climb over the bar counter had resulted in a massive amount of breakage and damage and, ultimately, a bill from the landlord to replace what he had broken. Prudence knew that the landlord was pushing for payment which would mean that they would all have to cough up because George had drunk all of his money. She needed the money she got from Martha and knew that she would have to put up with Martha's high-handed attitude or lose the only access she had to a bit of spending money for herself. But that decision didn't mean that she had to like working for Martha, far from it.

There was another person who was preparing herself for that evening's blackmailing and that person was Harriet Winters, the fallen-on-hard-times dressmaker who was totally innocent of the rumours about her. Once again, she had received a blackmail letter but this time she wasn't going to pay up and keep her mouth shut for the sake of her reputation. She had every intention of finding out who was blackmailing her and why and she knew that the only way to answer her questions was to still be near the hutch when the blackmailer collected their ill-gotten gains. She was making her plans that afternoon while she was sewing furiously at a new jacket for herself, in a style that she had designed especially for this evening. It was a reversible jacket which she could wear with its white side on the outside when she went to put her money into the hutch but she could then turn it inside out which made the jacket black and, therefore, much harder to see in the dark.

Harriet had also gathered pebbles from beside the railway line to put in a bag with some nails which, when jangled, made a sound as near to the music of coins knocking together that she could manage. She had no intentions of putting any money into it in case her plan backfired and she didn't get it back. She stitched away furiously at her new jacket, her anger growing with every beat of her heart that some wicked person wanted to ruin her life.

Well, she wasn't going to go down without a fight. The blackmailer might just get a shock that night.

Martha made her own meal and ate it in front of the empty grate in the kitchen. It was still far too hot to make her want to light the fire and she didn't need hot water because she could rinse out her plate under the cold tap. She had laid the fire ready to light when she got home because she knew from past experience that even sultry, hot days could turn cold in the wee small hours of the morning. She ate and then went upstairs to her bedroom to change her white blouse for a black one and to get her black shawl in case she needed the extra warmth later on. Black was the best colour for blending in with the background at night time. Then she checked her list of victims for that night and brooded over the timings once again, worried in case any of her victims were too early or too late and got tangled up with the previous or next victim. In future, she decided, she would only ever have one person at a time coming to leave money in the hutch. This worrying about victims meeting other victims was far too stressful and she was beginning to wonder if the money was worth all this planning.

Finally, her new watch crawled round past quarter to ten and she picked up her shawl and the leather bag she used to carry her payments in and set off for the shop. She knew she was early but she needed the walk to settle her nerves and she also wanted to be there before Prudence turned up. She didn't know if Prudence would have the sense to remain out of sight if she had to wait outside the shop for Martha to get there. If she stood outside in the street then anyone could see her and possibly put two and two together and make five.

Prudence was nowhere in sight when Martha reached the shop so Martha went round to the back alley and unlocked the yard gate. The hinges and the lock both worked smoothly and quietly now that Martha had spent time on them with some goose grease and some wire wool so not even a mouse would have heard the gate open. Martha opened the back door of the shop and crept into the kitchen, picking up the candle and matches which she had placed ready next to the kitchen door. She moved into the passageway between the shop and the kitchen before she lit the candle, knowing that its light couldn't be seen from outside.

Prudence joined her less than a quarter of an hour later and they both ascended the stairs and made their way to the front bedroom in order to look out of the window at the allotments over the road. There wasn't a light to be seen on the allotments as the last of the gardeners had left before it got fully dark, nor could they see any sign of life on the street so the stage looked set for their final showdown. Martha had placed two kitchen chairs in the window area so that they could be comfortable while they waited for the first of their victims to arrive and they both took their seats, one on either side of the window. Prudence opened her mouth to speak but closed it again when Martha gave a vehement shake of her head to stop her.

"We have to say as little as possible." Martha whispered, holding her finger across her mouth as she did so. "These walls are paper-thin and we have a house on that side of us where the people will be in bed. Don't speak above the tiniest whisper."

Prudence nodded her head to show she had heard and understood Martha's directions but, inside, she was fuming. She had intended trying to get more money out of Martha but, if she wasn't allowed to talk to her, she couldn't push her case. She was sure that Martha was doing this deliberately so that Prudence couldn't ask for more money and so her temper rose the longer she had to sit in silence. There were people living in the house on one side of the shop but, surely, the walls couldn't be that thin, could they? Would they be overheard if they tried to talk? Before Prudence had gathered up enough courage to question Martha, she saw Martha lean forward to look out of the window. Prudence turned her head to see what had attracted Martha's attention and then she, too, saw the lonely figure walking along the opposite side of the street, passing the allotments.

It was the unmistakeable figure of Robert Leigh, the Postmaster, who was very friendly with Olivia Westcott, the butcher's widow. His portly shape and his rolling walk made him stand out in any crowd but, that night, he seemed particularly short, probably because they were looking down on him from above. He was also doing his best to be invisible, which isn't easy when you are as round as you are high and you keep rotating your head to look about you in case someone is watching you. Never once did he think to look upwards, although he still wouldn't have been able to see the two watchers in their window.

Robert Leigh got closer to the hutch and slowed his walk. Martha, from the bedroom opposite to him, willed him to get on with it. She couldn't bear this dilly-dallying about. It made her want to scream in frustration at the stupid pudding-shaped man and she couldn't let her feelings go, trapped as she was in this little bedroom. The only release she had was to pull faces at Robert as he ambled past the hutch and then kept on walking. Martha released a pent-up breath and glanced at Prudence. She was still following the man with her eyes and Martha saw her face change when Robert turned at the end of the road and began walking back towards the hutch.

Martha's head felt as though it was on a string being manipulated by some other being, as her eyes turned towards the view of the allotment again. Robert was nearly at the hutch. Was he going to stop? Would he put his money into it or would he continue walking along the street without stopping? She let out another pent-up breath when Robert stopped next to the hutch and bent down, pretending to refasten his shoe lace. Martha's view of the hutch was almost completely covered by the huge expanse of black backside revealed to her and she couldn't see if he was actually putting anything into the hutch or not. Suddenly, the rotund figure straightened and Robert made off for the far end of the street at a speed which would have astonished any of his customers in the Post Office and made Martha blink in disbelief as she watched him hurrying along.

"Did he do it?" Martha hissed at Prudence, trying not to scream out loud.

"I think so, but I couldn't see much for his huge bum." Prudence replied, as quietly as she could when she had an overwhelming urge to giggle at the sight she had seen.

Martha heaved a sigh of relief and felt the tension streaming away from her body.

"We'll give it three more minutes and then you can go and collect it." Martha ordered. "And don't forget to go out of the back door so no-one will see which house you've come out of."

Prudence nodded in reply, her giggling fit gone as quickly as it had come. No matter what had happened, the worst part of the evening's activities now fell to her and she was dreading the walk out of the shop and across the road to take the money from the hutch. She always felt as though the eyes of the world must be on her and that, at any second, she would hear the deep voice of a policeman as he asked her what she thought she was doing. Or worse, the victim didn't go home but stayed around to see who was blackmailing them and Prudence got the blame for it all. A vision of herself standing in a courtroom next to a policeman swam into her head and she almost lost the courage she had garnered to get her through the next few minutes.

At this point, Martha lowered her arm from where she had been watching the hands of her watch as they traversed the watch face and nodded to Prudence to leave. With her heart beating a fast tattoo, Prudence went shakily down the stairs and let herself out of the back gate as quietly as she could before tiptoeing to the end of the alley and peeping round the last yard wall to see if anyone was about. The street looked deserted, so she crept along the house wall and peeped round the last corner into Station Road. It was dark and very quiet and nothing seemed to move in the still of the night. As quickly as she could without making any noise, Prudence edged her way along the street, clinging to the house fronts and the shadows to try and hide her presence in the street. That worked until she got level with Martha's shop, when she had to take her heart in both hands and step out into the road in order to cross over to the hutch. She always completed the last part of retrieving the prize at top speed because, once she had hold of the money, she was guilty of theft, in her eyes. She had money which didn't belong to her and she was moving away from where she had found it, making her a criminal. Her heart rate rattled through her body, making her pant and gasp as she shot back across the road and ran, silently, along the terrace of houses until she reached the corner. She hurtled round it and the next corner and found herself in the back alley once again, clinging on to the money and pulling herself along the yard walls towards the back yard of the shop. She slipped in through the gate and then closed it behind her, leaning back against its bulk as her legs began to tremble with the tension of the moment.

 She wasn't given long to restore some strength to her legs for Martha was standing in the back doorway, beckoning her into the kitchen and out of sight. Prudence staggered across the yard and squeezed past Martha into the kitchen and then waited for Martha to close the back door. Only then did her breathing return to normal and hands and legs stopped their shaking. She began to climb the stairs when Martha forced her out of the kitchen and into the passageway. Martha grabbed her by her skirt from behind and yanked the small bag out of her hand.

 "Wait while I check what's in it." Martha growled, still quietly but with a voice laden with venom.

 Prudence could hear the chink as coins moved against each when Martha opened the bag. She seemed satisfied with the result because she grunted, very quietly, and then began to climb the stairs behind Prudence. Prudence had no other option but to ascend the stairs and enter the front bedroom once again. The single candlelight had been enough to destroy Prudence's night vision so she had to feel her way over to the chair in front of the window before she could take the weight from her legs and rest atop the chair.

 Slowly, her vision returned and she could make out Martha sitting in the chair opposite to her, counting the money in the bag without taking the coins out of it. She grunted again which Prudence took to mean that she was satisfied with the total she had reached. She sighed silently in relief that the first collection of the night was over, but how many more drops were they expecting that night? She definitely wasn't being paid enough for all this worry. Perhaps it was a good thing that this was to be the last time. Prudence felt so alone and vulnerable during her trips across the road to the hutch to collect the money and tonight was even worse than ever before. She would have to find some other way of earning extra money, preferably one which didn't involve taking all the risks for Martha.

Chapter Twenty Five

The night dragged along, enlivened, in Martha's case, by the regular additions to her treasure pot although Prudence felt that the evening was boredom punctuated with intervals of sheer terror when she crossed the road to collect the money. It ran like clockwork. No-one was late, no-one was early, no-one appeared before the previous 'client' had left and no-one hung around long enough to see the next 'client' arrive. Martha was cock-a-hoop with the results of her labours. The leather bag into which she had decanted the money as it arrived was satisfyingly heavy and there was still one more victim to go.

Prudence was very quiet. She had made no attempt to talk to Martha after she had collected the first payment of the evening but had sat on her chair and stared out of the window, her face blank. Martha had been too taken up with collating her various caches of cash to notice that Prudence was even more jumpy than usual so she didn't comment on it. Prudence was hurt that Martha didn't realise that she was upset and that increased her anger, knowing now that she meant nothing to Martha at all. If Prudence hadn't accepted the position of runner for Martha, then she would have found someone else and forgotten that Prudence even existed. She was going to demand more money for her services, Prudence decided, while they were waiting for the last client to arrive. After the last drop, Prudence would tell Martha that she wanted ten pounds not five and then she would walk away from Martha forever.

Martha wasn't only contemplating the amount of money she had amassed that evening, she was also putting her mind to the problem of where Sarah might have hidden her treasure. If this was her last venture into blackmailing, she needed to have another source of income and Sarah's treasure was ready-made, waiting for her. She should take a step back from it and try and think where she would have hidden a fortune if she had been the confectioner, allowing for the fact that the woman had been very ill and half-blind.

As they waited for their final client, Martha's mind came up with and then discounted various places to hide money but she was dotting from place to place and not thinking about it methodically. If she put herself in Sarah's position, an old woman who was probably unsteady on her legs, not able to see very well and needing a place which was easily accessible - where would she turn?

Sarah wouldn't have put it in any of her furniture because she knew that whoever bought her house would probably throw the furniture away. The bureau, a decent article of furniture and too good for disposal, had been a suitable place for Sarah's papers but it had been sheer good luck that it had been kept in the house. Surely Sarah would have discounted any article of furniture as being either too small or too tatty in which to hide a fortune in coin? That left the house and the shop as the best places to hide her treasure and Martha knew that she had hit on the answer to her puzzle. She needed to think of a place in the building which Sarah would have been close to, all day, every day. A place which was always under Sarah's eye, so that she would know that her treasure was safe, hidden until the right person came along to find it and use it to its best advantage. Martha's mind roved back to Granny Lillian and her favourite places in their house.

Where had Granny Lillian spent the bulk of her time, the last few years of her life? Martha had the answer to that one immediately - the kitchen, of course. The kitchen was the hub of the house, no matter how many people lived in it, so that was where she would start. Where do most people spend time within their kitchens? Martha also had the answer to that one. People spend a lot of time sitting in a chair next to the range. The range! That was it! Martha needed to check out the range and she would begin the next morning while Edith was out getting her groceries and Martha would be alone in the shop.

At almost exactly the same time that Martha had her brainwave, Harriet shrugged her shoulders into her new jacket and examined herself in her hall mirror. The white jacket stood out spectacularly against the sober black of her skirt and it picked up the highlights in her hair and eyes. Harriet was satisfied with her workmanship and smoothed down her collar and then fastened the buttons, giving the hem a tweak as she did so. She picked up the bag containing the pebbles and nails, which chinked satisfactorily as she moved it, and opened her front door. She was early, according to the petite watch that she wore fastened to her jacket collar, but that didn't matter. She wanted to approach the hutch slowly to give her plenty of time to have a good look round. She needed a hiding place close to the hutch from where she could watch out for the blackmailer arriving to collect his ill-gotten gains.

Harriet didn't know it but, as she closed her front door, the blackmailer who filled her thoughts was rising from her seat to get a better look out of the window, to see if she could see her last victim approaching. Martha was bored with sitting still and was beginning to feel a slight chill in the air which came more from the dampness of the old house than it did from the effects of the weather. In reality, it was still a warm night, but Martha was feeling the effects of a cold bedroom without any form of heating, so she wanted to keep moving. She looked across at Prudence as she turned from the window and was dismayed to see the petulant expression on her face. She sighed, but knew that she had to speak.

"What's the matter with you?" she whispered. "Only one more and then you'll be finished."

"Yes, well I could do with more money if this is the last time we are doing this." Prudence leapt at the chance to make her claim. "It's all right for you; you get to keep all the money. I only get a few coins even though I'm the one taking all the chances."

Prudence would have carried on but Martha waved at her to pipe down as a movement outside in the street had caught her eye. There was a small figure of a woman walking along the far side of the road. She stood out like a beacon, dressed in a bright white jacket with a watch pinned to her lapel. Martha nearly groaned aloud at the picture the woman made. She couldn't have made a better display of herself if she had been carrying a lighthouse lantern atop her head. Did the woman want the whole world to know that she was depositing money for a blackmailer?

At this thought Martha was pulled up sharply and she eyed Harriet Winters more closely. The woman was doing it deliberately, that was the only conclusion Martha could come to, but why? Why would she follow a blackmailer's instruction for where to place her money, wearing clothes that made her stand out from the crowd? Martha knew that the only answer to that question was- because she wanted to be seen. And now why would she want to be seen? And Martha's answer to that was- because she was going to pull some kind of trick to stop herself from being blackmailed. At that thought, every nerve in Martha's body began to wail like the siren in the steel works. What could Harriet do to spoil Martha's game? The first and most obvious answer to that was that Harriet could hide somewhere to catch the blackmailer as he took the money and then face him with her accusations. The second answer which whizzed through Martha's mind alongside the wailing of her internal warning siren was that Harriet might not face down the blackmailer herself. She might go to the police with her information if she managed to follow the blackmailer home and nail his identity.

Damn! Martha whirled in the centre of the bedroom as her body tried to keep pace with her thoughts then she rushed across to the window as another thought struck her. She watched closely as Harriet approached the hutch and saw the bag swing as Harriet lifted it forwards to put it inside the wooden barrier. It looked heavy, almost as though it contained many coins but, with her warning signals flashing in her brain, Martha decided it looked too heavy, almost as though it was filled with rocks. Her last thought had been right! Harriet was trying to cheat her! She wasn't leaving money for the blackmailer, she was leaving a trap for the blackmailer to fall into. Martha nearly shouted out in her triumph at having seen through Harriet's ruse. Oh, she was clever, the little seamstress, but she was no match for Martha Coleman, even if Martha was having a bad day. She would always triumph over lesser mortals.

Prudence stood up, ready to go out and collect the last deposit but Martha stopped her with one hand.

"Wait." Martha ordered, still in a harsh whisper. "We aren't going to collect this one."

"Why not? Someone else might find that money!"

"They won't, because there isn't any money in that bag that she's just put in there. It's far too heavy for the amount of money I've told her to bring. She's filled it with rocks or something equally heavy. Just watch what she does next."

There was silence between the two girls as they both watched Harriet step back from the hutch and turn to her right. She walked rapidly across the road and entered the end of Coral Street, as though she was on her way home. Prudence went to move again but Martha held up her hand and uttered one word.

"Wait."

They craned their necks to see the house at the end of Coral Street which, truth to tell, was as normal as it always was. Prudence lifted her face to Martha and frowned in her ignorance of what Martha was doing. Martha lifted her finger and mouthed 'wait' once again. Prudence turned back to the window and then they both saw what Martha had been waiting for. A dark figure slipped out of the end of Coral Street and crossed the road to the allotments, stopping at the entrance to an allotment further along from the hutch. The figure crouched down behind what shelter the gate gave and turned her face so that she could watch the hutch.

"There. The slippery madam thinks she's going to catch us as we collect the money. She's turned that bright, white jacket inside out and she's now wearing a black jacket which makes it more difficult for her to be seen." Martha whispered with glee. "Let's see how long she wants to crouch next to an allotment gate which every passing dog has watered for the last fifty years, aye and many a drunkard on his way home from the pub as well."

Prudence couldn't stop the giggle which erupted from her lips, even though she stuffed her fist into her mouth to stop the sound of it. Martha smiled back at her, pleased to see that the sulky expression had disappeared from the girl's face although she knew that Prudence wouldn't forget that she wanted more money from Martha.

"What are we going to do, then?" Prudence asked. "I don't want to sit around here all night."

"Neither do I, but we can't leave until Madam Detective gives up. Don't worry, she's far too hoity-toity to spend a lot of time squatting amongst dog piss. She'll soon get sick of it and go home, especially if she doesn't see anyone at the hutch. Tell you what, I'll give you an extra five pounds on top of the fiver I promised you. That should be plenty to keep you going for a good while and don't worry, I promise I'll have other jobs for you to do which won't involve you breaking the law."

Prudence's face showed her changing emotions as she absorbed what Martha was saying. She hadn't thought that she would have managed to get a whole ten pounds out of Martha and here she was, offering it to her as though she waved ten pounds around every day. And she wouldn't have to do anything else which might get her into trouble with the police. The night was turning out to be one of the best she had ever had. Waiting around in this damp bedroom for a bit longer wasn't a problem anymore. She would happily wait another couple of hours if it meant she would have ten pounds in her pocket when she went home.

Martha was still watching Harriet watching the hutch, preening herself for her perspicacity as well as feeling relief that this nerve-stretching escapade was nearly over. She had meant what she said. She didn't fancy carrying out any more escapades which took her beyond the law. Not for a while, anyway.

"She's a right clever little body, that one isn't she?" Martha whispered to Prudence, not really expecting an answer this time. "She's wearing a jacket that is reversible, black on the inside and white on the outside. I bet she thought that she wouldn't be seen if, after she'd dropped the bag, she turned her jacket inside out and wore it with the black on the outside. Good job she made the other side white cos it was the way she stood out wearing it that made me watch her so carefully. She might be clever, but she isn't as clever as me."

Prudence agreed, although she would have agreed that Martha was the fairy on top of the Christmas tree if she had asked her to that night. She didn't really care what had warned Martha about Harriet's intentions, not now that she didn't have to go back to that dratted hutch. She was quite happy now to sit and imagine the joy on her mother's face when she gave her the money to pay the landlord in the Station for what her brother had smashed up the other night. Martha, also, was happy for silence to reign while she waited for Harriet to give up her quest and go home. She wanted to work out how she was going to pay Harriet back for trying to trick her and she couldn't do that if Prudence chattered on, even in whispers. Added to her desire for revenge on Harriet, she also wanted to think of a way to take the range in the kitchen apart because she still had to discover the treasure. She smiled to herself, thinking that life wasn't too bad in her little corner of the world, especially when she had so many ways to prove to the world that she was one of the cleverest people in it.

Time ticked by and Martha and Prudence were still sitting in the cold bedroom, waiting to see what Harriet would do next. Neither of them had any wish to leave the house until Harriet had gone and both of them had their thoughts to keep them warm. Harriet, crouching out in the open, surrounded by the detritus of years and the odour of all dogs' favourite watering hole, began to wish that she had found a better place to wait. As the minutes ticked by, Harriet began to wonder how long it would be before the blackmailer made his move. Surely he wouldn't leave the money in the hutch overnight, would he? Would she have to crouch here until dawn broke? The thought of staying where she was for much longer wasn't particularly attractive, but she had to pay that off against bringing the blackmailer to justice. For the first time since she had received the first blackmail letter, she seriously considered going to the police but her heart quailed at that thought. She didn't want to have to explain the reason behind the blackmailer's interest in her, not to a policeman who probably wouldn't believe that she and Michael met only to play card games and have innocent conversations.

In her mind's eye, she could see herself explaining her relationship with Michael to a policeman who listened to her with a leer on his face as he imagined exactly what she got up to when Michael called round. Would he then pass this knowledge around all of his colleagues so that she would never know how many people believed that she was having an illicit relationship with another woman's husband? Harriet felt her stomach contract with the thought that people would be watching her from then on, thinking she was a scarlet woman. She couldn't face that, even though she knew that it wasn't the truth. It was enough that other people would think it was the truth. No, she couldn't go to the police. She would have to stay where she was until the blackmailer arrived and then follow him to his home. She gritted her teeth and determined to stay where she was, however long it took.

Martha watched from the bedroom window, smiling every time she saw the dark shape shift as though to make herself more comfortable. She knew that Harriet wouldn't stay where she was for much longer. Harriet had been brought up in a comfortable home, cherished by her family and separated from the darker side of life. She may have come upon hard times but those hard times were relative. When Martha had been a child she would have considered Harriet's situation to be a paradise compared to her own upbringing and, if Harriet had any sense of smell, she would soon be overwhelmed by the odours which surrounded her.

Martha laughed when she saw the dark shape lift its arm and put its hand across its face. Martha knew that Harriet was trying to stave off the smell of ammonia which must be exceedingly strong around that gate. The hot weather would have dried it and exacerbated the strength of it so Harriet probably felt as though she was almost eating it. Well, it served her right for trying to prove herself cleverer than her opponent. Martha was the only one who was going to win in this battle of wills.

A few minutes later, the dark figure rose unsteadily to its feet and stared openly around it. Martha watched in delight as Harriet crossed the road towards Coral Street once more and then stopped again. She took one more, long look round and then shrugged her shoulders in defeat. Within seconds she had disappeared and the streets were empty again and Martha waved sarcastically at her retreating back.

"We've done it, Prue." Martha whispered. "She's gone. We'll wait a few minutes just in case she turns round and comes back but I don't think she will now. Here, here's your ten pounds. Enjoy spending it."

Prudence was happy at the night's outcome and didn't complain when Martha told her to go out of the back alley and go home Nelson Street way, even though it would add a couple of minutes onto her journey. It was worth it to have ten pounds in her pocket, especially as the Station landlord was only asking for two pounds. That left a substantial sum over for Prudence to spend how she wanted and no-one any the wiser. Martha promised to get in touch with her again when she needed any jobs doing, as she followed Prudence out of the back gate.

Martha walked rapidly home, the bag containing the money slung over her shoulder. The streets were deserted and the house in darkness when she got back. Good. It meant that Daniel hadn't returned home and she could take her ill-gotten gains indoors and hide them in her bedroom. Before going to bed, she mulled over an idea that had come to her while she was waiting for Harriet to abandon her attempt at waylaying the blackmailer. She had every intention of making Harriet pay in a different way for refusing to comply with the blackmail letter and she thought she had the ideal way. She could sabotage Harriet's dressmaking business. She grinned wickedly at the thought of the havoc she could cause but she would have to go and call on her, pretending to be a customer. That could wait for a few days though, because she needed to see if there were any loose tiles or bricks around the range in the shop kitchen. Her first task was to find Sarah's treasure and she had every intention of beginning that in the morning. Life was definitely good.

Harriet was in tears by the time she reached home. She hadn't managed to catch the blackmailer and she was absolutely filthy. The stench of the dogs' lavatory was still filling her nose and she was sure that her skirt had absorbed some sort of liquid while she had been crouching next to the gate. There was only one thing that liquid could be and Harriet's nose wrinkled in disgust at the thought. Once home, she stripped to her under clothes and dumped what she had taken off into the bath which usually hung on a hook on the back yard wall. She filled the bath with water and some soap and left it to soak overnight, before she mounted the stairs to go to bed. Her last thought before she fell asleep was to wonder what the blackmailer would do next when he discovered that she hadn't paid up. By morning, the whole of South Bank could be discussing her affair with Michael. As her eyes closed of their own volition, she wished that she could go to sleep and never wake again.

Chapter Twenty Six

The next morning, Martha awoke with the lark, humming to herself as she prepared her breakfast and then got ready to open the shop. Daniel still wasn't home, so Martha locked the doors against any burglars and made her way to Pearl Street, as sunny as the weather which surrounded her.

It was a quiet day in the shop, so Martha took the opportunity to check out the range in the kitchen. She closed the front door of the shop but left it unlatched, so that any customers would just be able to push it open. She left the 'open' sign hanging in front of the glass on the shop door so that anyone passing would be able to read that they were open and then made her way into the kitchen. If any customers came in, Martha would hear the bell jangle as the door opened and would be able to scoot through to the shop in seconds.

She stood in the middle of the kitchen and examined the range from that angle. It looked the same as any other kitchen range in any other kitchen in South Bank, but Martha wasn't checking to see how attractive a feature it was or even how clean it looked, although it was spotless because she had black leaded it herself the week before. Martha was looking for any signs of disturbance which she hadn't noticed when she had cleaned it, any sign that would tell her that something had been altered in it, on it or around it.

It was as she thought about the area around the range that her eyes roved over the brickwork of the walls and then the tiles of the hearth. She moved closer when she saw that the brickwork to the right of the oven door was uneven, as though someone had removed a couple of the bricks and then replaced them but hadn't managed to get them back in exactly the place that they belonged. The mortar was as dark coloured as the mortar between the rest of the bricks but it was uneven, obviously not put there by a workman who was proficient in his trade.

Martha's heart began to beat a little faster as she moved even closer and finally knelt in front of the uneven bricks. She laid her hand on the first brick and then traced the line of mortar between it and the one above with her finger. Her fingernail juddered over the ridges in the mortar and continued to do so as she ran her hand along the length of three bricks. From so close an angle, she could see that the uneven mortar now moved downwards until it reached a brick which was three courses below where she had started and then sideways until she reached a point which was level with the beginning of the bricks above. In all, nine bricks covered a section of the wall next to the oven. Her heart now beating a tattoo as she imagined she could hear the treasure calling to her through the wall, Martha leapt up and grabbed a knife from the pot next to the sink. She pushed the blade of the knife into the mortar at the top, right-hand side of her section and tried to push through it. Nothing happened. In frustration, she ran the knife blade along this uneven mortar until she came to the end of the next brick.

When she reached it, her knife blade slide between the mortar and the next brick of its own accord and the mortar moved forwards as a block. A piece of hardened, brittle mortar the length of the three bricks came loose in a chunk and Martha was able to grasp it between her fingers and lift it out of the wall. The three bricks the mortar had laid next to were now free and Martha lifted them out, one by one. She then dropped a row and began digging at the second row of bricks. She understood how it had been done now and she levered the knife between the mortar and the bricks below it. Once again, the mortar came out in a chunk, although the rather thinner end on this one did fall away from the rest. She removed the next three bricks and dropped down a row again, to begin working on the bottom row of bricks. The mortar came out whole and the next three bricks soon joined their fellows on the hearth.

Now there was a hole in the wall, exactly the right size and shape in which to hide treasure, as long as it was in the shape of money or gemstones. It wouldn't have been any use to hide an Old Masters' painting, but Sarah Salton hadn't possessed a huge oil painting, only a bag full of money; coins of the realm and a few notes, Martha hoped.

She reached into the black gap which was begging her to put her arm into it and groped about for the bottom of the hole concealed behind the bricks. She didn't have to reach down very far before her searching fingers encountered something hard although not made of metal or wood or even brick. Martha crinkled her brow as she tried to work out what it was, while her fingers grasped hold of part of it and tried to pull it upwards. It, whatever it was, didn't want to leave its hidey-hole and it slipped out of her grasp and landed with a dull thunk on the bottom of the hole behind the bricks. Martha tutted to herself and then swore under her breath when the bell on the shop door rang as someone came into the shop.

She rose to her feet and dusted herself down, sure that she would have soot sticking to her somewhere, before she made her way through into the shop. Mrs Leadley was standing next to a small chest of drawers, her hand laid upon it in a proprietorial fashion while her fingers beat a tattoo on its top. Mrs Leadley was in no mood to hurry her purchase and she insisted on Martha showing her every single chest of drawers in the shop before she went back to the original one and declared that it was the best one, but far too expensive for a poor old widow like her. As Martha knew that Mrs Leadley took in paying guests and was one of the richest women in the town, Mrs Leadley's complaint wouldn't have normally washed with her, but she was eager to get back into the kitchen and put her hand back into the hole in the wall. Without caring for her brother's profit margins, Martha told her she could have it for two pounds, which was three pounds below the ticket price. Mrs Leadley jumped at the chance to save so much money and she had slapped her coins onto the counter and picked the chest up as though it weighed nothing, before Martha had drawn breath to negotiate.

The 'poor old widow' woman left the shop even more quickly than Martha could have wanted, clutching her purchase to her side as though she was carrying a small bag of potatoes not an article of furniture and Martha was left shaking her head at the greed of the woman and at her obvious strength. Martha almost ran back into the kitchen and flopped to the floor in front of the fire again. Her arm shot into the hole she had made and, once again, she grasped whatever it was which was hidden behind the bricks.

It was heavy, very heavy. She almost dropped it a second time and would have done if she hadn't bent her arm at the elbow, bringing her face so close to the hearth she could smell the blacklead from the fire surround. Her face now scraped against the bricks as she gritted her teeth and used as much force as she could muster to pull the heavy object upwards and forwards to the mouth of the hole. She could see it! She took another huge breath and dragged her burden over the bottom bricks and dropped it onto the hearth. It was a thick canvas bag with leather reinforced seams and film of coal dust all over it. It had dropped like a stone when she had let go of it and the dust from the mortar she had removed rose in a cloud and floated around her head like a halo, although there was nothing angelic about Martha's state of mind at that moment. It was sheer greed which motivated her and made her eyes sparkle and her mouth open in a grin which had a touch of the devil about it.

There was a metal clasp at the top of the bag which was slightly rusty and difficult to open, forcing Martha to lose two fingernails as she tried to prise it apart but she managed to open it, eventually, and Martha could look down into the bag and discover the contents for the first time. What she saw made her heart race and the colour to flood into her usually pale cheeks. The bag was filled with coins of all denominations, even down to farthings, some with the old Queen's head on them. It seemed that Sarah Salton had started her blackmailing in a very small way originally, asking for pennies rather than shillings, but that she had gained confidence from her success and had gradually asked for larger and larger sums. That was the only way that Martha could account for the mixture of coins in the bag, the pennies and threepenny bits with the shillings and florins and half crowns. As Martha peered closer into the bag she discovered a pocket sewn into the side and inside this she found a bundle which was wrapped in paper and tied with string.

Her fingers couldn't undo the knots in this thin string and she cursed fluently in frustration at her inability to get into this bundle, tearing more fingernails and banging her hand against the hearth into the bargain. With another, louder, oath she grabbed the knife she had taken from the draining board and sliced through the string with ease, smiling again as the outer paper wrapper unpeeled itself from the bundle and proved to be another note from Sarah. It said -

'You've found it, you clever person. I hope you enjoy spending all my ill-gotten gains. Spare a thought for me - too old and weak to get any pleasure out of what I worked so hard to gather together.'

Martha threw this note to the floor, not at all interested in the old woman or her state of health, apart from thinking that she wouldn't wait until she was too old to enjoy the fruits of her labours. She was far more interested in what the note had been hiding, which was a rolled bundle of banknotes, carefully piled together in order of their value. It was more money than Martha had ever seen in her life before and much more easily acquired than the money she had raised with her blackmailing venture. She was now a rich woman and, to Martha, money meant success and a feeling of power, power over other people, starting with the little dressmaker who had tried to lay a trap for her the evening before.

Martha didn't bother to stop and count the money in the bag. That could wait until later. What she wanted to do now was to plan her revenge on Harriet Winters, although she wouldn't get in touch with her straight away because Martha wanted her to have a few days in which to worry about what the blackmailer would do next about the missed payment. The thought of Harriet worrying was a curiously satisfying thought and Martha rolled it round her mind, the better to taste the feeling of power it gave her.

Daniel had had a very successful day in Whitby, having picked up an extra load simply by being in the right place at the right time. He was still concerned about the overwhelming patriotism being shown by nearly every other person in the country, particularly as his heart sank every time he thought about the war. He loved his country as much as the next man, but he didn't want to have to leave his businesses in order to go overseas and fight, with the possibility of being injured if not killed. Being killed - that thought pulled him up sharp. He had missed out on so much that other children took for granted while he was a child and, now that he was finally leading a normal life, he didn't want to lose it so quickly. So many thoughts revolved around inside his head that it was no wonder that he failed to notice that Martha looked like the cat which had got the cream. At any other time, he would have been questioning her closely to find out why she was so happy, mainly because, if Martha was happy, it meant that some other person was suffering. But during those first few weeks of the war, Daniel had too much to worry about to care if other people were worrying too or to care if Martha had got her teeth into a new victim.

So Harriet was left to fret over her missed payment to the anonymous blackmailer, unaware that the said blackmailer had a nasty little plan in mind to make her pay in other ways for her supposed sins.

Martha began to execute her new plan exactly a month after the last night of her blackmailing life. She dressed in her best skirt and wrapped herself in a woollen shawl to protect herself from the cold wind which whistled down the streets and made her way to Harriet's little house. Harriet had worried constantly during that month, so much so that she had begun to lose weight from a body which had never carried any excess fat. Her clothes hung from her tiny frame and her face lost its rounded appearance and became very thin and long. Every time she looked in the mirror, she saw her mother's face looking back at her, in those last few months before her death from the terrible wasting disease which had killed her. But Harriet no longer cared what she looked like, even though she knew that ill-fitting clothes weren't a very good advertisement for her dressmaking business. In the past, she had always been immaculately turned out, so elegant that many people went to her to make their dresses and skirts purely because Harriet was so stylish and chic. Her regular customers noticed the change in her and many of them thought twice before calling to see her when they wanted a new dress for a particular social occasion.

Harriet knew that she wasn't as busy as she usually was and this only added to the anxiety she was feeling. As the summer finally passed over and the temperature dropped sharply, Harriet should have had a queue at her door, demanding she made them new outfits for the coming winter season, but her door remained sadly unknocked and she was reduced to making aprons to sell in Reed's shop on Nelson Street just to pay her bills. Aprons weren't a seasonal outfit, they were worn all day every day, to cover normal, workaday skirts so that they wouldn't stain or fade too quickly. They required no talent to make and Harriet wept again at the depths she had plumbed since that unknown person had discovered that she was regularly visited by another woman's husband, even though the visits were as innocent as the day was long. Harriet had always thought she was a strong, sensible woman who didn't need a man to make life easy for her but there were times over the recent weeks when she had wished that she had married one of the several suitors she had had before her parents died and she was reduced to living in this tiny house alone.

So when there was a knock on her door one blowy autumn afternoon, Harriet hurried to answer it, hoping that it would be one of her customers, coming to order a new wardrobe of clothes for the coming winter. When she opened the door and saw who stood on her doorstep, she was taken aback. Like the rest of South Bank, she knew Martha's life story and had never looked on her as a possible customer. She had forgotten that the girl's grandparents had died and that the small family had blossomed since their demise. She now had a vague memory of being told that Daniel was running two businesses and that they had abandoned the laundry work which they had been doing when Harriet first moved into the town. Certainly, Martha looked to be wearing a decent outfit and would pass anywhere as one of Harriet's customers. For the first time in weeks, Harriet smiled.

"Can I help you?" she asked, crossing her fingers behind her back that the girl would say that she had come to put some business her way.

"You are Harriet, aren't you?" Martha asked, with a smile which wouldn't have looked out of place on an angel. "I need a couple of dresses and some new skirts and blouses for the winter. Would you have time to make them for me?"

Harriet couldn't get Martha inside her house quickly enough. The use of the plural for all that Martha wanted made her head spin with joy and she virtually dragged Martha into her parlour. Martha continued to smile at her reception, convinced that Harriet had already lost customers now that she saw how worried the woman looked. Bad luck breeds bad luck and Martha guessed, rightly, that Harriet was on a downward spiral.

Martha actually enjoyed the afternoon, being measured and fitted for her new clothes and choosing materials and styles which would suit her. Harriet would have bent over backwards if that had been possible if it had meant that Martha wouldn't take her custom elsewhere, so she worked hard at displaying the various styles which would suit Martha and the fabric needed to make all the outfits. Martha had never been served in this manner before, but she was loving being the absolute centre of Harriet's attention. It seemed almost a shame that Martha was going to bring the woman down, so far that she wouldn't be doing anymore dressmaking in the future. Martha even considered not carrying out her plan so that Harriet could continue in business and Martha could come back again the next year but she soon put that idea aside. Harriet had to pay for not obeying the blackmail note and for trying to prove that she was cleverer than Martha. It was a shame though, because Martha would have enjoyed repeating the afternoon another time, but revenge came first.

Martha left rather late in the afternoon, promising to return at the appointed time for her fittings and made her way home, where her good mood was again not noticed by Daniel. When Edith called round to invite Martha and Daniel to Sunday lunch, she didn't notice how excited Martha was either, mainly because she was so much in love with her new husband and still living the romantic dream she had cherished for so many years, that she wouldn't have noticed if the sky had fallen in. If either Daniel or Edith hadn't been so self-absorbed, one of them might have realised that Martha was on the warpath because they had both seen how Martha behaved when she had her knife in someone and they could have recognised the signs. They could possibly have put a stop to Martha taking the road she had chosen but, unfortunately for Harriet, neither her mother nor her brother looked beyond their own thoughts.

Of the two people who could have stopped Martha, Edith was the only one who knew every detail of Martha's background. In the past, Edith had worried about the baby she had produced as a result of her own father's incest, but she had worried that the baby would be born with some physical defect, some mark that would show that she had been conceived against the laws of nature. It had never crossed Edith's mind that her baby girl could have inherited too large a share of her grandfather's and father's wicked, twisted personality. When Martha had been born a beautiful, perfectly-formed little girl, Edith had thanked God that her daughter wasn't going to have to pay for her father's and grandfather's sins and had stopped worrying about it, which had been a huge mistake on Edith's part. Martha was now well down the road to being even more wicked and twisted than her father/grandfather with a far greater level of intelligence and a greater ability to formulate methods of hurting other people. Where her father had stopped at physical cruelty, Martha had mastered the art of inflicting mental torture and was finding that not only did she delight in inflicting it but also that she delighted in watching the effects of it on her victims.

Chapter Twenty Seven

It took Harriet less than three days to make up one skirt and one dress, ready for fitting, and then she popped a note through the shop's letterbox, informing Martha that she could call at any time to try them on. Martha grinned when she read the brief note, slipping it into her pocket and deciding to call on her way home from the shop that evening.

There was a definite chill in the air now when Martha locked up that night, making her grateful for the woollen shawl she had brought with her that day. If there had been any trees in the streets that she walked, she would have seen by their leaves that autumn was already far-advanced but the massed terraces of housing had eaten the ground that the trees had grown in, leaving only a brick and concrete landscape around her. If she had walked across town to Normanby Road and looked south, she would have been able to see the hills in the distance and they would have given her proof of the continuing march of time, as they were covered in rusty orange bracken and almost shone in the late afternoon sunshine. But Martha's mind was set on the next stage in her revenge on Harriet and she didn't look about her as she hurried to Harriet's house.

Harriet was working on the second of Martha's skirts, her eyes barely lifting from the dark grey fabric that Martha had chosen, but she was aware of the chill of the day even as she pumped the treadle of her sewing machine. Her little house was damp and was always cold, even in the height of summer. The chill mist of the autumn day was making the house feel even colder and Harriet had to keep stopping in order to wring some feeling back into her fingers. She could have lit the fire, but she didn't know when she would be able to afford to buy more coal and she knew that the weather would only get colder from now on, so she preferred to keep the coal that she had to use when the frost made its appearance. She had wrapped her warmest shawl around her shoulders and fastened it across her chest with a brooch which had belonged to her mother, in a vain attempt to keep herself warm but she wasn't winning the battle against the chill in her joints. She was grateful that her nose was too cold to run because she would have been appalled if it had dripped on this beautiful material and spoilt it.

Harriet jumped when the knock came at the door and nearly fell over as she stumbled her way to answer it. She didn't want to seem too eager so she hesitated before she turned the latch but then rushed at it in case Martha tired of waiting and walked away. She couldn't afford to lose any customers so she ignored her pride which told her to stop being so eager and nearly knocked Martha over with the warmth of her welcome. Martha smiled at the woman's obvious need as it added to the sense of power which seeing Harriet always brought her and stepped inside the chilly house.

Martha tried on the skirt and the dresses which Harriet had ready for her, not appreciating the cold air which attacked her as she removed her own clothes. Really, the woman should have the fire going in this little room so that her clients didn't succumb to pneumonia while they were being fitted, but she didn't comment on the cold out loud. She was playing the role of rich customer and she enjoyed it almost as much as she had enjoyed choosing clothes in Reeds when Lucy Renwick had been forced to serve a girl she considered to be, socially, so far beneath her. It amused her that Harriet had no idea that she was dealing with the blackmailer who had been making her life a misery.

The work that Harriet had done had been done to perfection. The seams were all neatly finished off and the waistband on the skirt couldn't have fitted Martha any better if she had grown it as a second skin. The dress was faultless even though Martha checked every seam, stitch and hem, looking for any flaw. Harriet had even matched every pattern repeat in the seams so that the design of the fabric wasn't spoilt by any interruption in the tiny rose design which decorated it. Martha was amazed at the woman's skill but still had no compunction about trying to destroy her reputation. To Harriet's face, Martha sang her praises while Harriet marked the hems for both skirt and dress, promising to have them ready for Martha to collect the next day. Martha left Harriet to her work and made her way home by way of Reeds shop, where she bought yards of the self-same fabric of which Harriet was making the skirt she had nearly finished for Martha.

Martha went home and, after she and Daniel had had tea, she cleared the kitchen table so that she could spread out her new fabric and opened the pattern she had received in the post a few days before. She had seen the design for the skirt in one of the ladies' magazines which she devoured every time they were published and had recognised it when Harriet had shown it to her on her first visit to Harriet's home. That had been the moment when she had finalised every detail of her plan to destroy Harriet, knowing that Harriet didn't expect that she would have seen a copy of that magazine.

Martha cut out the pattern from the material and, by bedtime, had the whole skirt tacked together and ready to be sewn on her own sewing machine which had been a present from her mother before she had got married. That task was completed the following evening so that, when Harriet popped into the shop to say that her dress and skirt were now both ready for collection, Martha already had the identical skirt at home, waiting to see the comparisons between the one she had produced and the one which Harriet had worked on so devotedly.

Martha wasn't a bad seamstress but her work was nowhere near the standard of Harriet's work. Martha hadn't finished the seams in that professional way nor did her hand stitching stand up to scrutiny as she had frequently changed the size of her stitches, often not catching both layers of the fabric which she was attempting to sew together. This meant that the hems on the skirt that Martha had made weren't level and, in places, weren't stitched together at all. Martha was very pleased with the way that her skirt looked as though it had been made by a very untalented amateur and she smiled delightedly when she compared the two. This was exactly the result she had planned, even though it had gone against the grain to be so slovenly as she plied her needle.

Her next step was to hang the dress and skirt which Harriet had made for her in her wardrobe before she took the skirt she had made herself and went to light the fire which would heat the boiler in the laundry which was still in place in the back yard. It didn't take long for the fire to heat enough hot water for her to fill the poss tub, empty a bag of soap flakes into the water and then push her homemade skirt into the welcoming warmth of the water. It seemed overly-extravagant to fill the poss tub for only one garment but Martha revelled in the knowledge that she now had so much money, she didn't care about how extravagant she was being. The steam rose from the surface of the water and Martha's head was soon enveloped in it, before it drifted across the ceiling of the shed and began to condense on the cold walls. The smell from the soap flakes was a mixture of carbolic and lavender and Martha enjoyed sniffing it as she hung over the copper watching the skirt appear and disappear as she stirred the water.

She hadn't put the fire out underneath the copper, or even damped it down, so the water in the poss tub was getting hotter and hotter by the minute and the clouds of steam were now collecting across the whole ceiling as the shed grew warmer and the steam condensed more slowly. It soon became like a vision of hell as the temperature rose and the steam swirled with every movement of Martha's arm as she stirred the tub, grinning wickedly as the colour began to come out of the fabric of her skirt and dye the surrounding water. Martha thought it very amusing that, in the old days when she was a slave in the laundry, she would have been beaten for being so careless with the temperature of the water.

The water began to bubble in the tub as it reached boiling point and Martha, regretfully, knew that she had to remove the skirt before it not only lost its colour but began to shrink. That was the last thing she wanted to happen because she needed to wear the skirt in order to complete her plan. She fished the skirt out with the wooden tongs and laughed out loud at the amount of dye which poured from it, splattering down the sides of the tub onto the floor. A quick rinse in cold water soon got rid of the residue of the soap and she put it through the mangle, turning the handle with practised ease. Then she hung it on a hanger which she slotted onto the drying rack above her head.

It was perfect. Martha stared up at it and congratulated herself on the way the colour had run from the skirt. In parts, it was nearly as black as the original material but in other parts, it was a mixture of grey, rusty brown and a dirty red. Martha had heard that there was no such colour as black; that fabric was dyed either very dark red or very dark blue and she guessed that this fabric had been dyed a very dark red. It looked an utter mess although Martha knew that it would look a lot better when it was dried and pressed. She moved over to her left, the better to view the back and sides of the skirt and was rewarded with the sight of a broken thread hanging down below the skirt and a hanging hemline, puckered in a couple of places. Good! They wouldn't dry off or press out - they were permanent but didn't look as though they had been done deliberately. All in all, Martha considered it was a work of art and perfectly suited for its purpose- to destroy Harriet's business. Harriet had used her needlework skills to try and spoil Martha's blackmailing. It was only fair that Martha should use her needlework skills to destroy Harriet's business, admittedly with a dollop of Martha's intelligence as well.

Two days later, Martha invited Prudence to go with her to a fund-raising afternoon tea in the Church hall. It was being organised by a group of women at the Church, who wanted to make sure that all of South Bank's boys set off for war with at least some of the comforts of home. Autumn had arrived and everyone knew that winter wouldn't be far behind it, so these ladies had formed a group of knitters who were busy knitting hats and socks for the boys, but they were running out of wool. The afternoon tea party was intended to raise as much money as they could so that the ladies could provide at least one item for each man who had signed up for the army. Martha knew that a lot of the ladies who were Harriet's customers would be at the event and she intended to make quite a stir when she arrived in the Church hall.

Martha couldn't have chosen a better place for the last part of her plan. It was the first of what was to become a long line of fund-raising events which would take place regularly over the next four years at different places in South Bank. After the declaration of war at the beginning of August, many of the young men of the town had rushed to enlist in the Army, determined to do their bit for the good of the country. Then, all activity had seemed to cease, almost as though the declaration had been a false one and the whole town had held its breath, waiting to see what would happen next. Then, as the year moved closer towards its end, a flurry of activity broke out and men received their papers and their travel warrants and suddenly the town was plunged into a frenzy of preparations and the actuality of the war was brought home to all.

The afternoon tea was, therefore, very well-attended as every woman wanted to show the world how patriotic they were and how much they loved all of these boys who thought they were going on an adventure. It didn't matter what social background you came from, every woman was equal when she was worrying about her son or her husband or her brother and they turned up in their droves to prove their love to the world.

Prudence had been amazed that Martha was contemplating wearing such a skirt when she arrived at the York Street house to accompany Martha to the festivities. Prudence didn't know what to say in case Martha bit her head off so she limited herself to staring at the offending skirt, especially the front hemline which was trailing along the floor. It has to be said that Martha had been correct in her assumption that the skirt would look better once it was dried and pressed than it had when it was hanging, dripping wet, in the laundry, but it still didn't look good.

"What's the matter Prue? Don't you like my new skirt?"

Prudence hesitated as she tried to summon up enough courage to give Martha the truth, but she was wary of Martha's incredibly sarcastic tongue, so, in the end, all she managed was a mumbled 'Yes'. Martha roared with laughter at this reply.

"You can tell me the truth, pet. I won't bite you!"

"Well, it's a very nice shape, but you do know that the hem's coming down and it looks as though someone's thrown bleach at it."

Martha giggled again, much to Prue's amazement, and then she decided to tell Prudence the truth of the matter.

"You remember how Harriet Winters thought she would outsmart us and not pay for her dallying with Michael Lewinson?"

Prue nodded, still as bewildered as before.

"You know that Harriet is a dressmaker? Well, I've decided to make her pay for trying to be so clever with me. I'm going to ruin her reputation as a dressmaker. She doesn't know what I intend to do, so she'll be as shocked as the rest of the town when I spill the beans this afternoon. Isn't it going to be a great laugh?"

Prudence wasn't too sure that anyone would be laughing. She couldn't answer Martha's question because her mind was too busy trying to work out how anyone could be so callous. Dressmaking was Harriet's only source of income. If Martha ruined her business, then there was a good chance that Harriet would go hungry and Prudence had experienced that only too often when she was a child to wish it upon anyone else. She tried to remonstrate with Martha but wasn't strong enough to put her point forward properly.

"Don't you think you are going a bit too far? I mean, Harriet won't have any money coming in if no-one buys her clothes. How will she pay her bills and buy food."

Prudence's voice dropped to a whisper as Martha turned her gimlet eyes upon her.

"Do you feel sorry for her?" Martha hissed through clenched teeth. "Have you forgotten that she left a bag of stones and nails as payment for the shenanigans she's being getting up to with Lewinson for years? She doesn't deserve to have a business when she's sleeping with a married man behind his wife's back."

Prudence had forgotten this detail and, as she always did when she had to defend her position with Martha, she capitulated immediately.

"Yes, I'd forgotten about the nails and the affair with Mr Lewinson. I see what you mean."

Martha patted her arm to show her forgiveness and then flung her shawl round her shoulders.

"Come on then. We're off to put Miss Hoity-toity Harriet in her place."

Prudence wrapped her own shawl around herself and held it tight as though it would give her some comfort. She was worried over the way Martha was going to destroy Harriet and wasn't sure that she wanted to be with Martha when she was being so cruel. Why couldn't she ever say no to Martha and go her own way? Why did she always have to crumble when Martha turned those steely eyes of hers on her? Not for the first time, Prudence wished that she had never met Martha Coleman.

The Church Hall was heaving with bodies when Martha and Prudence arrived. Martha was deliberately late, wanting to make as much of a show as possible as she walked into the hall. It had to be said that a number of women turned to watch as Martha strode confidently to the front of the hall and asked for tea and scones for two, in a very loud voice. Mrs Trent, who was in charge of the tea urn, started to pour out the hot, strong tea while watching Martha over the top of her glasses. Martha knew that she was going to make some remark and waited with bated breath for the ball to be thrown into play. She didn't have to wait for very long.

"Have you come straight from the shop, Martha?" Mrs Trent asked, as she banged the cups down onto the table top and turned to take the two plates of scones from her helper.

"No, Mrs Trent." Martha answered in the same loud tone. "Why would you think that I've come straight from work?"

"Well lass, you certainly haven't dressed yourself up for the occasion, have you?" Mrs Trent replied. "I've seen you wearing better rags when you were at school."

Martha's face paled because she didn't like Mrs Trent's referring to her childhood like that but she lifted her chin and spoke the words which would damn Harriet Winter's career.

"Rags!? I'll have you know that this is my best skirt. I've only just received it from the dressmaker. If you've got anything to say about it, I think you should say it to her, not me. Rags indeed!"

Martha motioned to Prudence to collect the plates of scones and she picked up their teacups and made for a pair of vacant seats at a table at the side of the room. A buzz, like a hive of bees full of heather pollen, followed them as they walked across the hall until one lone voice suddenly sounded louder than any other.

"Who's your dressmaker then?"

"Harriet Winters, of course." Martha answered the unknown questioner. "Isn't she the best in the town?"

Prudence tried to hide her face in her teacup while Martha sat, straight-backed, and lifted her buttered scone to her lips. She acted as though she didn't have a care in the world, dabbing her lips with a lacy cotton handkerchief and nodding to various acquaintances as she looked around.

There was a sudden silence and then the hum of noise began again, louder this time as the ladies in the hall discussed their views on Harriet's skills as a dressmaker. Martha ignored it all, drinking her tea and eating her scone in as ladylike a fashion as possible, while she cheered inwardly at how easy it was to get these sheep to do and even think what she wanted them to do and think. Prudence didn't utter a word and refused to look at anyone else in the room, wishing that she could be anywhere else in the world but here in the Church hall with Martha. She was never going to go anywhere with Martha ever again, she vowed to herself as her cheeks coloured up and her hand started to tremble. She could also feel a matching tremble in her bottom lip and prayed that she wouldn't show herself up by bursting into tears. Martha would kill her if she did that now.

The only bright spot that Prudence could see that afternoon was the fact that Harriet hadn't attended the party as she was busy finishing Martha's second dress, desperate for the money she would receive for it. She was hoping that Martha would spread the word around her friends about Harriet's skills because she might get some more of the younger girls of the town as customers. God knew that she needed more customers and this could be the break she was hoping for. Poor Harriet.

Martha and Prudence didn't stay long in the hall, As soon as they had finished their teas, Martha rose and prodded Prudence to rise also. They carried their pots to the table at the front of the hall and then Martha made sure that everyone knew that she was leaving by shouting across to Mrs Trent.

"Thank you very much Mrs Trent. Lovely scones and the tea was just as I like it. Bye."

Now that she had the attention of all in the hall, Martha took a five pound note from her bag and ostentatiously waved it around a bit before she dropped it into the donations bucket which stood on the end of the serving table, then turned and marched out of the door. Prudence trailed along in her wake, not meeting anybody's eye, in the hope that she would be invisible. Once outside, Martha turned and grinned at Prudence but Prudence couldn't stomach anymore of Martha that day and set off for home at a rate of knots, leaving Martha standing alone on the pavement. Martha shrugged and then made her own way home, hugging the memory of the shocked looks and the intense conversations to her as she walked.

It was only a matter of days before the subject of Harriet Winters' skill as a seamstress had spread across the town. One or two good, honest citizens had made it clear that they weren't going to be swayed by the evidence that Martha Coleman had given in the Church hall, but the bulk of the gossipers were ready to paint Harriet's reputation as black as they could and they found plenty of people who were agog to hear about Martha's skirt. Martha thoroughly enjoyed the sensation she had caused and found it very amusing to watch people turning to each other to spread the gossip as she walked past them.

It was another couple of days before anyone let Harriet in on the secret. She had sent a note to Martha to tell her that her second dress was ready for collection but Martha didn't turn up to collect the dress and didn't make any payment for it. Another lady who had ordered a winter jacket also didn't arrive to collect or pay for it and Harriet began to panic. At first, she didn't dare send out any more notes, worried that something had happened that she wasn't aware of and it was only when a young girl shouted something rude at her in the street that she began to realise that her worst nightmares had come true. She finally got the truth out of her next-door neighbour, who was one of the few who had defended Harriet when the rumours about her workmanship began to circulate. The neighbour felt that it was only fair that Harriet was made aware of what was being said and passed on the information as gently as she could, but there was no hiding the dreadful results of Martha's statements made in the Church hall.

Harriet sank onto her little sofa after her next-door neighbour had left and stared into outer space. She was ruined, there was no doubt about it, and there was nothing that she could do about it. Martha Coleman, for her own, unfathomable reasons, had delivered a death blow to Harriet's business, a blow that would take years to recover from. And Harriet didn't have years. Her finances were now so precarious that she would never manage to rebuild her reputation because she had nothing to fall back on. Poor Harriet never managed to work out why Martha had done what she did. She knew that it was Martha who had worn one of her skirts which looked as though it had been in a railway accident but she couldn't work out why or how that had happened. She didn't discuss the subject with anyone else but, very quietly and with as little mess as possible, and using her dressmaking shears, opened the veins on both her arms as she was sitting on her little sofa and quietly allowed her life blood to seep away from her. To make her passing even more tragic, no-one realised what had happened until a week later when the milkman called round to her house for payment and Harriet didn't answer the door. The milkman tried again the next day and the next and, after the fourth try, he informed the police that he thought there was something wrong. They broke into the house and found Harriet still sitting on her little sofa, surrounded by her needlework paraphernalia and as dead as her business.

Prudence heard the news of Harriet's suicide from one of the customers of the Station Hotel when she was gathering up the dirty glasses and tankards. Her face drained of colour and she swayed where she stood, alarming the customer who leapt to catch her as she fell. Although deeply shocked and feeling guilty over her part in the affair, Prudence was touched by the young man's concern over her health and a relationship began that night which would lead to the pair's marriage after the war ended. Martha told her that it had been down to her that Prue had found her life's mate but Prudence never remarked on that comment. She used her new relationship as a way of getting away from Martha's influence and her life became a lot easier after that. She never lost the guilt that she felt over Harriet's suicide.

Martha found out about Harriet's suicide from a customer in the shop. The woman, who regularly spent quite a bit of money in the shop, asked Martha outright if she felt that wearing the ruined skirt had contributed to Harriet's suicide but Martha laughed it off. She told Mrs Court that she wasn't responsible for Harriet's desire to kill herself. It wasn't her fault that Harriet had been such a bad businesswoman or, let's face it, such a bad seamstress. She must have been a weak person, Martha concluded, because no amount of complaints about her furniture would make Martha kill herself. Silly woman.

The best part, of course, was that Martha had another skirt, absolutely identical in design and shape but made by a perfectionist so it was beautifully sewn and hemmed. She was going to enjoy wearing that skirt.

The End

Coming soon - the second part of the Coleman Chronicles - Daniel's Way.

Printed in Great Britain
by Amazon